HOPE

of

REALMS

HOPE
of
REALMS

BLOOD OF ZEUS: BOOK FIVE

ANGEL PAYNE

WATERHOUSE PRESS

Copyright © 2023 Waterhouse Press, LLC
Cover Design & Images by Regina Wamba
Interior Cover Images: Shutterstock

ISBN: 978-1-64263-352-8

For Leo

You are the hope of all my realms, the pride of my soul,

and all the best parts of my world.

"If you believe in me,
I'll believe in you.
Is that a bargain?"

— Lewis Carroll,
Alice's Adventures in Wonderland

CHAPTER 1

Maximus

S INCE THE DAY OUR fingers first touched, Kara Valari has changed my life in a hundred incredible ways. A million surreal moments.

But never so much as this one.

I'm still in my own apartment, surrounded by all my familiar things—but my world is upended. Catapulted to someplace far different than the hell I traversed to rescue her or the magically cloaked ashram in which we both tried to recover from the ordeal.

My mind battles to grasp an announcement that overshadows either of those experiences. Larger than falling in love with her in the first place, and then the moment I learned, from the king of the gods himself, that I'm his bastard son.

That was all before learning everything about *her.*

That nearly from the second she was born, she was promised in marriage to another. An incubus who'd help her make more demons for the glory of Hades and the underworld. But because of the extra element in her blood, she was saved by her witch sisters for another destiny.

The path of falling in love with me.

But she and I didn't need the help.

I'm sure of it, down to the marrow of my bones, as I gaze at her now. Her beauty has never sucked away more of my breath. Her hair shines brighter in the late-afternoon sun streaming through the big windows. Her skin is practically glowing. The edges of her lips, caught by uncertain quirks, have never been more captivating.

Even as they open to stammer out words at her brother. The exact same words screaming through my mind.

"*Pregnant?* Jaden. Come on. This isn't a fun way to take revenge for the fantasy pony decals on your Daytona car."

"You think that's what I'm doing right now?" the guy volleys, glaring at her through thick swaths of his hair. "About a subject like this?"

Good point. One that has my legs finally giving out, sending my ass down to the cushions of my couch. With one hand, I beckon Kara to join me. As soon as she does, I look back up at Jaden.

In the same sweep, I include Kell, who's communicating more with her silence than any vocal message. Like Jaden, the woman has extrasensory abilities imbued by her demon DNA. Clearly, Kell's able to smell something extra about her sister while their brother hears it.

No. Not something extra.

Some*one* extra.

A new life, growing inside my woman this very second.

The concept feels too huge to fathom. Too miraculous to embrace. It crowds my senses, huge and hot and looming, tempting me to roar aloud from the pressure.

I've never been so grateful for the self-containment skills that have been like a sixth sense since childhood. They've never been more useful than now, as I return Kell's and Jaden's gawks with determined purpose.

"We need the room, you guys. Please. If you want to stick close by, Jesse's probably home by now. He's three floors down, basically the same unit location. Look for the door knocker that looks carved by a depressed German viscount."

"That supposed to make us feel better?" Kell snaps.

"Well, now I'm intrigued," Jaden adds.

Either way, I'm grateful they're already headed toward the door. I'm even more glad for the warmth of their sister in my arms.

But like before, that only scrapes the surface of what I'm truly feeling. *Glad* is reserved for when Jesse and I finish grading term papers. It's the satisfying conclusion of a good book. The gratitude for sunshine on the beach in the middle of January.

This…is far beyond all that. At least a thousand words past that hill and the twenty behind it.

This is the build-up of all those words behind the massive knot in my throat. It's impossible to whisper everything I planned into Kara's ear. At this point, I can't even pluck *one* out. Nothing feels right enough. Vast enough. Life is suddenly a panorama of possibilities, made even more beautiful by the vision of sharing them with this amazing female.

The center of my soul.

The bearer of my child.

"Maximus?" Her voice, barely a sough, pushes her breath to the front of my left shoulder.

It sounds shaky and unsure, raising alarms along my senses, but the last thing she needs right now is me acting like king melodrama. There'll likely be plenty of time for that soon, if I'm remembering things right from witnessing two Alameda colleagues count down to their own new family additions.

Under normal circumstances, I'd laugh at myself for the thought but manage to smooth it into a warm-toned reply along the curve of her nape.

"Yeah, beautiful?"

She barely moves. If anything, her limbs are tensing against my embrace.

"Listen. You have to be honest with me."

"Have I ever been anything but?"

She gulps hard before stuttering back. "Are you...happy about it?" But then, before I can form half a glower, "I mean, we don't even know if Jaden and Kell are right!"

I forget about what to say. What I *do*, tightening my hold with unmistakable force, is more meaningful. I watch the gratitude in her eyes, despite the new element that's invaded her tone and my nerve endings. What is it? Desperation? Insecurity? *Fear?*

Again, not the time for melodrama. *Get your shit together, man.*

I push my energy forward, focusing everything on her. I soothe the back of her head with a steady hand.

"What's your gut telling you?" And perhaps other anatomical parts—though I obey common sense and keep that to myself.

"I don't know."

"Don't know?" I murmur. "Or don't want to admit?"

I hate being the cause of her new startle but refuse to be the guy watching her head disappear deeper into the sand.

"Kara?"

The better part of another minute goes by. I give her the pause, acknowledging I haven't exactly asked her for a comment on the weather. I can't just focus into her soul and figure out what she's thinking, but she *can* do that to me, and she has to be basking in nothing but the radiance of my joy and the fullness of my giddiness.

But now, so sharply, the jab of my puzzlement.

As I feel her shoulders tremble from soft sobs.

"*Kara.*" I cup her upper arms and extend her away by several inches. My neck cracks from bending over so fast to peer into her eyes, now a bright sienna from swelling tears. "Little enchantress. What's all this?"

She sniffs heavily. "Not *all* this, Maximus. Just…*this*. A *baby*. It's so singular. And incredible. And…irrevocable."

Against my strongest will, the edges of my lips twitch. "I'm aware of how that works, sweetheart. I helped with the process. With all my heart and soul, I might add."

She glowers. It's adorable. I bite my tongue to discipline the lip quirks, but not fast enough. Kara side-eyes my subtle mirth before batting at my jaw.

"Heart and soul that are like my air and water, Mr. Kane. But we've got a bigger picture to figure out right now. Like what this is going to mean to a lot of different…entities."

"I understand." Probably more than I want to—though that part also stays buttoned behind my pressed lips as I tuck her close once more.

"I don't want to tell anyone." Her words are soft but resolved, now heating my right shoulder. "I don't think we *can*. And Kell and Jaden should probably sign nondisclosures."

"Right." Too late for reining my sardonicism at that one. "Hold on. I've got a stack waiting in my kitchen drawer."

Kara pushes away, already shaking her head. "They're already in danger just for knowing. If you and I were just a couple of humans announcing a visit from the fictional stork—"

"Hey. We *are* humans." By fewer degrees than most, but it's still a fact.

"But less than two hours ago, you were facing off with Megaera, an *actual* stork by any other name. She was more than happy to fill you in about why her mistress, the queen of freaking Olympus, ordered her to stay in this realm and keep watch on us."

I push my head forward. It's not a confirming nod. But not a denial either. "Meg's a harpy, okay? Historically speaking, she gets off on fear and terror. She could've been stringing me along—"

"Even when *you* were the one to first broach the subject? Because you overheard my wannabe cool witch auntie talking preliminary war strategies with her wingwoman because they were…what? Preparing to dominate in Iremia's weekly Battleship tournament?"

I frown, wishing she were referencing any two females besides Hecate and Circe. I also wish I could find half a line of laugh-worthy stuff about her sarcasm.

But there's a higher commitment for me here. A larger truth we have to dig into, even if the real story simply doesn't exactly match what Megaera revealed to me during our chance face-off back in the Alameda University library.

A lot of my brain cells devote themselves to that hope.

But a lot of my instincts are already ordering me to give up the mission.

"I'd like to confirm nothing better than that, sweetheart," I tell Kara, combing a tender hand through her hair. "Would've enjoyed a tournament like that. Nobody enjoys sinking a few plastic warships more than me."

Her eyes darken. There's a thick, sad sheen in them. "Maybe we'll need that strategic genius sooner than we thought."

"Whatever's in store, we'll do it together." I flatten my free palm along her belly. "Especially this."

Kara drops her head between her stiffening shoulders. She flattens her hands atop mine. "This," she whispers. "Oh, God, Maximus. I'm so scared."

I curl my fingers upward, enforcing our clasp. "If you weren't, I'd be worried. And for the record, I am too." I don't hide my deep frown. "My comfort zone is self-control. But I already love this jellybean more than I ever thought possible." And just like that, my scowl is gone. And my eyes are brimming with as many tears as hers. "And I love *you*, woman, for creating him."

Her face lights up with a watery laugh. "*Him?* You're that sure, huh?"

"Fate wouldn't screw with me by tossing in the extra chromosome." My pulse already edges toward panic from the consideration. What would I do with a girl? How huge could my heart stretch—or my self-discipline shatter—to handle the protective love for her?

Kara's sweet lips brim with a full smile. Though my thoughts remain as concrete lines of logic, there are gallons of emotions behind them. Energy that I pray she sees. That I send to her heart and soul in gigantic waves. I have my answer as soon as she lifts one of her hands to the side of my face. Her touch is gentle but meaningful. Vocalizing nothing but saying everything.

"No matter *what* fate decides, *we're* deciding on love," she whispers. "Even if that means fighting for it. Against *all* of them."

I breathe in, determined to sew her declaration into my senses as fast as possible. I show her my commitment too, copying her motion with my palm along her cheek. "Them," I repeat, locking my gaze to hers. "You mean Hecate and Circe? Or Hera and Megaera?"

"All of them," she says. "But just to start with. With everything we know now, I'm not crossing Hades off the list anymore. By extension, even Arden and my mother. Or your father."

A low growl twists up my throat. "Zeus won't mess with us. He wouldn't dare."

There are new shadows in her gaze. "He might not have a choice, Maximus. Not if all your suspicions, and Megaera's confirmation, prove true. If there's a war coming and Hecate is going to risk the stability of all the realms—"

"Then we're walking the DMZ," I insist. "Down the middle, no questions asked. Nobody gets our commitment. I refuse to compromise the safety of our family just to help any of them make a point."

She flashes the barest traces of a smile. "We may not have a choice, Maximus."

I don't want to be so instantly defensive, but I am. At once, I recognize the reason. She may be right.

She's *probably* right.

"Oh, hell, sweetheart." I can't conceive anything more poetic, no matter how hard I try. "You really are scared."

"Scared in one book is prepared in another."

Though Kara looks ready to speak exactly that, it's been given volume by a much different voice. Someone capable of lower registers and, at least in this moment, steadier authority.

My front door opens, facilitated by the only person besides the super who possesses a spare key. I'm smirking big before Jesse North is finished crossing the threshold, rolling his wheelchair with more game than a rock star at a fan con. Even his stretchy rubber hand toy has come out for fun, smacking up and down from one of his palms like a yo-yo.

Fortunately, he keeps all the arrogance below his neck.

From there up, despite the half grin he's flashing, he's clearly focused on our freshest announcement.

"These two crazy kids filled me in on the way up," he explains, gesturing to Kell and Jaden. "So no congrats gift right now. But don't worry. I'm good to shell out for the nursery's six-foot teddy bear."

Kara rises. "It's all right. And you do understand, more than most, that it hasn't exactly been a normal week for us."

"When a Valari says that, feel free to cut your imagination loose," Jaden inserts.

"Professor North has a really big imagination, J."

There's obvious—and uncharacteristic—awe beneath Kell's comment, bringing bug-eyed doubletakes from both her siblings.

I'm mildly stunned myself, but for a different reason. My worldly buddy is alarmingly oblivious to the woman's admiration. Unless Jesse's gotten better at the aloof Mr. Darcy thing? Or—more likely—that he already sniffs Arden Prieto's claim all over Kell?

If so, I don't blame the arrogant succubus. If Kell is already under Arden's skin as swiftly as Kara burned beneath mine, I understand in too many ways to admit. More ways than I ever want to fight.

Jesse's close enough to extend a friendly hand toward Kara. "Hey. Congratulations." And then toward me. "To you both."

I clap a hand on top of his. "Thanks, man. It means a lot."

"But?" he prompts.

"But it's a little complicated."

"More complicated than wondering how you'll handle a hotter Uncle Jesse than the one from that cheesy TV show?"

"Considerably." I throw in an eye roll as a token thanks for his levity. "And regrettably."

Jesse nods, unoffended. "So…it's complicated. The kind of *complicated* that's connected to your little head-butting fun with Erin Levin back at the library?"

He's scoffing, of course. Or so I think—and hope. But there's not enough cynicism in his reference to Erin to ease my mind. *Damn* it. How much of the truth is he really starting to piece together?

"We weren't butting heads."

He snorts. "Are you seriously throwing syntax in my face? The room had glass walls. You remember that part, right?"

"And now who's evading their point?"

The rubber rope hand *thwack*s his palm for the final time. After tucking the thing away, he stabs me with the full force of his gunmetal grays.

"Who is she, man? I mean, who is she *really*?"

There are moments in which I both love *and* hate my best friend for that brilliant brain of his. I rip my regard from him to check for Kara's approving nod about disclosing this to Jesse, and I don't waste time once it comes.

"*Erin Levin* is the name for her human form. She's actually a harpy and a member of Hera's inner circle."

"Hera?" His stare isn't so intent now. That tension rolls back into his shoulders, which slam against the back of his chair. "As in, Z's righteous queen? The one who basically

11

hates your guts for simply being born?"

At once, I yearn for the eye-rolling good times of five minutes ago. "That'd be her."

Jaden adds his own grunt to our mix. "And I thought casting directors were brutal."

Jesse crunches a frown. For reasons beyond my fathoming, the expression always emits a swoon-now-or-die signal to every eligible female in his sphere. Apparently, for better or worse at this point, that description still includes Kara's younger sister.

She grips the edge of the dining table as he hurls a new question toward me. "So back at Alameda, you requested that confrontation alone with her...why?"

I dart another look toward Kara. Her idea about the nondisclosures was wiser than I gave credit for. We're essentially asking these three to keep some cosmic-sized secrets. But she gives me another solid nod, so I quash the wariness and move on.

"We thought she'd transported back to Olympus after revealing herself the night after Hades's earthquake swarm. She found us on the patio outside the crisis response center while we were signing the discharge paperwork for Kell."

"What?" Kell is the first to tee up with a startled look. "Why?"

"Why not?" Kara's injection is threaded with sister-to-sister subtext. My theory is confirmed when the women expel matching huffs. "Mean girl by proxy," she elaborates. "Hera wants us to stay out of her neighborhood, and Megaera is making sure the message really sticks."

"Damn." Kell parks a full hip against the dining table

now. "And I thought the *Daily Spill* blog writers were brutal."

Jesse steeples his fingers, still steadily regarding me. "And you thought, with her mission accomplished, that she flitted—or whatever—back to Hera's side."

I nod. "She dissolved into glitter dust before our eyes."

Kell wrinkles her nose. "Flashy exits only work in Vegas."

"And don't stick in LA at all," I say. "I already got wind of the fact that she hadn't taken as huge a powder as we'd hoped, but I still didn't think I'd see her at McCarthy's side on campus."

Jesse presses his fingertips together. "What'd she say when you asked about her realm loitering?"

"She's a good little soldier," I offer. "She was probably ordered to."

"A clear given," Jesse concedes. "But why? Pretty sure Hera didn't just tell her minion to hang with the locals and try to overhear conversations in the coffee shop. There had to be a clearer directive. A much bigger campaign, to warrant the extended stay. Did she even drop any hints about it?"

I hesitate before answering. There's a thing such as communication with my best friend, but then there's dragging the poor guy into an informational vortex that might be the first stroke of a signature on his death warrant. Do I want to be the jerk with that symbolic pen in my hand?

"That's an astute question, Professor North. Perhaps I can be of some help in answering it."

But now I see, as soon as my eyes adjust from the voice behind the new light burst in the room, that I never held the pen in the first place.

"Oh no!" Kara rasps, though she's nearly muted by Kell's concurrent comment.

"Now *that's* too flashy for an *entrance*."

"What the—" Jesse blurts. "Who are you?"

"Oh, my word. Where are my manners?" our new arrival murmurs, stepping forward in an ensemble that's still flowing with her typical earth mother theming. Though I have no idea how she's accomplishing that with the strands of gold chainmail draped over her long purple tunic. Keeping her mane of curls contained is more of the defensive steel, crafted into an elaborate headpiece that culminates in a triangle-shaped gemstone at the center of her forehead. The setting for the black opal is ornate and ancient, but not so old that the seven spokes that radiate from its top aren't visible.

The rays that match the eager beams in her eyes and the odd charisma beneath her preternatural smile.

"I am usually called Goddess Hecate," she informs Jesse with the same strange serenity. "But to my friends, I am simply Goddess."

I've probably never been more impressed by my friend, who receives that information with barely a blink of reaction.

"And to your enemies?" he asks.

Hecate returns his droll brow notch with a contraction of her gaze that would send most people into instinctual retreat. When Jesse holds his line, one side of her mouth inches higher.

"Well, that depends, sir. Which are *you* exactly?"

CHAPTER 2

Kara

I COVER THE FOUR steps to Maximus's side before any other thought intrudes. But once I'm there, the temptation to wrap both my arms around one of his becomes another instinct entirely.

It's not my normal need to burrow against him.

This is stronger. Scarier.

A visceral necessity to push him back and then step in front of him. In front of Jesse, Jaden, and Kell too.

"Hecate."

But my voice emerges as a minor, mealy plea. It's paltry and pathetic, yet somehow enough to dial back *her* demeanor. The attitude she's brought to match her new outfit accents.

Her whole look, from the thick velvet of her gown to the war wear that's masquerading as jewelry, is on purpose. She has to know that I see it all, though I'll be damned if I fully acknowledge it. Especially not with this new secret Maximus and I share. A truth we have to bury, from her more than anyone, for as long as we possibly can. Every thread in my senses affirms it. Screams it. But luckily, at least right now, doesn't have to focus on it. There are more pressing worries to claim the majority of my mind.

"What's going on?" I demand. "Hecate? Are you okay? Is everyone else at Iremia?"

Through every syllable, I order my sights not to veer from the confidence across the goddess's face. If I flick even one glance to the area past her, where her sacred grimoire is carefully hidden under a leaf of the dining table, she'll surely detect what I'm up to. Her certainty will match *mine*: the knowledge I hold, deep and defining, that she must be kept apart from that book.

Another hateful wall I'm erecting against her—it's the compilation of *her* spells, after all—but my belief is as blinding as it is illogical. Maximus and I haven't survived the last three weeks because of *logic*. If anything, it's been the exact opposite.

And it won't be forever.

My soul repeats it to my needy heart, another two then four then six times. I believe it because I need to. Because I have to hope that I haven't been wrong about the goddess all this time. That everything I sensed in her at the start, all her earnest peace and passionate integrity, weren't just a sorceress's sham.

That somehow, in some way, she'll see that truth again.

For the sake of the realms.

For the hope of the life I'm bringing into this one...

"Hecate?" I prompt again, helped by Maximus's firm hold

around my middle. In the space of those two seconds, I fall twice as in love with him as before. I never thought it possible, but just one vision of our baby's hand, one day grabbing his outstretched pinky, and I'm emotional mincemeat.

Our baby.

As soon as the words slam my brain, I banish them—along with the urge to flatten a protective hand against my belly.

Hecate can't know. She won't know. Certainly not by looking at you. Get it together, Kara. Keep it together.

"Oh, sweet one. The size of your heart…" The goddess flows her arms out as if inviting me over for a hug. "By all of Pan's nymphs, it continues to dazzle me."

I force myself to step over and into her embrace. It's so tight and warm and authentic that I know—*I know*—not everything about her is a ruse.

Not everything. But not nothing either.

How do I tell it all apart?

How much of her affection, care, and pride have been real? And what part has been just her dazzling cover story? The façade for her real spell, beneath everything she's done and said, from the beginning?

You're a bridge now, Kara. The bridge between worlds. And so much more.

How much of *that* was real? Because I believed her. All of it. Every serene syllable delivered from her magical aura atop the whitecaps on my family's swimming pool.

But why not? Right or wrong, the statements themselves were true. For better or worse, I *am* a bridge. A crazy crossover of DNA that'll probably open a lot of doors for her.

So which one of us is making the bigger mistake right now?

She sang the song, but I bought the melody and lyrics. The kindness and inclusiveness of her tone, which dug all the way into my spirit. I was so desperate for someone to just understand my confusion, to help me make sense of what had happened in Hades's dark cage, that I believed *her* performance from the start.

What part of it did she mean? Or was the whole thing just another pretty show, luring me into becoming her war machine headliner? And if that's the case, what will she do with my child? Will my pregnancy buy us some time to thwart her plans, or fuel her ambitions in new and strange ways?

Suddenly, I don't *want* to learn any of the answers. It's all I can do not to shove her away with a scream. Instead, I maintain a calm but concerned stare while forcing a steady reply to my lips.

"Iremia," I prompt once more. "Everything's all right there? And every*one*? Circe?"

The sorceress's name is my selfish addition. Circe's exceeded the boundaries of grace since we met, becoming a fast friend when Maximus and I stayed at the hidden witch enclave in Trabuco Canyon. In her hands, my insecurities and fears became gentle quips and uplifting atta-girls.

But most importantly—and alarmingly—she was a needed accomplice yesterday when Maximus and I had to sneak out of Iremia. She twisted the truth to Hecate so the two of us could make a clean getaway and race to Rerek's house. Though Hecate eventually found out and all seemed okay between them, there's no telling how the winds have changed since then. If so, would Hecate even be forthcoming about it?

"Circe is fine," she swiftly stresses. "Probably catching up on the last few episodes of *Hathaway Harbor* as we speak."

I let my concern tighten into confusion. "Then why… and *how*…did you…"

"My dear one." She flows a hand up, fingers playing the air with balletic boldness. "I always know how to find my most precious treasures."

I jolt. Not a lot, thankfully. But enough to scramble for a wobbly smile as a fast masquerade.

"Ummm…treasures? Like what?"

My smile is genuine, blasting out my relief as soon as Hecate breaks out a laugh.

"Like *you*, sweet Kara," she chastises. "A mother always knows where to find her diamond girls."

"So, you remember she has an actual mother?"

Before Kell finishes the peeved bite, I'm startling.

Nearly word for word, she's echoed Mother's defense of a couple of days ago, after breaking into Iremia with Arden. A trip, I now realize, that must have been agonizing for Veronica to take. Humbling herself to seek the help of witches with whom she had such strained history. Doing it because she was desperate to help her daughter and had nowhere to turn. Enduring it despite the reception she was given, the social equivalent of an ice floe.

A glacier from which I willingly waved to her, as well. Because I held a stupid grudge, seeing nothing past my dismay at being ordered out of the room during her last confrontation with Gramps. At the time, I'd thought she would tear him apart alive. Her own father!

But eventually, I saw the truth about Gramps. The amazing strength he always hid so well. The courage that bolstered him to be Maximus's guide in rescuing me from the ninth circle of hell.

So why didn't I give Mother the same consideration?

I'm disgusted by the answer to that, coming from the brutal honesty of my psyche. I didn't do the right thing because it was simply easier to stay mad at her. To lump her with the rest of the underworld and its politics instead of pondering—maybe even knowing—that she was as helpless as me to control Hades's scheming.

I'm going to correct my mistake. Starting right now.

With an equally audacious game plan.

A tactic that won't work if I choose to follow Kell's call on this exchange. She's spent enough time with Hecate to know some basics, but I have to follow my gut on the ones *I* know too. A scorpion doesn't like to be cornered, even if it's rocking shiny goddess curls and an outfit worthy of a *Mad Max* Vegas revue. And if we poke this one too hard and fast…

Hecate's new expression, with a smile that's as fixed as her *see me here, see me now* gaze, already fills that answer in. With chilling clarity.

I don't dare glance away. Not for half a moment.

I just stand here, mired in the same adhesive, and desperately hope that Kell gets it. Somehow, I have to convince Hecate that her arrival is surprising but delightful.

"My sister hasn't painted the box quite right, goddess, but the contents are still correct," I finally say. "You and I both know how trepidatious Veronica can be. And once the underworld party lines light up, she'll know that I was the one who sprang Kell and Jaden from Rerek's hex, as well as who helped me to do it."

At last, the goddess flinches. It begins in her multicolored eyes, the ruling shade now a stormy green instead of a summer blue, but fans across the tense set of her shoulders then down to the new clench of her hands.

"So…she'll return to Iremia," she supplies.

"Likely." I coerce my composure to penetrate past my skin, dictating even the calmer pulse of my blood. One factor I *don't* know completely yet: the sorceress's abilities to read energies. Perhaps even hear heartbeats.

"Not a wager we can merely conjecture, sweet one." She lifts a hand and taps a contemplative finger to her chin. "She'll do it fast, too. She'll try to bribe the new incubus on many levels, getting him to help her back to the compound."

I nod, not about to fill her in on Maximus's update from fifteen minutes ago. The news that Arden spent the afternoon at Alameda's research library with him, digging up background information about *her*. It's much better that she sweat from the concept of Arden and Veronica pounding into Iremia's *sala* any second—this time with the large dining hall in a more vulnerable state without her there.

"Now you understand why we decided to leave, and so quickly." I sweep a finger to indicate at Kell and Jaden, grateful for the chance to look away from the goddess's earnest stare. My actions look natural, instead of a liar looking for a chance to break eye lock.

"All right, then," Hecate concedes, and I wonder if she's already trying to smooth wrinkles with her own set of lies. This feels too fast and easy, even from the goddess whose best interest is rooted in keeping me compliant. "That is…admirable. And appreciated. But when will you be returning?"

I knew it. I didn't want to, but I did. Now I'm fighting anger because of it, steeling myself from turning and asking how she was able to survive the last ten minutes without dropping the demand on me.

I almost do it…but don't.

I'm stopped by the new incision of her stare.

I brace harder, letting her peruse as deeply as she wants. I'm still in media confrontation mode, meaning she wouldn't detect even national security secrets if that was her plan. Part of the trick is believing the act for myself, even temporarily, which makes my answer an authentic experience.

"I'm afraid it won't be right away. I'm going to need a few days here in the city if you truly want to keep Veronica off Iremia's doorstep."

"She's right," Jaden inserts, his slow saunter adding to his easy demeanor. But even if he's feigning the vibe, I'm grateful it's soothing the room's tension. "Mother will back off your game if she gets a few days to play hers. This weekend kicks off the pre-EmStar Awards events around town, so she'll be in heaven if the five of us are flanking her at some. But we'll have to get to her fast, since it's already Thursday. She'll have to activate the fashion army and—"

"Wait." Maximus is as stiff as his interruption. "The *five* of us?"

Jaden squints as if he's asked why photo filters exist. "Me for the smolder. You, Kara, Arden, and Kell for the happy family factor." He raises both palms with a no-offense pose. "I didn't write the code, man. It is what it is. The media's going to feed on us no matter what, so we should beat them to the narrative."

"A big, happy Hollywood family is the juiciest meal on the red-carpet platter." The comment, ridiculously right, comes from Jesse's end of the room. He's been abnormally still and watchful, a factor I haven't overlooked, so I'm grateful for the mirth if not its truth.

Maximus isn't on the same bus. His shoulders sag, as he's likely already accepting his deficit on this matter. But the moment carries one positive, giving me an excuse to settle back to his side.

As soon as I do, I release a small sigh of gratitude. My heaven is right here, and now I'm sure of it. Having to heft so many shields for Hecate, physically and mentally, has tipped my energy toward the red zone.

Thankfully, Maximus knows what my body language is saying. He ropes a fortifying arm around my waist before dipping a nod toward Jaden and Jesse.

"I really hate it when you guys make sense," he mutters.

"Especially because it means I'll be taped into a billion gowns for the next week," Kell adds.

"Taped?" Jesse scowls. "Do I even want to know what that means?"

"Probably not," Jaden laughs out.

Despite Maximus's physical support, my psyche continues to weaken. It's not easy to see my loved ones in such doldrums. But my light isn't snuffed yet—a good thing, since I've still got to deal with Hecate's dejected scowl.

"Very well." She adds a purse of her flawlessly balanced lips. "Do what you must, sweet one. I'll relay your generous act to the other diamonds."

"And give them huge hugs for me too?" I don't have to feign a syllable of sincerity now, helping me look her straight in the eyes for our farewell.

"Of course." But she continues pouting like I've handed over a basket of scorpions for her to carry. "Come back home soon. Hopefully we'll see you too, Maximus."

"Thank you, Hec—"

He stops as I jostle back, realizing I'm now hugging nothing but iridescent glitter. The sparkly motes cling to the silhouette of where she just stood.

I step back and brush my clothes as if the spectral residue is actually craft glitter, loitering everywhere. Despite that weirdness, it feels good to release all the tension from my lungs. Still, I pull a three-sixty one direction then the next, certain she's only phased herself a few feet and is now hiding in a corner, waiting to eavesdrop on our unattended reactions.

"Really, people?" Kell folds her arms and cocks her head. "If I wanted sparkles and sizzles, I'd be hitting back at the cute special effects director from Piper's premiere party."

The sarcastic mention of her movie star bestie should have me cracking at least half a smile, but I'm still too busy checking the dark corners around the bed. During Hecate's little house call, night has fully fallen over the city. I'm relieved when my search of the messy blankets, bookshelf headboard, and both nightstands brings me nothing out of the ordinary.

"Okay," I finally mumble. "Maybe she's really gone."

Despite that, I order myself to breathe in deep again, knowing it'll help me pick up any nearby vestiges of her aura. I can still feel my siblings and Maximus, so I know there's nothing wrong with my special senses. If anything, I feel them too much.

Kell and Jaden are still pinning the psychological needles for fascinated but fearful, while Maximus—my amazing but beleaguered man—is all over the place at once. At one end of his scale, he's battling anger and agitation. But at the other there's euphoria and excitement. The wonder of considering himself as a father-to-be.

I need more of that. A lot more. Every minute of every hour of the next nine months, if possible.

But that's not going to be possible.

Not even right now.

Not even as I cross to the walk-in closet to confirm Hecate isn't lurking anywhere in there either. Or the bathroom, pantry, or tiny storage room.

But her absence doesn't dim the lingering complication of her. Or the situation, and its climbing complications, because of her plans.

Supposed plans.

At least we can speak freely about it all again—for now.

Kell's the first to understand that assignment. As I step back to the dining table and take a needed plunk into a chair, she wastes no time in tracking me with a jerked her chin.

"Time to clean the griddle, sister. You're not really planning on going back there, are you?"

Maximus strides forward with a defined growl. "Of course she isn't. Kara?" The prompt comes after too many seconds of my pensive silence. "*No.* Absolutely not. You're not going to entertain one more *thought* about—"

"Why?" I push to my feet but far too quickly. Once again, my vision swims. I mask the weakness with a tighter glower. "Because you said so?"

His nostrils flare. "Because you're carrying my child, damn it. And next time, Hecate might not keep her perimeter—or her watch over you—so casual."

I bristle. "We don't know for sure if I'm—"

"Oh, we're sure," Jaden interjects.

"Surer than sure," Kell adds.

"Even so, I won't show for a while. And if this is really going to happen, and we need to learn more about Hecate's plans—"

"Then we'll find other ways," Maximus snaps, only to shake his head as if apologizing. "Kara. Please. This isn't something I'll negotiate on. Not after watching that witch peer at you like the Codex of Leicester."

"Whatever the hell that is." Kell already brandishes the expression she gets before silently reversing our birth order. "Regardless, I'm with the big guy on this one." She thumbs toward Maximus. "If you go back to Iremia, no way will you leave just as easily. Hecate's already reeking of raw ambition—believe me, it's not an aroma one forgets— so she'll make good and sure you're under her complete control next time." Her eyebrows hitch a little higher. "Your choice, of course, but do you really want to go down in history as the witch queen's warhead?"

I spin away from all of them, pacing toward the big window. "I don't want to go down *anywhere* in history."

A sigh spills as my gaze tracks across the rooftops, toward the place where full nightfall is encroaching on the last lavenders of the sunset. Those last holdouts of the daytime are like the places inside that I can still identify as *me*. How long will they hold out?

"I just want…"

"What?" Maximus's murmur is close enough to brush the fine hairs along my nape. He steps closer, pushing back the weight of my hair so he can rub the back of my neck. "What do you want, Kara? Just tell me, love. Tell me, and I'll move the universe to make it happen."

It's not just his words that squeeze my heart until my chest pangs. It's my surety that he'll do it. Whatever I ask. However quickly I need it.

That conviction, of simply knowing it, brings the

wildest joy—and fear—I've ever known. Do I know how to live in a world where my value isn't about my silhouette in an evening gown or the few years of orgasms I'll bring an incubus? Can I define myself past the life I've been trained to live for over two decades?

Hecate made me believe that answer was *yes*.

And in that affirmation, so many worlds started opening for me. My spirit gained wings, translating into the ability to do the same thing for my body. Levitation. *Flight*. Despite the fear of the situation, when I soared high over Rerek's rooftop and looked out over the ocean...for just a few seconds, I was exhilarated. A creature of incredible power. My heart was one with that endless sky, stretching into an endless horizon of possibilities and ideas...

So was that it?

My only glimpse of all the dreams?

Did Hecate free me from my cage in Hades's wasteland, only to be hiding the gilded one in her mystical sanctum? Was she wooing me with the view before locking me back behind the bars? A place where I'd have to sing for my proverbial supper—and likely Maximus's too.

"I just...want it all to be over," I finally rasp in reply to him. I can whisper it like that because the man hasn't moved from my side. Nor will he ever. I know that with aching completion, abiding joy. He's the love of my world. The destiny of my soul. In so many ways, *he's* already my dream spun to life. "Or back to the place before it began." My hand moves up, drawn to the magnificent line of his jaw. "So that we know what's coming now—and to just run before it finds us."

Maximus releases a formidable sigh. He pushes his face against my palm but slowly moves away again. Not far. Just until our gazes are fully fixed with each other.

"We wouldn't run," he utters. "You already know that. We wouldn't do it then, and we won't do it now, because we're doing it together." He leans in, making sure I'm really looking now.

How can I *not* be? His blues are infused with the last purple light in the sky, shot through with frissons of his unmistakable electricity. I know it. I feel it. And in this moment, I cherish its chaotic kinship.

I push up on tiptoes while tugging at his beard, compelling him into my long press of a kiss. Best move I've made all day. His arms encircle me in possessive ferocity. His mouth becomes pure command, ordering me to feel every degree of the commitment behind his words.

Stopping feels like another faraway dream, but we somehow—barely—manage it. Maximus releases only my lips. The rest of my body is still wrapped in his blissfully bold grip—most especially my stare, fully enthralled by the lightning flashes still reflected in his. I'm going to drown in his stormy, sexy cobalts—and I'm going to love every tumultuous second of it.

But when he speaks, his murmur is velvety as spring rain—with an underline of thunder that halts all the breath in my being.

"So, what do you want now, Kara?"

CHAPTER 3

MAXIMUS

"**Y**OU REALLY GOING TO make her answer that while we're still in the room?"

Kell's quip has me vacillating between a grin and a glare. I'm grateful for how her sarcasm has brought a small giggle to Kara's face, but that same action has me craving to kiss my woman again. So much deeper than before. Twice as hard.

Until we're both thinking of doing other things.

Thinking that needs to become *doing*—about ten minutes ago.

I clear my throat, trying not to think of the last time I had to summon self-control this intense, but it does finally kick in.

"Maybe it's time I offer to walk the three of you out."

Jesse doesn't waste a second to join his smirk to those of the Valari siblings. Still, the wicked gleam in his eyes doesn't measure up to theirs. Thanks to their extrasensory perceptions, the siblings know things he never will. No doubt Jaden's aware of how my heartbeat has tripled, and Kell is scenting much more on her sister than the baby's talc and strawberries. Doesn't mean that the guy isn't observing it across their faces or even extrapolating a bunch of meanings from mine.

"Yes. Damn fine idea, pal," he says, popping a small wheelie in order to spin around and lead the way to the door.

As Kell and Jaden follow him, I'm given a few seconds to seize a fast opportunity. Without hesitation, I grab Kara by one hand and tug her the opposite way. Once we're clear by a few feet, I lower my mouth to fit against her ear.

"I'll only be a minute, beautiful," I whisper. "And when I get back, I want your body between my sheets and your fingers between your legs. We clear?"

"As the skies in your eyes," she sighs out, stroking along my eyebrows. Her sweet mouth beckons me lower until our lips are tenderly melded.

"Now I *really* need to get out of here," Kell grouses. "Come on, J. Get me home so I can rest this earthquake casualty again." She indicates at her knee with an efficient chin jog.

Jaden chuffs. "Anything you want, diva, as long as it's not another rant about the pissing match with Arden Prieto that led up to everything."

Before they're finished, or I can thoroughly access the recall about said pissing match, Kara's jerking away from me. "Home," she practically stutters. "Uh, yeah. I guess…that has to happen."

"Perhaps sooner than later?" comes Jaden's quick comeback—along with a pointed look to make me notice what's going on with *Jesse*. More specifically, how much effort he's driving into his focus on Kell. Desperately, I hope I'm wrong about the new leaps of his brows and the eager lean of his torso.

"Hey…uhhh…if you guys don't want to wait on a ride, I can drive you up the hill."

Nope. I'm not wrong at all. And I almost swear aloud because of it. Especially when Kell pivots with a sparkling smile, expanding the play time on my friend's worshipful gawk.

"Seriously?" she says. "You'd really do that?"

I step over behind her, trying to snag the guy's gaze for myself. *No, no, no!*

Jesse spreads a wider grin. It conveys only one answering word. *Oh, yes, yes, yes.*

For Kell, he has another reply. "Well, now I'm going to insist."

"Well, I think we've got to let you." Jaden leans over, smacking a palm to one of Jesse's. "With a shitload of gratitude."

"Happy to help. Really." Though as Jesse's words flow to Jaden, his gaze tracks over the guy's shoulder—to the one target I'm still dreading.

A desperate glance back to Kara leaves me stranded. She doesn't notice a second of the silent—and increasingly dangerous—exchange here, taken to new levels by Kell's lopsided smile and consuming blush. My poor woman is wrapped in a mire of her own, which she keeps struggling to push through.

Finally, the shroud gives way enough for words. "Home," she repeats, hopping an unblinking stare between her siblings. "That means…Mother."

Thankfully, that tugs Kell's attention back over. "What about her?"

Kara steps forward, twisting her fingertips. "You guys aren't going to tell her everything, right? I mean, you *can't* tell her—"

"Of course we won't," Jaden assures. "It's your news to share, in your own time and way. Our lips are sealed, Kara. We promise."

"Mark this moment in history. I actually agree with the brat." Kell shoulder-bumps her brother, reveling in the chuckle it evokes from Jesse. "But not without doling some advice too, sister of mine. *Your own time and way* might be wiser on the *sooner than later* scale." She taps a finger toward Kara's middle. "That little twiglet is a custom DNA delicacy. You could be showing by tomorrow morning—"

"Oh, my God," Kara stammers.

"Or popping them out next year."

"Next *year*?"

"Tomorrow morning?"

As Kara and I stammer our tandem reactions, Jaden's forehead furrows. "Mother had normal human pregnancies with all of us, so there's that. But if Kara's demon or witchy sides were flowing strong at conception, along with Maximus bringing the Olympian nectar to the mix—"

Kara flings up a hand before I can. "Okay, Sisyphus, roll that stone down to earth."

"Or back up the hill?" Kell quips. "Because seriously, I can hear my pillows screaming my name all the way from here, kids."

Jesse taps one of the pouches on his wheelchair, causing its definable jingle. "Let's head down to the garage."

"Yesss." Kell playfully pumps a fist before circling over to hug Kara goodbye. During their clinch, I overhear her whispered promises about forcing Jaden to go blow off steam with some friends and a motorcycle ride. Though the idea sounds like heaven to my own senses, it doesn't come close to the need to return to my woman's side. To connect in full with her again.

But first, there are the private words I need to have with her siblings—and my best friend.

Once I've flipped the deadlock bolt to hold the door open by an inch, I follow them into the hallway. Even now, I turn my back to the entrance and hunch my shoulders as an instinctual volume guard for my voice.

"You guys meant it, right?" I say to Jaden and Kell. "You're going to keep this thing out of Veronica's orbit for now?"

Jaden's shoulders stiffen. "You don't think we're good for it?"

"Hey. Chill," Kell admonishes him. "We're all dealing with post-underworld PTSD in one way or another."

"But you also have a support network to help out," Jesse comments, rewarded at once by Kell's good-natured grin.

"As in, making an extra stop so I can adopt a therapy cat?"

"Sure," Jaden scoffs. "Because *that's* a fantastic idea. Cain and Abel will be loving that so much."

I frown. "Cain and Abel?"

"Our nicknames for our mother's dogs," Kell fills in. "And there's something *you* can keep off of Veronica's radar."

I chuckle. "Secret's safe with me."

"While we're back on that subject..." Jaden folds his arms and cocks his head. "Kell had a point back in there. You could be helping Kara into maternity clothes by next week."

I stab a hand back through my hair. "Shit. And there's really no way of knowing?"

"Doctor Doug might have some educated theories," Kell offers, looking contemplative. "But more than that, he'll be able to run some necessary tests on both Kara and the baby."

I frown again. "Doctor Doug?"

She nods. "He and five others service the worldwide demon population. They rotate to different locations around their designated districts. I can ask around about when Doug will be in LA next."

My scowl deepens. "*Five* physicians? To service every demon on the planet?"

"It's a special gig," Jaden states. "Requiring nearly a century of study. If a demon chooses the calling, they agree to go through existence-extending blood transfusions. From what I hear, the procedure isn't comfortable."

"Existence extensions," I echo. "Like vampires."

Jaden chuffs. "Well, the other parts of the contract demand total abstinence and sobriety."

"So, vampire monks."

Jesse's drawl gets him fast chortles from the other two, but again I'm not missing that Kell's reaction is the fuel for his fresh preen. And now, my new discomfort—spurring my need to react quickly but calmly.

"Fascinating as we could make *that* subject…" I address to my buddy's quip, "I'm proposing a new plan." That part is addressed to the siblings. "If any of the media did track you guys here, maybe it's best that you two take the stairs down. Jesse and I will throw them off at the garage elevators and text you when the coast is clear."

Neither of them are fully buying it, but they're not calling bullshit either. "There's just enough paranoia there to make sense," Kell replies. "J, give him your digits. I'm still not sure if our friends in the *Hysminai* have totally given up on tracking my phone."

"*Hysminai*," Jesse echoes. "The fighting spirits? They're real?"

Poor Kell. The prologue of her reply consists of a visible shudder. "Real enough," she croaks, prompting Jesse to cover her shaking hand with his comforting one.

I don't let him keep it there for long.

Doesn't mean he's happy about the foreboding shake of my head.

Not happy all—as he clarifies the very second after Kell follows Jaden into the stairwell.

"If I were a friend who kept score, I'd call that a solid cock block, amigo."

I answer his cutting bite with a new—and stern—head dip.

"And I'd call it saving your hide, *adelfos*."

The man has studied enough astronomy, cosmology, and meteorology to properly translate the word, which I've certainly used with him in English form before. But I've purposely saved the original Greek version of *brother* for an occasion in which I'd need it for extra emphasis. A lot of it. That time has finally come.

"Listen. I'm not trying to be your locust rain. But if you don't order your libido to change its weather forecast about Kell—"

"Okay. Got it," Jesse retorts. "Clever metaphor gets you five points on the board. I hear you—"

"Do you?" I cut in. "Because *clever* shouldn't be your main take-away here. Nor should Kell's phone number. You remember the part about Veronica negotiating Kara out of the mating contract with Arden, right? And the fact that the underworld let it slide because there was *another* Valari to take her place?"

His eye roll is eerily casual. "Fine. Yeah. I remember," he mutters like a dating show contestant who's had one too many beers.

"All right. Then act like it."

"Like *what*?" He drums a couple of fingers against his chair's armrest. "You think I'm going to sneak into the mansion and grab a quick bang beneath Veronica's nose?"

I drop my head back, letting it *whump* the wall. If he thinks I'm losing my patience, he's right. "I think you're getting hooked on how that young woman looks at you. Looks *up* to you. And those angles in her sails feel a lot different than your normal cruise with a woman, so now you're intrigued with how to best conquer the wind on this one."

"Conquer the…" He fumes. "What the hell are you—"

"Uh-uh. You don't get the insulted pout on this one, North," I interject. "You already know the full GPS on this. That if Arden even gets a whiff of your interest in his mate, you won't get even three seconds to tap out an SOS signal."

"His *mate?*" His sulk billows into a full snort. "And that's a viable thing right now…how? Last time I checked, the man's leash was nowhere near her neck. His ring isn't on her finger. So unless he's stamped his brand on her ass—"

"How about we don't go there and you just believe me?"

The verbal slam isn't my preference, but it's faster than option two: a full explanation of how Arden already did put a ring on it with Kell, only to drag that jewelry off of her finger and hurl it into the Pacific.

Even in that moment, a little over twenty-four hours ago, I winced when Arden let his temper override his logic. But I refrained from total blame. His emotion spoke volumes about his passion. In his admittedly bizarre way, the incubus already cares about Kell. But that's not why I'm here now, in a glare-off with my best friend about it. Arden's heart gets a drop of my concern. Jesse's life takes up an ocean.

"You know what?" my buddy prompts, bringing me back to the moment. "That's a great idea. Let's really not go there—and *you* just believe that I'm actually smarter than one of your freshmen?"

I shove away from the wall. "Jesse."

In the same three seconds, he's popped his wheel locks and begun a rush for the elevator.

"*Jesse!*"

Shit. It's a supreme effort not to bellow that part too. Even more of one not to sprint after him. When the man insists on retreating, he's full lone wolf Clint Eastwood about it. Two decades of friendship have earned me expert status about that.

In all that time, we've survived plenty of spats—but not a single one has been about a female. Especially not one who's been promised to an arrogant incubus in the name of preserving her family's standing with the underworld.

In short, a woman who's going to get Jesse in way over his head.

"*Shit.*"

And there it is anyway. Kicking my ass—with proper justification. Because when did I turn into the guy with full rights for that call-out? Aren't I the one who's in way over my own throbbing head?

The head with the brain that's still struggling for some awareness here. A list of words that are still defying my comprehension...

Papa.

Daddy.

Father.

Words that were never a part of my world. That were

never defined for me, except in the made-up stories that Jesse and I consumed in comic books or action movies. To us, fathers only fell into three categories. Evil taskmasters, elderly mentors, or deceased icons.

"Well, there's a lot to go by," I finish in a low growl, already conceding the psychological corner into which I've trapped myself. The place where I've got to face the large, looming facts—mostly the one having to do with the arrival of my real father in my life.

I yearn to smile sagely and enjoy a private *aha* moment here, as I'm magically illuminated with new wisdom about his powerful presence.

No to the power of ten. If anything, Z's intrusion has only complicated a number of things. Okay, more than just that. I don't dare try to enumerate the quote, because I'll probably need room for higher figures.

For now, I'm determined to leave *complicated*, and all the words that go with it, outside my front door. Beyond this portal, there's no more thoughts of *Iremia*. Or *Olympus*. Or *harpies* or *secrets*…

Or *war*.

For tonight, the atmosphere in this apartment will only filled with one collision of molecules. Mine and Kara's.

The mesh of our hearts.

The lock of our bodies.

The fusion of our souls.

The commitment to our powerful little twig.

I smile, silently thanking Kell for the assignation. It's already a perfect fit. Bright and sweet but bold and brilliant, exactly like this new miracle is going to be. So much like their mother…

My gorgeous little demon.

My blazing, daring soulmate.

The woman who already lifts a smile back across my face, even as I lock the door and look back up. I'm grinning as if the sappiest soundtrack is permeating the air, with my eyes stinging and my cheeks aching—

Until they're not.

Until they're moving into a new look, somewhere between stupefied and stunned, once I swing my gaze all the way back up to the bed.

And see that Kara isn't gleefully complying with my sensual directions. At all.

She's still fully clothed and perched on the edge of the mattress.

Her head is bowed. Her hands are twisting. Her shoulders don't stop their adamant jerks, belying her ongoing sobs.

My shoulders stiffen. My gut clenches.

So much for *complicated* staying behind tonight.

CHAPTER 4

"HEY, BEAUTIFUL."

I startle for a second, wondering how I missed Maximus coming back into the apartment, let alone onto the bed platform and then by my side. Has all my emotion dragged me that far under?

No. Not just emotion.

This is worse than a puddle of nerves.

This is a tidal wave of terror. A panic so deep, I'm positive my bones are rattling against each other. I can practically hear them, knocking in time to the wild poundings in my brain. I wouldn't mind it by half, if only the beats made sense. But it's all chaos, a desperate tumble that makes me long for an old-fashioned fetal position sob fest.

Fetal position.

There's *that* motivation killer.

Which triples my gratitude for the man now wrapping

his powerful arms around me. For the kiss he presses into my temple, as casual as if we're sitting at a park and feeding the ducks. How I wish that were the case. That all I had to worry about was a little gaggle of waddling birds.

Waddling.

Clearly, I'm determined to shred more than the positive thinking posters tonight. My scattered mind is now responsible for cranking open the spigot of my tears, which I dump all over his shirt through too many tense minutes. All too soon, he's going ask why I'm losing it like the duck who can't stop sticking its backside up in the air, and I won't have a single word of an answer. But the calamity is inevitable. His mounting confusion is palpable. I feel it, rising and thickening...

But he doesn't say a word.

Hardly a sound wells from him except a rough sigh. Another. Just like that, we're psychologically switched. I'm the one with a baffled gawk, and he's the guy with no words. Not even in the moment before he sets his expression with determination and then turns and gathers me closer. At once, he circles his arms tighter. He swaddles the back of my head in his massive but gentle hand, his fingertips so soft and reassuring along my scalp.

Oh, *damn.* In all the best ways there are.

I've never dwelled much on the concept of heaven. Never saw the need. But this moment... Oh, I've arrived. This is it. And he's my saving angel.

I burrow in, whimpering in open delight while working my head against the plane of his shoulder. I still feel all the bafflement biting at him, but there's something else in his spirit now. Something that confirms I really have discovered the meaning of heaven.

It's his compassion.

His own acknowledgement—of *my* feelings. Not because he can sense or smell or hear them.

Because he simply knows them.

Because he knows *me*.

He knows that I don't need all his words right now. Not his questions, and not his responses to my answers. No pretty words or reassurances. No talk of rushing out for baby books or doctor's appointments. Nothing but his loving silence and ongoing understanding.

Nothing but the fortitude of *him*.

I'm not sure if it's minutes or hours that pass, but throughout every second, his warmth and strength subside. It's not just around me, but inside me. There's not a moment that I'm not drenched in his tender love.

But eventually, I have to pull back and reach for a tissue. Once I'm done blowing my nose and wiping my eyes, I force out a laugh. What other option is there when knowing I must have a Santa-red nose and darker eye rings than Catwoman after an all-night fight?

"Well. Still happy you knocked me up, Professor?"

To his credit—probably more than he knows—Maximus gives back a full chuckle. But as he smooths his long fingers across my damp cheek, his mirth fades just as fast. The summer sky lights in his eyes are replaced by a dozen deeper hues. They range from rich indigo to the dark cobalt that always steals every molecule of my breath. This time is no exception. I'm motionless. Boneless. Beyond enthralled.

"Oh, my beautiful sweetheart. I've never been happier in my life."

And now, I'm beyond in love.

I had no idea there was such a realm for my heart and soul, but I'm there now—and determined to stay—as this incredible man pushes in at me more. My sights are consumed by his broad, proud torso—but that's not half the joy of letting him dominate my breath with his sizzling sweep of a kiss.

But damn it, that's all it is. A brush so fast, it's hardly contact. A kiss that's hardly a kiss—but so much of one.

Because it makes me want more. Need more.

I tell him so. *Right now.*

By vibrating the inches between us with my urgent moan. By twisting an urgent hand into the front of his T-shirt.

By exploding the moan into a frustrated chuff, realizing that this is one of the T-shirts that the *magistra* conjured for him at Iremia—so it's two sizes too small. The cotton snaps away as soon as I tug at it.

I'll have to do this the old-fashioned way.

"Show me," I plead in a throaty husk. My other hand rises, cupping his face as he's doing to me. But pressing in harder. Craving him more. Every drop of the oceans in his eyes. Every zap of the intensity beneath his jaw. Every coil of the strength in his body. "Show me how happy, Maximus."

His brow crunches in a silent question, but I'm prepared to give him the answer. In the greedy rush of my own kiss, working against his mouth with a hungry thrust. In the demand of my hands, scoring his scalp and shoulder with passionate digs. In the new sound that travels up my throat, high and achy and unrelenting, telling him I won't stop until he responds.

Oh, how he does.

With the sensual snarl that vibrates through his own system, so powerful that it possesses my bloodstream.

With the force in his own grip, now raking along my sides—until he's pulled off my main layers of clothes.

With the expression that takes over his face, unspeakably sultry and meaningful, as he stares at me in nothing but my underthings.

My bloodstream still approves. And now, much more of me too.

It's a blaze I've never felt before, making me double-check my limbs with assessing grabs. Am I still all here? Or has he thrown me into his demigod incinerator and torched me to pieces? Everything still feels in place…

Until he introduces a new fever into every inch of my nervous system. An electricity that sings on the wires of my senses, zinging into my extremities as he seizes my elbows. Hauls me closer and tighter. And then plunges his mouth back over mine, not settling for a brief brush this time. Not even close.

It's one of the most passionate possessions of my existence.

And I *am*…possessed.

By him, with him.

Obsessed…

For him, because of him.

So maybe that makes me a total mess too—the opposite of every glam, go-getter girl boss that Mother's pushed for my brand since I hit puberty. But what it also makes me is *honest*. And brave enough to confront that truth. And broken enough to accept it. To know I can't set it all back to right by myself.

I need help.

I need *him*.

And isn't that part of being a boss too? Knowing when it's all too much? Knowing how to admit it? Knowing how to offer everything I am to help fix it?

I don't look around for an answer. It's already waiting, right here inside me, bursting with my love for this man.

Blessed…by so much of him.

He has to see all of that on my face, but his stare still rakes my features like he's seeking the message out. He grabs me by the corners of my jaw, holding me in place as he peers further. Deeper. I'm not allowed to escape a second's worth of his stare.

"Now *you* show *me*, Kara," he grates. "But not the happiness. We'll get to that. What I want is all the rest. What you're still trying to hide from me. Show. Me."

I shake my head, fighting his hold. Not hard yet but with a clear directive. "I'm not holding anything—"

"You are," he insists. "I glimpsed it. Right after I walked

in but before you noticed me. I saw it, Kara."

"What? Me sobbing my eyes out? As I remember it, I *did* show you. Every last humiliating detail."

At least he acknowledges that with a small nod. "All right. You did," he acquiesces. "But you still tucked something behind all of it. Deeper feelings that you thought I wouldn't notice or care about. But my beautiful woman...I care about it *all.*" He squeezes his hold a little tighter. His palms are firm against my jawline. His fingertips drill into the curve behind my ears. "About all of *you.*"

Frustration knots in my chest, sending a matching huff past my lips. "All of me. That's...well, I'm not opposed to that. I mean it. But..."

His cobalts narrow, examining deep into me. "But what?"

I hesitate longer. It's not because I'm resisting his push. It's figuring out the right way to respond to it. Or at least a way in which I make some semblance of sense.

Finally, I come up with, "But what if, this time, there's not an *all* to see?"

He drops his hands. Rocks his head back. Only by an inch but far enough to notice. "What are you saying? *This time?* For how? For what?"

"For this."

I grab one of his hands and press it across my stomach. I swear there's already a responsive leap from somewhere inside me there. From our incredible some*one.* I want to rejoice about that but don't. I *can't.*

"Him," I croak, tears swelling once more "Or her. It

doesn't matter. It won't change anything. Not…the way it needs to."

"It won't change anything about what?" Maximus prods. "In what exact ways that it needs to?"

I slide my hand along the top of his. But even the hills of his big knuckles aren't such a staunch comfort anymore. How I wish they were. How I continue stroking, hoping my brain will borrow a shred of their fortitude. It's no use.

"I have no idea how to do this, Maximus. Not a single shred of a clue."

I don't hide the wobble of my voice. But it doesn't stop my desperate check on his searching stare and furrowed brow. He's not saying anything, for which I'm really thankful. The words aren't coming any easier, but his patience is helping a little with my search.

"I guess what I mean is…I have no real-life reference points about this. Zero. You've probably already filled in some of the big-picture blanks on your own. How we were raised, and by whom. So needless to say, Kell, Jaden, and I weren't exactly the kids on the block being called in for dinner after racing our bikes through the secret dirt paths."

He doesn't flinch. Not that I expected him to. It's a nice observation anyway. "Hmmm. Too bad. Dirt is a good look for you."

And now it's better than nice. Especially as he rubs a thumb into one of the mud smudges on my arm. I try but fail to cloak a small smirk.

"Regardless, this isn't a road I've mapped at all. How do I figure this out? Veronica never did bedtime stories or even nagged us to floss our teeth. We didn't have park picnic days in the summer or bake Christmas cookies in the winter. We didn't bake or cook at all. I barely know how to boil water!"

Well, that takes care of the smirk. And any other glimpse of happiness in my confession. The helplessness is back in all its desperate glory, clutching my self-esteem with ruthless glee. The man doesn't help by intensifying his stare to the point of pure gorgeousness. But when he keeps it up, I have to take pause.

"What?" I prompt. "You don't get it? How is none of that making sense to you?"

"Because it doesn't, sweetheart."

I'm ready to be peeved with him. Actually, I want to be seething. But his sweet rebuke and matching gaze are the blitz I can't ignore. I'm putty under his new embrace, as he traces tender little circles into the balls of my shoulders.

"You were raised to fit a brand, Kara. But everything you just mentioned…you know it was *also* stuff that was fabricated to fit certain molds. Christmas cookie time is an image for selling flour, sugar, and the hottest holiday movies of the year. Picnic days are for pushing hot dogs, macaroni salad recipes, and whatever the new outdoor sports equipment is."

I let some of my tension go. But not all. "And what about teeth flossing?"

"Did you need your mom to remind you after getting your first cavity or two?"

Time to let the smirk back in. "I've never had a cavity."

"Probably because you didn't gorge on Christmas cookies."

"All right, then. And how about the bedtime stories?"

"Hmmmph." Maximus cocks his head. "Fine. You get half credit for that one."

I tilt mine in the same direction. "Only half?"

"As long as we're airing the semi-dirty laundry...you weren't the only one who didn't ever get a tuck-in story. The nights my mom wasn't at work, she was doing stuff to get prepared *for* work. She was either down at the laundromat, making sure we both had clean clothes to wear, or in the kitchen doing meal prep."

"Packing your lunches...complete with home-baked cookies?"

"Maybe," he hedges, cracking a small smile. "Yeah, probably. But I helped when I could. And it's not that hard. I can teach you."

He means well, but the effort doesn't stop the giant lump from invading my throat again. "I know you will," I manage past a newly emotional choke. "But it's just another thing on the list." *Dear God, such a huge list.* "So many things I don't know."

He rolls his hands in, over my collarbones, until he's bracing the sides of my nape. "And so many things *I* don't either. But sweetheart"—he presses his fingers in, compelling my gaze to lift and twine with his—"we're going to learn it all together, okay? Probably more than we ever want to."

I join a soggy chuckle to his self-effacing one. It feels so good, being in this emotional place with him. Looking into his eyes and seeing that he's as clueless as me but not going anywhere. He *wants* to be here with me.

"Just tell me you're not planning on any pop quizzes for any of it." I'm only half-joking, but he delivers with an amused smirk.

"If I did, you'd ace them. Because even if you burn the cookies, you'll do it with all the passion in your spirit, the love in your soul, and the colorful brilliance of your amazing mind." He slides a hand up and flows his fingers across my forehead. "You're going to be the most incredible mother in the world, Kara Valari. In any and every realm there is. I know it already because I know *you*. Because I see all of you. The beauty of your heart. The shape of your character. The light you shine beyond the confines of your world… seeing beyond that pretty bubble to what really lies beyond. You've chosen to be so much more than the walls that were dictated to you. You were terrified about it, but you did it. And I'm still in awe about that. Complete, consuming awe."

I sit in silence, absorbing all that, for a long beat. Another. I probably need at least an hour to process it all, but no way can I wait that long to answer him. To give him the truth of my soul, begging to be let out for him in response.

"I was only able to do that because of you, Maximus Kane. Because of loving you and experiencing all your love in return." I climb over, inserting myself totally in his lap. "If you're in awe of me, it means you're in awe of yourself too. *You're* my light. My strength."

My profession becomes a verbal magnet, drawing our mouths together. We kiss because neither of us have a choice. Because we're air and wind. Fire and rain. Even flour and sugar. Alchemy. Destiny. Cosmic intention.

And now, a perfection of passion.

Blazes that combust, mingling our breaths and infusing our blood. Stretching our awareness. Sizzling along our skin. Winding around our muscles and fueling our hunger for even more.

Yes.

Yes.

I'm barely aware of it bursting from my lips as soon as we part, because it hardly matters. My next words are the more important ones—and I make very sure that Maximus hears them before we get enough air to mesh our mouths again.

"Please. Show me more, Maximus. *More.*"

CHAPTER 5

Maximus

I DON'T NEED TO hear anything else. I already know what she's referring to. I already know it because I feel it too. Just as deeply. Just as intrinsically. To the same center of my being. The place where my feelings aren't just feelings. They're truths as vast as the oceans and as endless as the stars. They're the connection I get when sailing on the former or lying beneath the latter. Realities too huge to be afraid of because they just *are*.

My love for this woman…it's one of those axioms. Unfathomable. Unfightable. As much a part of me as my hair and eyes, my blood and bones, and more.

All the parts of me that burn for her now.

Yearn for her.

That clamor and scratch and singe, wrapping greedy flames around my muscles and marrow, until I'm clamping her like a wild, desperate animal.

She feels it too. Every degree of the swelling, frantic burn.

I see it in her eyes, already nearly full of their photorealistic flames. I feel it in the planes of her exposed skin, like silken sun rays beneath my urgent caresses. I hear it in her sighs, shaky but searing, as I scrape along her back, around her buttocks, and down her thighs.

She helps me out with that part, moving around and then up before mounting me in full.

"Oh! Maximus!"

And just like that, I'm incinerated alive. Yet there's room for more of the flames, twisting at my muscles as I do the same to the side panel of her panties—and then pull.

"Fuck." It bursts up from the center of my chest as Kara plants her hand there, returning my favor by tearing down the front of my shirt.

As the cotton gives way, her fiery touch takes over. Exploring my pecs. Thumbing the peaks at their centers. Raking over my ribs…

And lower.

"Oh *fuck*, Kara."

While playing at my waistband with one hand, she dives the other into my hair. She's not gentle. I don't want her to be. My every instinct is bellowing about how much she needs this. To be in control of something, *any*thing, if only for now. If I can be that something, all the better. In so many ways…

Starting with what her mouth is doing to mine.

Plunging without remorse. Smashing without faltering. Tangling and taking, but then licking and giving. Moving her lips as if they've never known mine and never will again.

It's rushed but relishing, cruel but kind, hurting but heated. Almost as if we're one-and-done lovers—or so I imagine, from what Jesse has told me.

She finally pulls her mouth away, but not by far. She trails her lips to my neck, where every nip and bite is like a private message to my cock. One of those signs with the yellow triangle and the exclamation point.

Open me now. Arousal incoming!

I'm unable to stay upright. I fall back, dominating the center of the mattress. As soon as Kara follows me down, her teeth gouge along my Adam's apple.

"*Unnnhhh.*" It's a joyously primal grunt, erupting as I brace a hand behind her head again. I savor her answering sound, a heavy hum mixed with her rough need.

She's not shy about fitting her lips against my right ear. A good thing, since her new sough is one of the sexiest sounds I've heard in my life. "What do you want, Maximus?"

Which makes my initial gulp one of the most painful feats of the same existence. Finally, I get past it to form words.

"Same thing as you, beautiful. More of it. All of it." I tug her hair, urging her to meet my lust-clouded gaze. "All of *you*."

Slowly, she smiles—in tandem with the measured shake of her head. "Ohhh, Professor. You've got to do better than that."

My lips twist up. My eyelids tack the other direction, dropping beneath the weight of my desire. "I want you to set me free."

As if I've waved a prison pardon in her face, a sigh

shivers out of her. Her smile teeters, but only for a few seconds before she stops with the flirty fidgets along my waist.

This time, she grabs at the button there. And then the zipper.

And then clutches inside my jeans.

Over me.

Around me.

Until that groan is rising from my gut to my lips again, and I'm thrusting my hips to meet each stroke of her hand. The sound roughens as she again sinks her lips to mine, twining our tongues and clashing our teeth.

My hands lower to her hips. I grip her hard, guiding her core to where I need her the most. I work her body back and forth, increasingly commanding, ensuring she feels how fast my flesh is tightening…growing. Her lips part, shiny from how she's fiercely licking them. My mouth waters, wanting to kiss them again, but I'm mesmerized by the blazes that have truly taken over her eyes. The same fires that take over every inch of my erection. Higher. Hotter. Fuller.

I dig my hands in harder.

She gasps and rocks her head back.

I watch the wild pulse at the base of her neck, coinciding with the primal tattoo from her intimate channel. The beat that eagerly greets my cock as I notch our bodies together.

Another thrust more. Then another.

"*Maximus.*"

There's a soft whine beneath her rasp, hinting at a plea but not fully surrendering yet. I push up a little higher, encouraging her to chase the pleasure. As she does, with quickening breaths and hypnotic hip rolls, my own arousal climbs.

Higher. Steeper.

Until the air thins and my lungs ache to catch enough air. My veins are thrumming. My limbs are protesting.

But it's so good. So right. As complete and right as the new life we've created together, already adding a new dimension to our passion. New colors to our energy. New heights to our flames.

Stronger than ever. Brighter than ever. Until I'm blinded to everything…except her.

The amber halo around her form is reflected in the centers of her eyes, now turning nearly white. It's as if I've finally breached my metaphorical summit and am voluntarily peering into the sun for too long. But if this is what dusts my vision and is the last physical sight I remember, it's worth it. Until the end of my days, I'll never forget this brilliance. The blistering perfection of my breathtaking Kara.

"Maximus!"

I have to shake my head to force volume back to my lips. Some parts of the room come back into focus, but not without a price. My head pounds. My cock throbs worse.

"What is it, beautiful? Tell me." But it all hurts a little less as I kick up a teasing grin. "Tell me what *you* want now."

Kara drops her head. Hunches her shoulders. Taunts me back with the most stunning smirk that's ever lifted the lush curves of her lips.

"I want you…to set *me* free."

I chuckle, but not for long. I swivel my hips, goading her with the head of my shaft, but also not for long.

Because what the woman asks for, she gets.

With all the force of my fire. With all the vigor of my hips. With every inch of what I can offer.

Again. And again. And then again.

Until our breaths spill from us at the same rhythm of our passion. Until our bodies are rocking, our moans are tangling…and our climaxes are colliding.

"Oh!" she screams.

"Damn!" I mix to it. Beyond that, words aren't happening. My mind gives up and my body takes over. I'm surrounded by need even as it all spills from me, racking my psyche like a hailstorm from the cosmos.

The stars that were physically shifted for us.

The secret constellations that Hecate herself pushed around, aligning our fates to meet that much sooner.

A miracle I'll fully accept.

A marvel that takes me a couple of degrees past dizzy when I try to comprehend how I existed in a world without this woman. How I perceived myself as anything close to happy or fulfilled. How I went about my days as half of myself, thinking that was all there was. Worse, that it was all *okay*.

I'll never be *okay* again. And I never want to be.

I want this. To kiss and crave and crash with her. To sweat and stroke and move with her. To be blinded and inflamed until I'm bursting inside her.

To be overwhelmed with the joy of thinking about

forever with her. As an *us*. As a *we*.

As a family.

I swaddle my soul in the thought even as our passion slows and mellows. Even as Kara descends and presses against me, mingling our sweat and meshing our heartbeats. Beyond that blend of our pulses, all is quiet. I use the silence for roaming my hands along her spine—and for giving some heartfelt thanks to my maker. Not just my father—though he's undoubtedly in that mix somewhere—but to the bigger force beyond him.

He—or she—exists. I'm positive of it. And they deserves my praise because this moment is nothing less than sacred. A jewel of time, precious and powerful, needing its own shrine. I build the whole tower of it in my mind, imagining Kara inside its crystalline perfection. Resplendent. Radiant. But most of all, protected.

Not a reality I'm going to get. Not anytime soon, at least.

So for now, I have to accept that the intention is enough. And, yet again, hope that it will manifest into more.

Until that day, a man can certainly pray.

I'm still at the mental genuflections a half hour later when Kara rouses.

"Mmm… Oh, *my*… Did I doze off? Maximus?"

I lean my head up by a few inches to press my lips to her temple. "Right here, Mama Kara."

"Because where *else* would you go?" She's obviously

diving for the sardonicism to avoid my last two words. "Sorry. Guess I was a little tired."

"And *I* guess you had a reason to be. No apologies, okay?"

"Oh, dear God. I drooled all over your chest. Maximus, seriously—"

"You do remember the part about no apologies, right?"

She sighs heavily. "I must've really been out."

"As I'm well aware," I say with a casual chuckle. "But I also don't mind."

It's amazing to hear her echoing the sound, as soon as she rears up enough to sneak a glance toward my groin. "I wouldn't believe a single word of that, except for…*that*."

I'm not normally the guy with the roguish grin, but it breaches my lips without shame this time around. "Well, now." I roll my hips with sultry suggestion. "Guess it's true what they say about demigods and staying power."

Her head swings back up, revealing the fresh flames in her irises. I grin a little more as their orange light dances along my face.

"What *do* they say?"

I lower my hands to scrape rough trails around her gorgeous back cheeks. "Want me to tell you…or show you?"

My little demon lowers once more, sliding her chest along mine. The beads of her nipples are like stones along the pond of my composure, rippling entrancing light beams to the edges of my awareness.

"How about…both of the above?" she whispers against my lips. I part them, already licking at her—and reveling in the answering undulations of her sweet little body.

"I think...that can probably be arranged."

"Of course it can." She nibbles along my bottom lip. "Because Papa Maximus can do *anything*."

At once, I'm blinded again...by happiness. Suffused with so much gratitude and awe, all I want to do is prove her right.

Beginning with giving her the most incredible orgasm of her life.

CHAPTER 6

Kara

SUNRISE OVER THE DOWNTOWN LA skyline is like a magic trick in slow motion. At first, in the minutes after the streetlights turn off, the heavens extinguish the stars too. The shop lights become a curious patchwork, some turning off while others turn on. The headlight beams of delivery trucks and on-call cars are still brighter than the sky, a rich mix of tangerine, mustard, and thistle—until the moment the sun clears the western hills and bathes the city in a warm golden glow.

The sun bath that, to my delight, includes Maximus's balcony.

I'm curled up in one of the rustic chairs on the landing, sipping on some herbal tea in yet another borrowed boyfriend T-shirt, when a sleepy grunt fills the doorway behind me. I absorb the sound with as much gratitude as the daybreak on my face. It escapes back out on a wispy sigh, which prompts Maximus into a gruffer sound. Yet another sound I won't take for granted as long as I live.

"Hey, beautiful," he adds to it in a sleepy rasp.

"Hey there yourself, Professor."

"What're you doing up? It's not even seven."

"Just couldn't sleep."

And there's the irrefutable truth of the morning as soon as I twist around to look fully at him. And then all the way up and down him, devouring as much of his fresh-from-the-sheets glory that I can. The flawless V of his torso, with the twin rows of muscle leading below the waistband of his track pants. The breathtaking bulge that takes up the spot between his legs. And his legs themselves, as tall and strong as the support beams for this whole building. Even his feet are captivating, the mighty planks and regal toes dusted with enough tawny hairs to add definition to his flexors, plantars, and accompanying tendons.

So much for any thoughts I had left of going back to bed. Well…to sleep.

As I continue my gawk, I run my tongue over my whole bottom lip. Honestly, how am I this turned-on by his *feet*?

Luckily, he doesn't give me time to worry about the answer. He's already paced over to kneel in front of my chair.

"Are you feeling all right?"

I move my tea into the chair's cup holder before sliding my whole body down, straddling him. I can already sense the follow-up queries in his senses, but questions are the last thing I want or need. Not with him so close once more, smelling so good and radiating such warmth.

"I'm fine," I murmur. "*Very* fine." I emphasize it with

a soft kiss to the corner of his mouth. Then another, a little farther in. Yet another, closer to the center of his overly worried moue. "I'll be even…ermmm, finer…if we can negotiate *this* as the sunrise special."

I take my next cue from his inspiration, intent that he's not allowed half a second to dream up a comeback. I'm defined and swift about where and how to slide my eager hand. It's down between our bodies before he can interpret the intent in my gaze—and once I'm there, stroking and squeezing, a deliciously dark sound vibrates from his throat. It only gets better when I squeeze him tighter. His balls are already hot and firm, a recognition causing my own aroused moan.

"I assume you're not talking about omelets and fruit?" Maximus teases into my ear, sending vibrations down my neck and then across my chest. My nipples, already engorged and erect, stab against the cotton of his LA Marathon T-shirt. Thankfully, the breadth of his chest shields the evidence from any eyes that might be prying at this height and hour.

"Well, breakfast usually isn't my thing. But today I'm suddenly…ravenous."

Heavy air pushes from his newly parted lips. I waste no time in taking advantage, sliding my tongue in for a deeper taste. Right away, I thank myself for it. Turns out that his mint toothpaste is the delicious chaser for my tea, though the real secret ingredient is the fiery spice of our combined desire.

It only gets better as he spreads his hands to the tops of my thighs, where he discovers that his borrowed boxer briefs are just as strange a fit as his event tee. Yet again, that's pure serendipity. My parted legs have caused the fly in the underwear to open, allowing full access to the inward sweeps of his masterful thumbs.

"You mean…right here?" he rasps into the sensitive skin at the underside of my jaw. "And right now?"

I shiver against him before swallowing and finding my words. "Oh come now, Professor. You've never had breakfast *al fresco*?"

"Not while wondering if a crafty cameraman is positioning for a good shot of my eggs."

I'm sigh-laughing into his neck. "I'll never think of eggs the same way again."

His growl-and-groan omelet is hotter than both of his feet. "You already give new meaning to a hard scramble, beautiful."

I cup his cock even tighter. That last pressure is enough to set his velvet knob free.

"Well, we'll make sure your…yolks…stay under wraps," I whisper. "Nobody will think we're doing anything but necking in the sunshine."

"Necking?" He utters it like a foreign words while yanking back far enough to stare at my whole face. His own features are tense but alive, his cobalts full of lust and his nostrils full of air. "Not with how hard I plan to take you, woman. With how far I need to be inside you…"

He barges in on his own words with a lusty snarl. It's just seconds ahead of his sweeping, heart-halting kiss.

A brand-new mewl spills from me in return—overtaken

only by my aching sigh as soon as my man pulls my soaked center atop his waiting shaft. After one gasp-worthy lunge, he's fully embedded. And I'm already clinging to him with sweaty but greedy hands. Wiggling to work him deeper.

And so ready with my desperate, panting reply.

"I'm…uhhh…also fond of breakfast in bed…"

His chuckle blends with my fresh moan, which comes courtesy of his sweep up to a full stand—with me still attached. As I instinctively lock my legs around his waist, incredible friction invades all the sensitive tissue I have. I'm so hot. So full. So unbelievably blissed out. The feeling is so intense that I almost order him to stop and let me ride him like this, paparazzi cameras be damned.

Only one factor holds me back. The thrill of hearing more sexy syntax from him. The knowledge that I turn him on as equally as *he* does *me*. When it comes in his own words, from his own aroused lips, it's a better aphrodisiac than his eyes and abs and touch combined.

"Oh! My word!"

My shriek is a fifty-fifty mix of surprise and delight, layered with how the man swoops us back to his bed. At once, we seize each other with openmouthed abandon. We thrust tongues and lips in a ravenous, voracious rhythm. The same fast tattoo our bodies eagerly adapt.

The comforter and sheets are billowing and caressing. Maximus is bold steel and unrelenting lust. Beneath it all, I'm wildness but softness. Passion but submission. The most grateful lover in any cosmos that exists.

Until all those constellations home in and become… me.

And those stars are expanding. Then exploding. Flaring into brilliance I never thought possible. A climax that soars me into white-hot heavens, without thought or limits, until the only halves of my existence are this whole man and my grateful screams.

I never want the flight to end.

But something has thrown a rope around my mental rocket ship and is hauling it back to earth like the planet's survival depends on it. Someone shouting my name over and over again.

Someone who's not Maximus.

He's too busy joining me in mad grabs for the sheets, using his long arms to get us covered below the waist. I take care of towing the comforter up to my armpits while hurling a scowl over the mountains of his shoulders.

"Kell?" Her messy ponytail and lounge attire are magnets for my attention—and concern. It's not like her to throw on the first stuff in her closet, even for casual morning errands. "What—the—freaking—"

"Won't bother asking you kids the same question."

My sister has the nerve to drawl it with the hint of a smirk, which brings me to a new—and harder—glower. In this case, Maximus and his stores of self-control are perfect gifts from the universe. I reach my psyche into his, borrowing from his deep well for a much-needed composure check.

He offers another dose of that good stuff with his wry drawl across the apartment.

"And I won't bother asking how you got the key to my front door."

It's an interesting but weirdly welcome challenge to Kell's ongoing urbanity, which defines her quirk of a head tilt. "After last night, Professor North understood the assignment. And I'm grateful."

"The assignment?" Maximus visibly stiffens despite his steady echo of the assertion. "In what way, specifically?"

Kell squints as if he's brandished a gun and dared her to guess if it's loaded. I have to admit, the edge in his second charge pulls me toward the same impression.

Luckily, Kell doesn't waste much time on the discomfort. With the grace of a Bond girl, she cocks a hip and offers, "Now that Veronica knows we're all back and ready to roll, *she's* ready too." She rolls her gaze to me. "Do *not* say you didn't see this coming."

"This…what?"

Before Maximus finishes the prompt, I'm rolling a reassuring hand along his shoulder. Or perhaps a placating hand. I can't pick it apart right now. Not with the thoughts I *am* able to construe from the look on my sister's face.

"The plan we discussed last night," I say. "So, Veronica's bitten on the distraction bait?"

"Hook, line, and sparkly sinker," Kell returns.

I twist my lips, unsure whether it's from relief or regret. "Which also means we're being summoned to the mansion for media-blitz prep."

"Summoned?" Kell scoffs and shifts to the other hip. "Dearest, if it were only that, you think she'd have sent *me* all the way down here to fetch your pretty little ass? Which *is* quite pretty, by the way."

"Shut up." I drop my hand to wrap myself tighter in the comforter.

"Most gladly, so long as you two untangle yourselves from each other and get downstairs like sweet little captured convicts. I even brought you some new clothes, which makes me the world's most awesome sister." She pulls a pair of my favorite velvet joggers and a faded Stevie Nicks tee out of her big messenger bag. "So hop to it. Miles is waiting in the car."

"Miles?" I let a frown replace the ambiguous look.

"Dalton's replacement. He's very sweet."

"So was Dalton," I volley. "If you overlook the whole secret-spy-for-Hades-and-not-telling-us-for-years thing."

"Hey." Maximus's touch is as tender as his tone, rubbing over my now-white knuckles. "I'm sure they've vetted this guy in full. If not, he's likely to think twice about messing with a son of Zeus. Because I'm not leaving your side."

"For which I'll relay my gratitude this second," Kell puts in, "because my instructions were to return with you both. I've already been threatened with horrific repercussions for noncompliance."

I hate myself, if only a little, for how that makes my lips jerk up. "Should I demand details?"

She blows out a heavy breath. "Only if you're ready to learn them without that special sheet around your bum." She hitches a shrug in time to my protesting gasp. "Details from me, details from you. Everyone's even. At least it'll give us fun stuff to chat about during tonight's party for the city's earthquake relief fund."

"So that's going to be the family's first event?" I return. "Interesting choice."

"The *only* choice," she returns. "Every A-lister in town RSVP'd at once."

"For what it's worth, I'm glad our posse has, as well," Maximus adds.

"Excellent," Kell murmurs. "So can we fire up *this* part of the posse now, or what?"

I push out a resigned sigh. "*Now* as in you're going to wait in the hall while we throw on clothes and shoes? Or as in you'll be a love and chill with Miles while we grab fast showers and coffee?"

"Ohhh, nice swing for the fences," Kell laughs out. "But that's barely the first half of a spare, darling."

Maximus grunts. "You mean that's barely a base hit?"

"Sure. Whatever." She waves a hand while sauntering back toward the door. "You two have ten minutes, and you've already wasted thirty seconds of it." She lifts her other hand, wiggling the phone in it. "Timer's on!"

"What? Are you kidding—"

Maximus slides his hand to my elbow, halting my retaliation before it becomes a regret. He's still gracefully composed. My own reclining lion.

"*Breathe*, beautiful. She's doing this for you."

"Because she's the world's most awesome sister." My drawl is only half a joke, and he knows it, proven by his warm buss to the top of my shoulder.

"A sister who knows what it'll take to keep your mother at peace," he states. "A circus I'll gladly perform in too if that means it'll buy us some time to figure out our next steps." He curves a finger beneath my jaw, gently guiding me to turn and meet his gaze. "I'll do a can-can on top of an elephant and let it go viral if it'll keep you and the twiglet safe."

A giggle spills from me until the point that my lips press up to his. As soon as our mouths meet, my intent is serious again. Dedicated. With the surrender of the kiss, I give him my trust. With the high sigh in my throat, I give him my soul. With the wrap of my hand around his neck, I give him all the conviction in my spirit. The commitment to remain by his side. To stay there until we have a workable plan for all this—if such a thing exists.

Can we actually do it?

Thwart Hecate's war cries while staying out of Hera's crosshairs? At the same time, protect my siblings—in Hollywood *and* Iremia—from the fray? And the other people that Maximus and I care about, like Reg, Sarah, Nancy, and now even Arden…by a fractional margin. How is all of this going to affect them? We're confronting the task of stopping an inter-realms *war*…

Kell and her timer can stuff it. Right now, I need a long and tight embrace with the most important person of my existence. I tell him so by roping both arms around his neck and burying my face in his hair. The thick strands still smell like sunshine, surrounding my senses in warmth and my mind in longing.

"What if the twig and I just want to jump in your truck and drive somewhere no one can find us?"

Maximus, returning the urgency of my clasp, exhales hard into my ear. "I'd say that you and our amazing offspring were on to a great concept—in any other situation except ours."

He doesn't elaborate. He doesn't have to. I tell him that by resting my head against his pectoral and savoring the low thrum beneath my ear. The heartbeat of the man I love more with every passing second. More importantly, the incredible human being I'm committed to despite the fact that his father can drop a pin on us wherever we go in all the cosmos.

It is, as Maximus has perfectly said, just part of the *situation*.

CHAPTER 7

Maximus

AFTER A DAY FULL of fittings, fashion consultations, and even a full facial—which, I admitted to Kara during our rare moments behind closed doors, was unexpectedly close to a religious experience—I thought I'd be heading for the darkest corner of the trendy restaurant on the Pendry Hotel's rooftop for some much-needed solitude.

I should have known better. And definitely should have remembered that when Veronica Valari's running the show, there's no such thing as solitude.

Still, it's impossible to be miffed at the woman, who's thoroughly in her element while guiding Kara and me along the wall of floor-to-ceiling windows overlooking a tonier section of Sunset Boulevard. She's dressed in form-fitting leather that's in line with the casual-elegance fashion dictate for the event, which hasn't stopped boggling my mind. Casual *and* elegant?

Admittedly, I don't dissect the subject too deeply. Not

when I'm getting away with an untucked button-up, fitted jacket, dark-wash jeans, and a pair of obscenely comfortable boots. Without a tie closing in on my windpipe, I'm actually enjoying myself a little between the photo ops to which Kara and I are being brisking shuttled. Unbelievably, I'm actually smiling for those cameras too.

But the biggest reason for my perpetual grin is the woman by my side. And, more than I expected or hoped, in my arms. The photographers don't have to push hard for us to moon and peck at each other as if the romance Christmas movie season has come early. There's an awesome freedom in obliging them.

No. More than that. It's amazing. Exhilarating. The most magnetic female in the building, rocking a dark-red pantsuit with a frothy black blouse beneath, is the woman I can now openly worship with the rest of LA's elite—and, via all their social media, with the world. There's so much we're still hiding from all of them, but the enormity of our love isn't one of those elements anymore. For now, I can and will be grateful for that.

Veronica turns us toward another lighted photo-op area, where there's a large display with drawings and three scale models of buildings complete with working lights and "guests" in all their two-to-three-inch, formal-clad glory.

Jaden's already standing next to the display, fielding questions from at least a dozen reporters.

"All three of these theaters, historic landmarks in the city, suffered significant damage in Monday's quake," he tells them. "Part of the funds from tonight's event will be dedicated to historically relevant renovations and retrofittings for them. In addition to job opportunities for hundreds of Angelenos, we're preserving key parts of the city's history. Movie theaters are as vital to LA's heritage as the Broadway houses in New York, the jazz clubs in Chicago, or the—"

"Kara! Maximus!"

The reporters bellow it so many times, I wonder who they're clamoring to drive the point into. Remembering my own name was only a problem during the first minute I beheld Kara in her finery for the night. It's not an issue now, even with the photo flash storm that erupts from every angle.

"Whoa," I mumble. "Wow." And realize, several seconds too late, that the other photo stops were mild warmups for this main show—which, in my dazed opinion, Jaden was handling just fine on his own.

The poor guy obviously agrees, though I'm probably the only one to catch his disappointment before he throws a smooth mask across it.

"What are *your* thoughts on it all?" one of the correspondents directs at Kara during a lull in the din. "Should these buildings be rescued despite the risk of them crumbling worse during another quake, or should their history be sacrificed in the name of modern safety codes?"

Well, there goes Jaden's facade of civility. Good thing, since that means I'm not alone in the irked glare department.

There's no way Kara can pick a winning answer to that, though she seems determined to try with a sweet cant of her head and a charming quirk of her lips.

In the same moment, a fascinating aura settles over the throng. My stunning sorceress already has them all in thrall—and Jaden and me, as well. But the marvelment doesn't stop us from indulging gloating smirks because of it.

Kara's take is different. She looks at the reporter with merciful contemplation. Her voice is even more diplomatic.

"Wow. That's such a good question, Greg. But I guarantee my answer wouldn't be as informed as the one my brother started."

It's officially my favorite moment of the event. A segue that embodies my woman to perfection, as humble and disarming as it is smooth and sassy. No wonder I yearn to kiss the woman into oblivion for it—if only I weren't occupied with glaring down a good chunk of the crowd, guys *and* girls, looking ready to do the same. I even wonder if Jaden's about to join my end of the throwdown, until he opens his mouth to continue with the talking points—only to be verbally stomped again.

"As long as we're on the subject of *starting things...*" A new reporter steps forward, casually tossing dark hair that's cut in a glam rock pompadour. His look is finished with gold eyeliner that stands out against his terracotta skin, though the makeup isn't necessary. His bright-green gaze brings a stab all its own. "You two... Our Greek gladiator professor and the Valaris' shy girl... You two interested in issuing an official statement here?"

And that's it. Less than twenty words from this smartass, and Kara's cool confidence evaporates into mist. It's a dark fog, taking over every inch of her face as she pushes physically closer to me but lets loose at the bold little rock star with startling volume.

"Official? You demanding a signed affidavit?"

The reporter smirks while subtly directing his photographer to focus on Kara and switch to video mode. "You offering one, Ms. Valari?"

"Would it change your story angle at all, Ellery Gentry?" She steps forward and folds her arms. "Since that's the pointless rhetoric for the night, why don't we all move on to what really matters here tonight?"

Gentry flips the front of his pomp from one side to the other. "To a lot of people, you and Maximus *do* matter."

"*Enough*," she bites out. "Your verbal gymnastics aren't amusing, Ellery. Especially not tonight. So step aside and let someone else—"

"Ask the same question?" The taunt blares from someone at the back of the group. "Come on, Kara. This time, Ellery gets a pass. He's just being nicer about it than the rest of us."

The reporter to Gentry's left is a diminutive redhead who raises her hand. But even from here, I know the gesture's just a formality.

"Kara. Maximus." She intones it while swinging her stare between us with the tact of a wrecking ball. "We're not asking for a half-hour sit-down with wardrobe changes. Can we just get something, *anything*, for the record, please? Are you two doing this publicly now, or not? If so, where are you pinging on the commitment radar?" She takes a small breath, but her personal pendulum is still in dramatic motion. "Because if that number's anywhere below five, I've got a proposition for Professor Kane…"

I'm confused about the item she holds aloft, as well as the hefty group laugh it stirs, until Veronica rushes forward and snatches it from the reporter's hand. In nearly the same movement, she sweeps around to stuff the thing—a cocktail napkin with a name and phone number scrawled onto it—into a newly filled glass of white wine.

The cheerful guffaws are reduced to nervous snickers. Though it's not my first time today, I look to Veronica with new appreciation. The media isn't called an animal of its own for empty reasons, yet the beast bows instantly and collectively to Mama Valari. This, coming from a band of skeptics with incomplete knowledge of her ancestry. It's enough to double my own awe. Even by this realm's simple standards, the woman's a full force of nature.

With, fortunately, a daughter who knows how to balance her out.

Kara's light laugh emerges with ideal timing. "Well, thank goodness I know you're kidding, Leeta," she offers to Napkin Woman with a serene smile. "Because the fight wouldn't be pretty if you weren't."

Just like that, everyone's back to easygoing party chortles. But on many faces in the crowd, I glimpse more than the basic mirth. I see it because I'm feeling it too. A wagonload of sheer relief.

Though all too quickly, my wagon's pulling back out to the big prairie of nerves.

It's not the way Kara steps back over to snuggle close

once again. It's that *now* the words beneath my breath are a total match to the truth I'm living.

"Deer, meet headlights."

Not even Kara's commiserating giggle can dim the cacophony we're subjected to. The wild surge of overlapping shouts. The primal din of jostling bodies and clashing cameras. But most of all, the sci-fi strangeness of their rapidly flashing bulbs. To their lenses, the way I resecure my grip on their princess is another sign of the affirming affection they're digging for. Only Kara knows the truth. She has to. She's got to know that *she's* giving *me* a lifeline in this endurance test, not the other way around.

Whatever it is, we must be giving the horde what they're looking for. They're bellowing with praise now, like we teamed for a game-winning Super Bowl play, despite how we've barely moved for several minutes. My bewilderment about it goes gut deep, manifesting in a growl that vibrates against Kara's hand, now splayed to the middle of my chest.

"And now you know why they call it Holly*weird*," she mutters past her tight smile. As I groan and chuckle, we're doused in more strobing lights and the football stadium yells.

Veronica flows back into the photo area just in the nick of time. "So, everyone's clear about the commitment radar now?" She eyeballs Leeta the napkin girl. "Good. For those of you with platinum access to the event, Maximus and Kara will be down in the hotel's social club in a few minutes for a fun face-off against Jaden and Kell."

"A face-off?" I speak for Kara and myself with the lower-registered query, thrown to Veronica as soon as we step away from the chaos. "Should we be excited or scared?"

Veronica laughs and flutters a hand. "It's all in good fun. I promise. The hotel's new owners want to show off the private social spaces downstairs, so they've pledged five hundred thousand dollars to the targeted earthquake relief fund of the winning team's choice."

Kara's posture tightens. "The winning team...at *what*?"

A new flitting motion from Veronica. "Oh, they have all kinds of things down there. I mean, a swimming match just isn't possible, and the virtual reality studio will muss your makeup even more, so they'll likely have you in the VIP bowling lounge."

"*Bowling?*" Kara's blurt slams the air before I can rustle half a chuckle. "What I mean is, how are we supposed to make that work?" she adds in a worried rush. "Kell and her leg... She's been on it all night, so the injury has to be barking at her by now. Has anyone asked her about how she f—"

"Your sister was the one who suggested it, dear."

Kara chuckles despite a small groan. Thankfully, Veronica is pulled aside by some friends and hardly notices either. Though I sense an eyeroll is next from my beloved, it never manifests.

"Of course she did," she mutters instead, even making a point to throw out a few cute *sister showdown* jibes at the reporters who linger long enough to follow our stroll to the hotel's service elevator.

Her private gripe lends enough strength for half a smile and an approving wave when Veronica is pulled aside by some friends just before we get to the elevator. She lingers for some obligatory chit-chat with them, meaning we get the sudden treat of a private elevator ride.

Outwardly, the situation lightens Kara even more. But once it's really just the two of us in the lift, heading down to the social club level, I pick up on the deeper layers of the woman's energy. More of the unsettled nerves. The tension, stronger than before, that skims just below the surface of her composure. This clattering steel box likely isn't helping things, either.

"Hey." I tug her close, doubly grateful that Veronica had to hang back with the gabby gal-pals. Kara and I are alone except for a small security camera and a linen napkin that must have escaped a room service cart. I don't care about either as I pull her all the way in, not relenting until her sweet curves are flush against me. "Your mom had it right, you know. This is supposed to be some good fun."

"Fun?" She's only half teasing, though I grin when she tries for a punctuating laugh. "You do remember the time I told you that I suck at bowling, right?"

I push my chin against her forehead. "Full disclosure. So do I." A few inches down, and our mouths are aligned. I lift her face by cupping her cheek and then cover her with a tender kiss. "But now we'll suck together. And for a good cause. And you'll still be the hottest woman in the lanes. And after we're eviscerated, you'll still have the right to crow. Because everyone will know what I plan on doing with you *after* the game."

New light dances in her gorgeous brown eyes. But my

heart waits to stop during the moment she winds her hold around my neck, gifting me with a meaningful smile across her lush lips.

"You're taking me out for a chocolate malt and fries?"

I kiss her again. Longer. Deeper. No male on earth would blame me if they heard what this woman's rasp does to the word *fries*. Just the mental replay of it has me plunging my tongue between her lips and shifting my hold to the perfect swells of her backside.

And now, contemplating if anyone would miss this elevator for ten minutes if I leaned back and pressed the elevator's Stop button…

CHAPTER 8

I DON'T HAVE TO see into his spirit to know the intention of his desire. It's apparent in more obvious places.

Better places.

The thick blue flames in his eyes. The searing breaths from his slightly parted lips. And best of all, the growing ridge between his thighs. The place I work with my own burning center, stirring the brew of our lust into an elixir we won't be able to deny. Or stop.

Stop. Stop. Stop.

I program the word on a loop, messaging it to him without mercy. Out loud, I give him the orders to back it up.

"Maximus. *Please.* Push the button."

Now, now, now.

Stop us. Stop this. Stop the whole damn world.

"Please...push it..."

My husks are rough and low and aching, drenched in

the need that overrides my manners, modesty—and even my sense of duty. And how is *that* even happening? No matter how deeply Mother digs her fingers into arrangements at events like these, I never lose track of the real reasons they exist. My onus to the organizations they help. The people who are out there on a daily basis, giving and doing for others. But right now…

Oh God…

It's so much harder to remember.

Not when *giving* and *doing* suddenly mean such different things.

Urgent, pulsing, impatient things.

I need to give it to you, Maximus.

I need to do it with you, Maximus.

To whatever force of the cosmos that interferes, making his throat growl and his eyes dilate, I pledge a lifetime of loyalty.

To whatever additional power that steps in, coiling through his arm to make him reach out and whomp that magical red button, I pledge my afterlife fealty as well.

At once, alarms clang around us. I owe them a fidelity ceremony too, since their clamor easily absorbs my long groan once Maximus swings me around and slams me onto the railings that meet in the lift's corner. I moan again, wondering if we've dented the steel wall, before realizing I don't care. The repair bill will be worth it. As Maximus moves in, making room for his hips between mine, I already know that as total fact.

He drags his head up, exposing me to the full force of

his stare. Thick clumps of his hair are in our way, making his lust look like safety beacons through thick fingers of tawny smoke. But right now, he's feeling everything but safe. I see it in those pure blues and absorb it in his primitive need.

"They could find us any second," he growls, his lips half a breath from mine.

"I know," I rasp back.

"They could see me pinning you in like this."

"I know."

"Fucking you like this."

"I know!" I twist my grip into his beard and haul his mouth back down upon me. His mouth, tasting earthy and peppery and lusty. His mouth, doing everything it can to blatantly mash on me…and punish me… "I know, damn it. I don't care. I *won't* care. Just…oh, please…Maxim—*oh!*"

Ahhh, those glorious alarm bells, wrapping around the full force of my shriek—as this incredible male forces my body to do the same with his erection. And then again. And again. Each time, I cry out louder. Screams of confusion—*When did he unzip me* and *himself?*—but also of obligation. Sheer, primal gratitude. Bowled over, dragged under, catapulted across.

And spread so wide.

And nailed down hard.

And loving him even more for it.

Every thrust he can't be gentle about. Every drive he doesn't dare take slow. None of this can be about that now. We're here for the totality of our connection. The hot, hungry rush of awareness that we fought when our fingers touched for the first time. The battles we waged against doing exactly this. Tangled in each other. Pouring out to each other. Losing every boundary we possess. Finding every height we can soar to.

And oh, how we do.

Even in an elevator that's headed down, we're surging up. Stretching higher. Lunging through the clouds and then past the stars. Rocketing past Mars and Jupiter and the rest, until we're flaring to life in an uncharted galaxy…

"Kara."

"Yes. Oh, Maximus."

"*Kara.*"

Oh…*wow*. It's a new solar system entirely, exploding into all its colors just as my body goes supernova around his. *With* his. As he pumps me full of liquid starfire, my blood already turns it into the real stuff. We float through an incredible galaxy as one blindingly bright orb, marveling at its quiet beauty despite the earthbound clangs that still riot around us.

Until, suddenly, they don't.

In their place, there's a voice. A strong, slightly accented baritone.

"Miss Valari? Mr. Kane? Are you all right?"

"Uhhh…yeah. All good here." Maximus bellows it loud enough to mask the rustles, clanks, and zips as we hasten to correct our clothes. Since Mother invited the whole press pool down from upstairs, we'll surely be outed for any discrepancies between then and now—though at this point, I still don't care. In even better ways than before.

I had no idea that fast and naughty elevator climaxes were as good as the other kinds. I'm as woozy as if I've just left the spa after a brutal massage. My muscles are like artisan bread loaves, my limbs like well-done noodles. In short, the best kind of woozy to have—despite the giant carb craving I'm fighting on top of it.

"Oh, that is quite a relief to hear," says the genial baritone. "Ermmm...my name is Namazzi Wood, and I'm the manager on duty this evening. Please be assured that I've contacted engineering, and they will be here soon with the elevator repair team. Miss Kell Valari has been very clear about the urgency to get you out of there quickly—"

"I'll bet she has," I slice out with equal emphasis.

"So we are working diligently to make that happen," the man finishes, not hearing my interjection. Or perhaps not choosing to, which makes him as sensible as he sounds.

"For which we're grateful, sir," Maximus responds with a furtive glance up at the security camera's lens. I have no idea why that has me bursting into a giggle, since there's a tiny chance that little camera picked up some viral-worthy footage, but my amusement can't be helped. My boyfriend is *blushing*. And being adorably surly about it.

"Please. It's just Nam," the manager rushes on, exposing his serrated nerves. I surrender the giggles to a grimace, already envisioning what Kell's put the poor guy through. Oh, no. Not just Kell. If Veronica's gotten the time to arrive on the scene too...

"Yeah. Okay," Maximus returns before I can give a proper gasp of sympathy to Nam. But his assurance sounds more like distraction, delivered as he eyeballs the camera again. As soon as I realize he's deliberately positioned himself between the lens and the panel with the control buttons, he's already pushed the red one again.

The car lurches. Around us, pulleys and gears whir back to life. We're on our way again, making my man a hero for Nam and the engineering team. He's spared them from any more of my sister's and mother's impatience, though he's now on the hook for a chunk of *mine*.

Doesn't he know that his nobility is one of the quickest ways to rekindle my hormones? That's when they're operating at *normal* levels.

But now…

Hormones might not be the right word for them anymore.

But searching for that replacement isn't my main concern. Holding myself back from smashing that red button again… *That's* a priority. Shoving down the craving to make him take me again, so wicked and fast and fierce… Major priority, part two. Twice as huge as stressing about Kell and the victory smirk she's undoubtedly prepared to wield as soon as the lift doors slide back open…

Sure enough, here she is. Already tricked out in a pair of classic bowling shoes that actually look cute with the punk-influenced threads that were her choice for tonight, though not straying too far into Rizzo territory. Yet shouldn't she be? Where are the sassy smirk and bowling scorecard she should also be accessorized with?

Why do I practically sprint out of the elevator, taking

the briefest of seconds to acknowledge Namazzi's greeting before dragging my sister to the far side of the elevator landing?

"What is it?" I demand, my psyche crackling with her tension before my gaze registers the taut brackets of her mouth. "Has someone already downloaded the elevator footage? Has Mother seen it?"

Her stare pops wide. "And there's the news flash I needed but didn't. Thankfully, Nam's already on my side of the paid secret box for the night. I'll put him on scrubbing the footage just as soon as we're all clear."

"All clear?" Apprehension rises, all mine this time. "From what?"

Or from *whom*?

But while that feels like the more accurate comeback, the words won't compel themselves to my lips.

"Kell?" I prompt instead. "Come on. A little context for the cagey mystery, Jessica Fletcher?" Though as old-school references go, I much prefer my callback to the beauty school dropout. "What am I not getting yet?"

She still doesn't answer. Not unless a bunch of glances out into the club's public area are considered answers. But she staves off my exasperated huff with an upheld hand, which drops only after a spatter of applause from the main room.

"Okay…good," she finally rasps. "Jaden's here. And Piper too."

"Piper?" My head tilts, weighted by confusion. "I didn't see her earlier. Isn't she supposed to be in London, promoting the new movie?"

"She changed her plans because of this fundraiser."

"I heard that," Maximus inserts. "A couple of the hair stylists were talking this afternoon," he explains to my perplexed glance. "Piper's parents' place collapsed during the quakes. Her mom is okay, but they had to pull her dad from the rubble. He's still at Cedars-Sinai and not doing well."

I shut my eyes, wincing from the emotion that squeezes my heart. "Ugh. Piper's really close to her parents." When I reopen my eyes, it's to throw a more intense look at my sister. "Is she doing okay?"

"Good as can be expected." Kell's lips twist a little. "I think she was happy this party came up, if only as a temporary diversion. She was only supposed to be doing a quick stroll for the cameras out on the step-and-repeat," Kell states. "But she changed her plans again, for us."

I raise a hand along with my eyebrows. "So, officially still the clueless sister here. You're clearly including *us*"—I wag a finger between Maximus and me—"in that *us*, but our immediate plan is a few friendly rounds of bowling so the paps can have fun watching me look like a total dork, and—"

Maximus interrupts me with a rough nibble to the column of my neck. "No dorky Kara on my watch," he growls. "Especially after my invincible pro tips."

Kell wheels back around. "Not going to happen."

And earns herself my instant startle.

The words themselves aren't the issue. They're typical Kell. But everything they're wrapped in…it's not her usual sleek and smirking package. She's issued it as an order. A serious one, at that.

I have no idea how to rebut it, except with a follow-up challenge. "So, you're just wearing those pretty shoes to start a new fashion trend?"

"Was considering it. But then my phone buzzed, and I had to get fake-whiny about some residual pain flaring up in my leg. Piper came to my rescue. She's filling in for me. For you two, as well."

"Huh?" I blurt.

"Why?" Maximus demands at the same time.

"Because the text on my phone was from Doctor Doug." She swings her head to directly meet the new surprise in my gaze. "He's in town. And he wants you to see him right away."

CHAPTER 9

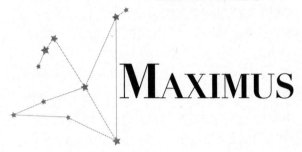

MAXIMUS

WE'RE ABLE TO LEAVE the event with no more major hiccups, and I'm glad about that. What I'm *not* breathing easier over is the ongoing weirdness in Kell's demeanor, which Kara seems to be absorbing at an exponential rate.

Finally, after pretending to be interested in all the stretch limo's fancy features, I swing a pointed glance between them both.

"Okay. What memo did I not get here, ladies?"

Kell cocks her head and narrows her eyes. "Maybe the same one *I* didn't get. Kara? You holding out on us, sister?"

"Hmmm?" Kara looks up and around as if a fog bank has invaded everything between us and the sliding divider. "No. Of course not."

But she's saying one thing with her syntax and another with her testy tone. A direct callout on it won't be my wisest choice. Instead, I wrap a hand around one of hers and gently murmur, "This is supposed to be a happy thing, right? Isn't that still the general consensus for new baby news? Did I get it wrong? Are you feeling otherwi—"

"I'm fine, okay?" she bites out. "Let's just…get this over with."

Apparently, I'm out of touch about the proper definition of *fine*, as well. It's not remotely what she sounds like, but I shelve the point for the greater good. And, frankly, my own. Reconnecting to my inner calm and strength will ensure I can help her in whatever way she'll need. Or, more accurately, allow.

Our driver turns down a side street, heading south off Sunset. Our route zigzags at Santa Monica and then San Vicente Boulevards, taking us past the different-colored behemoths of the Pacific Design Center buildings. In the buildings' reflective glass, I can see details of the early evening scene in the neighborhood. Guys on bikes, girls on phones, dogs tugging at their leashes in the park across from the Center. But what's still so dark for me is the source of my woman's tension.

She was less fidgety than this during the approach to the party. But I'm resigned to my pledge. Silent support and steady strength. Bombarding her with needless questions makes me no better than the mob back at the Pendry, especially that glammed-up douche in the cologne he probably got in a press junket goodie bag. What was his name?

"Gentry." I grunt at myself. It'll have to stand in for the self-inflicted backside kick. "Damn it," I mutter with a triple

underline of apology. "Didn't mean to say it out loud. Just…
remembering."

Kell arches a brow, exposing her glitter-covered eyelid
to a flash of gold streetlight. "You mean trying to shoo the
bug out of your brain so you can flush it for good?"

I'm still determining how to match the excellence of
that metaphor when Kara erupts with a giggle. Not a huge
one, but just as amazing to hear.

"Unbelievably, Gentry did dial back on the obnoxious,"
she says to Kell. "At least a little bit."

"Not what I heard," her sister grouses. "Piper had barely
entered the building before he cornered her with questions
about her dad."

"Oh, my God," Kara utters. "I should have guessed
there was a reason for the bump in his preening game."

Kell's face contorts. "Can we bribe Hades to take *him*
back to hell?"

"Why was he even allowed to stay at the party? Didn't
Piper report him?"

"Oh, she tried," Kell mutters. "But he started citing
constitutional rights. He played back video footage, told
them he hadn't harmed Piper physically, and was just *doing
his job.*"

As soon as Kell tacks air quotes around her last three
words, Kara looks ready to throw her own free hand through
one of the windows. Thankfully, she ramps things back to a
silent fume, glowering out at the busy city streets as we close
in on Beverly Grove. I connect the dots, imagining we're
headed toward one of the medical buildings near Cedars-

Sinai Medical Center, where Dr. Doug's office is likely tucked at the end of some discreet hall.

The conclusion supports the subject my brain has tracked to—one that does deserve a few words of conscious voice.

"You know, both of you—and your whole family, actually—are amazing to me." The sisters' startled stares get my upheld palm in reply. "You've got all the labels and adulation about being the chosen royal ones of Hollywood," I explain. "You're the anointed family. But that lifts you so high onto pedestals that you're no longer human. Incapable of having faults or needing forgiveness for them. It's not like you can book a prime-time interview and come clean about the big family secret."

Kara sighs. "The secret that doesn't do anything to make up for itself."

Kell sneers. "Oh, come on. There *are* the super-keen superpowers, right?"

"Valid point," I interject. "You guys could've inherited halitosis and dandruff."

"Or god-sized biceps?" Kell's crack earns her my darker glare, though Kara's new laugh is worth it. "Uhhh, yeah. I *really* see how lucky we are now," she snarks as follow-up. "Especially because Jaden's too far away to have heard any of that by now."

I relax against the cushion with an easygoing grin. "If he's that keen to build some mass, he's welcome to join Jesse and me at the pit in Venice. It's more tolerable with friends to yell at you."

No more than three seconds after I'm done with the magnanimity, I'm regretting it—as soon as I catch the new sparks that transform Kell's gaze into a miniature force of nature. "Wow. That's so cool of you to offer. Which days do you guys do that?"

"Ermmm…" My hesitation isn't feigned. "We're not tied to a set schedule." And then throw a puzzled stare out the window. "Doesn't look like our driver knows how to set stuff, either. Like his GPS."

"Huh?" Kara frowns. "Why?"

"Because…we're at the mall."

The pause in my answer is from the temptation to phrase it as a question. Her shrug confirms that intuition.

"Oh, right. That *is* perplexing." She swings a glance at Kell. "Didn't Doc Doug pick this one last time?"

Now it *is* time for me to question. "This one? For what?"

"Late summer sales," Kell remarks to her sister. Fortunately, her gaze sobers when it hops to me. "For obvious reasons, the underworld docs don't have traditional, or even permanent, offices. They rotate their covers in every city. The businesses that barely get attention are the best ones, which is why Doug usually goes for his bunker underneath the country club around this time."

A fast snort from me. Can't be helped. "*That's* staying under the attention radar?"

"During seasonal reseeding and marketing for film awards contenders, it is. But lucky for us, Doug likes a hot deal on Gucci better than a martini overlooking the sixteenth hole."

During her explanation, we've rolled to the front of the queue beneath the Beverly Center's gleaming valet rotunda. She presses the button to roll down the window beside her seat, already prepped to beckon the guy with a Benjamin between her outstretched fingers.

"Hi there." She acknowledges his flash of recognition with a serene smile. "We're here for the VIP car detail. And it needs to stay private."

The valet tips a respectful nod. "Of course, Miss V—"

She pulls back on the tip. "Remember the part about *private*?"

"Yes." He flushes. "My apologies, miss."

To our right, a section of the marble wall slides away into a pocket slot. Once the car is all the way inside, the door closes, and we progress through a dimly lit tunnel. After another fifty yards, the light gets better. We arrive at a private lobby that reminds me of a Klimt painting crossed with a silent movie set. It's gaudy and gilded but oddly cool.

Kell crosses the space and knocks on a large, ornate door. Less than a minute later, the portal is pulled back to reveal the one thing I *have* expected from this trip. A clean, wide hallway. Fluorescent lights overhead. Several doors along the corridor, denoted by different numbers.

As soon as we enter, a tall man emerges from one of the rooms. He's wearing a spotless lab coat with a round badge at one shoulder. Well, what I think is a lab coat. It's a well-fitted, double-breasted style, with a black silk tie with a crimson dress shirt beneath it. His thick trendy glasses match the color theme.

"Ahhh. Well, well, well. Look what the expeditious feline has brought to my fancy den," he drawls. "So good to see you lovely girls. Very good indeed. But the daredevil bucko couldn't make it, hmmm?"

"Sorry, Doc." Kell uses the chance to rear back, away from the guy's overeager loom. "We brought a decent substitute."

"Ahhh. My goodness, better than decent. The famous professor, in the flesh. How do you do, sir? How do you do, indeed? They call me Doc Doug, but I'm sure you know that already."

I'm pretty sure I haven't forced out a smile like this since Mom coerced me to be her date for a co-worker's wedding. I was promised prime rib and cake. I got two hours of awkward dancing with bratty girls.

"Maximus Kane. Good to meet you as well, Doctor."

I manage to sneak a glance around him, which gets me a double dose of Valari-style giggles. They're savoring the fun of watching me commiserate with their mystery jitters from the car. So much for hoping either one of them will take pity and throw me a safety line from the Dr. Doug Zone.

"Well, then." He turns from affable social salon host to all-business physician in a couple of seconds. Now more than ever, my brain compares him to the genius scientist from *Jurassic Park*. Nicknaming test tubes one second, breaking down velociraptor genes the next. "Shall we figure out what's going on here, Kara Beara?"

I seize my chance to get even on the teasing chuckles.

"Kara Beara?"

She glowers. "He's known me since I was a kid, all right?"

"And it's way better than the one he has for me," Kell whispers.

"And how have *you* been, Mademoiselle de la Kell? You didn't say much in your text."

Kell stuffs a moan into the depths of her throat. "You can say I told you so, but only without laughing."

Kara catches her from following the doctor down the hall. "But what *did* you say in the text? Everything? I mean…the thing you and Jaden suspect?"

Kell rolls her eyes. "On a phone that Veronica may or may not be tracking? I didn't even say the issue had to do with you, though I think he snagged *that* hint as soon as we walked in."

"Of course I did." Though Doug's a good ten feet ahead, he's already stopped and opened an exam room door. The tiled corridor has likely become a megaphone for Kara and Kell's exchange. "Not to say that it didn't come as quite a stunner. But the perspicuities are plentiful—and, I might add, endearing."

"Wait," I cut in. "Perspicuities? So, you can already tell?"

I work at keeping calm about it. No need to get riled if the man's just drumming to his own beat and experimenting about who'll follow. But if he's already seeing evidence of Kara's condition, has anyone else noticed? Anyone like that weasel, Ellery Gentry? Worse, to spies we might not have seen? Was Hecate there, lying low along the walls? Or even Hades?

"Ssshhh. There, now. Let's all take a second and go to our peaceful trees." Doug smooths the air with a reassuring hand. "I only had a vague inkling based on mademoiselle's urgent text." He ignores Kell's grimace, continuing the explanation while waving us into the exam room. "Requests for immediate appointments are usually due to one of a few health concerns. As soon as there's a strapping but terse boyfriend along for the visit, the list gets whittled."

At least that prompts Kell into a spurting laugh. "Strapping. Ohhh, yes. I'm going to borrow that one."

"Don't you dare," I snap.

"Terse is the more important part," the doctor adds. "That's a warning as well as an observation, my boy." A one-two punch that's given with his assessing gaze down my stiff form. "Demigods can keel from coronaries too. On the other hand, demigods aren't supposed to be capable of *this*."

"Huh?" Kell demands. "Why not?"

"What facet of that answer do you want?" the doctor flings. "Biblically, hell and its denizens are solid *no no nos* for the heavenly ones. Socially, there are a lot of awkward extra layers. But most logically, there's the biological factor. Demon females are as fierce and formidable as lionesses, but even a lion will collapse if an elephant tries to get busy."

Kell gives up her confusion for a sharp snicker. "Hear that, mister? You're an elephant. Now *that* sounds better than *terse*, right?"

"Yes, but your sister's also a hybrid," Doug says. "That changes up the dynamic, I'm thinking."

"Thinking?" I break in. "Or *knowing*? The signs you're seeing. What are they?"

Dr. Doug extends a gentlemanly hand to Kara, helping her onto an elevated chair. The thing looks more like a bar stool than an examination apparatus.

"The instinctive hand on the stomach, already protecting what's inside," he replies. "And of course, your own posture toward her—attentive and focused…"

"But Doctor," Kara says, reaching for me. "He's always like that."

"Hmmm." He's as clinical as if she's commented on my insomnia. "Well, there's always…*that*."

I'm not sure what words spill out of my mouth once I follow the direction of his nod toward Kara's middle. My muteness is inconsequential, since Kell's eruption is better at expressing things for us both.

"Holy. Shit."

Another assessing hum from Dr. Doug. "I really don't think *that's* it."

"Okay, then. What is it?"

My syntax seems confrontational, but the look on Kara's face holds me to a civil tone. The O of her lips and wide circles of her eyes are painted by the red and purple light that's thrown up onto them…

Reflections from the glow that sneaks past the seams of her button-front blouse.

A light that begins in the center of her belly.

A gleam that intensifies as her shock becomes a smile. And that smile, a delirious laugh. "Well, talk about *wow* factor."

CHAPTER 10

Kara

"**W**HAT PART OF THIS do I get to call the weirdest?"

Kell's quip percolates a response from deep inside me. From the same place that my little twig has suddenly gained some blooms, sending a spectrum of color up to my ribs and down to the crests of my thighs. One moment, I'm a blue butterfly, soaring above those beautiful new branches. The next, I'm as brilliant as one of its flowers, my orange petals blowing in a summer wind. Then I'm part of that wind, carrying purple clouds and golden rain over the landscape of my spirit. A valley that's filled with so many of those amber drops I'm bathing in all their incredible warmth.

And hope.

And life.

And love.

A love I've never dreamed of—or dared to dream of—before. A fulfillment I've never imagined. A union I've never conceived. The only magic that comes close to it is my memory of when I knew I'd fallen in love with Maximus. I was in my car, stopped at a red light between Beverly Hills and his place in South Park. It was the first night we'd spent together, though I had yet to know that. I was only hoping he'd let me in—though not just to his apartment. He was already a part of *my* heart and soul, and I was desperately hoping he'd accept both from me. My heart raced and careened, preparing to see his glory again...

Now, my heart races with a different love. A new kind of connection.

I'm smitten with nothing but...light.

With *everything* that is *this* light.

The glow that grows stronger once I slip out the bottom three buttons of my shirt.

Beneath the fabric, the shape of my stomach is unchanged—a truth that's slightly strange because I'm tempted to look for the colored halogen light that's undoubtedly been shoved under my skin. But if that were the case, the light wouldn't be widening as I run my hand over it. Nor would it be doing the same for Maximus's cautious touch, only to shrink and fade once Dr. Doug pressed in.

"Ah!" he exclaims. "Ahhh...haaa! Seems we have a shy one here, folks."

"A shy *what*?" Kell demands. "You're seriously not going to declare this diagnosis now. You haven't done an exam or run any tests."

"Sister. My sweetness." I reach out and wrap my hand over hers. "He doesn't have to."

She snaps a sharp glare. "Excuse me?"

"Nothing to be excused for." When my attempt at glib only gets me more of her stern pout, I wrap my fingers around hers. "Hey. Come on. Where's the let's-get-excited bandwagon you and Jaden were riding last night?"

"Stopped in its tracks," she retorts. "Because there's something on them—like an offspring who's already decided the rave has started and has popped open the glow sticks to prove it."

Dr. Doug jabs her with an amused side-eye. "You're really not aware that you did the same thing to your mother?"

Kell's eyes are wider than an electrified lemur's. "Huh?"

"Oh, yes. All three of you," he emphasizes. "Except the glow was strictly red." He shakes his head with a quiet laugh. "The poor thing. By her last few months, she was wearing corduroy and velvet in public to keep everything hidden."

"Oh, dear," Kell mutters. "And that was before either of them were trendy again."

He arches both bushy brows, sage as a skinny owl. "That woman has made innumerable sacrifices for you three."

"No shit," Kell rasps. "I had no idea."

"Me neither," I say. "But why only red? What does that mean…about this?" I gesture toward my middle.

"Undoubtedly, it's royal blood," the physician says. "A bloodline that stretches up to the All-father." He hardly pauses before barreling on, almost as if remembering an important point. "So your mother really never told you about the *floga moro*? Why?"

"The baby glow," Maximus quickly translates.

"Which *is* pretty incredible," Kell finally admits. "But again, why were we never told about it?"

"*There's* a real mystery." Maximus follows it up by cocking a puzzled glance my way. "Veronica never said a word to you three? Ever? Not even teasing you about it? Not guilting you into doing the dishes or emptying the trash because she had backaches for months because of you?"

"Okay, okay," Kell grouses. "Maybe it's time to get back to the subject at hand. Like the fact that our little sprout can't wait to get to his first rave?"

"Huh? *Oh!*" My gasp layers atop Maximus's grunt, as our baby decides that two glow sticks aren't enough for this brilliant light show. The new shade is a dark but lush gold, stranding through the reds and purples with defined purpose. Like smoke that's about to form a shape but never does so.

But the message is still clear—with an intent that twists my gut in six new ways. Probably more, once I dare to look back up at Dr. Doug.

The man has no more soft chortles for us. Not even a slightly pleased smirk across his wide, gawky lips. His deep-set eyes take on a buggish life of their own as they ignite with curious light. No. I can't even call it that.

He's no longer curious about this.

He's anxious.

Unsettled.

It's an energy I've never experienced from him before, so my senses are unguarded against it. It's violent and strange, as he suddenly stares like his stethoscope has turned into a snake and sunk into his carotid. I lean back, overwhelmed to the point that I can't feel anything from Maximus or Kell. My senses are swallowed by the weird viper that's latched on to my doctor. The demon who's never hit me with anything but warm reassurance and dorky doctor humor.

There are no jokes to laugh at now. And, despite the summery shades continuing to rise from my belly, my blood is the temperature of a glacier.

Even as my gaze locks into the thick caramel of his.

His eyes, normally soft and melty, are now sharp-carved and hard. But he saves his most incisive blade for his next determined question.

"Is there something *else* you want to tell me, young lady?" He kicks up his thick brows. Then hitches them even higher. "Something that's not listed in your medical file quite yet?"

Without thinking, I spread both hands across my middle. I have nothing to hide but everything to protect. I tell the doctor as much with my head held high and my spine held straight.

"Well. A funny thing happened between the ninth circle and downtown LA."

His mouth falls open. "The ninth circle? You were in Hades's castle?" The air snags in his throat before I'm done with my nod. "Why? And when? And how are you back in this realm afterward? Don't tell me the bastard simply let you walk free? No, no. Of course he didn't. There's got to be another glitch…"

"Close," Maximus inserts. "Not a glitch so much as a

book. With gold binding…pretty similar to that shade." He points at the gilded swirls that sneak up between my fingers. I fan them out a little, allowing a small smile to break free.

"Books *are* magic, you know," I murmur.

"Books…are magic." Doug's iteration is a softer sough than mine, though his whirring energy slams me like he's brandished a pair of nunchaku. He jerks his head back up, indeed looking like a fascinated ninja. "Do you mean a *book*? Or are we talking a grimoire here?"

Kell shifts from one foot to the next. "How honest do you want us to be about that?"

"You ever hear the expression about not keeping secrets from your doctor? Although in this case"—he backs up and shucks both his coat and stethoscope—"if my suspicions are correct, I'm no longer speaking here as your doctor."

Air leaves Maximus in a brief but harsh rush. "Which is what kind of a development, exactly?"

Doug frees an equally rough snort. "One I hope you'll take seriously."

Once more, cold snakes slither through my nervous system. I clutch my stomach tighter while noticing a similar glower take over my sister's face.

"And I thought I was digging my brain out of a quarry before," she grouses.

I push off of the exam table. "We're listening, Doc… errr, Doug."

I don't know how we couldn't be. I've watched this demon keep his composure zipped tight through a lot of rattling circumstances, including Mother's bout with demon-exclusive malaria and at least five of Jaden's broken bones, to know that whatever's sputtered his wick has to be a daunting gale. It's almost why I didn't prompt him for more but also why I forced myself anyhow.

What's worse than a doctor brandishing a *fatal diagnosis* stare like this one?

When he's pulling out the same look *without* his doctor stuff on.

"Please," I urge again. "What is it? I mean, you've now got all the important details from this end, so—"

"No." Doug doesn't alter his expression even as I pin him with my flummoxed one. "No, I don't have *all* the important details."

I let my brows pinch tighter. "So, what else do you…"

He drops his chin but reinforces his stance. His response comes with equal deliberation to each syllable. "How did you get out of hell? *Exactly* how you did it?"

Maximus leans forward. "We already told you. The book—"

"You mean the grimoire," Doug points out.

"Yes," I say. "It was a grimoire. It…spoke to me."

"Spoke to you," he echoes. "As if it were *calling* to you?"

I squirm, feeling as if he's peeling back veils from those hallowed moments of my life…in my head. Times that feel intimate. Special. Too rare to be discussing while sitting on a table covered in paper, beneath lights that illuminate my pores like mineshafts.

"Yes," I finally stammer. "That's a lot like how it felt, I guess. The letters on the cover were glowing, and the air around me was practically vibrating. The feelings intensified as I got closer to the book."

"You weren't even touching it at that point?"

"No."

He closes his eyes like I've confessed to watching the sky fall. "And it had Hecate's name embossed on the cover?"

I'm still too fixated on his features to answer right away but then I realize I don't have to. Yet again, he's already detected my answer by simply studying *my* face. But also again, he's brought out the mental fighting sticks to flick my way. It makes me flinch this time, but Maximus ropes an arm around my waist to keep me from falling off the slippery table paper.

"Oh, my, my," Doug mutters. "This *is* getting interesting."

"Interesting?" Maximus retorts. "Or troubling?"

"A bit of both, to be honest."

"Which means what?" Kell asks.

"What'd you do with the grimoire when you returned?" he asks Maximus and me. "Assuming it came back with you?"

I wince. "Yet again, how honest do you want us to be about that?"

His hands, down at his sides, start to flex against the air. "To be clear, you don't have room to live in lies about this."

"It's stored safely," Maximus states without fanfare. "Only Kara and I know where it is."

"Good," Doug says. "Keep it that way. Don't even tell *us*." He indicates between Kell and himself with a finger, though returns right away to nervously flexing his hand in time with the other one.

Kell goes for an opposite vibe, tightly folding her arms. "I'm probably going to regret asking, but why? Is that spell book all that important? Or powerful?"

"Both," Doug replies at once. "That grimoire is potent. It's imbued with the energy of ages past. The forces that can only be gathered from centuries of siphoning its content from the human race."

Kell angles her head up and away though maintains a steady regard at the doctor. "Excuse me, but *huh*?"

"Beings like us—demons and gods, ghosts and angels, mages and witches, and even semi-breeds—we're awesome and amazing, but that's because we've been *allowed* to be through the dominion that the humans have handed to us since the beginning of time."

As he circles his scrutiny around, some of the color returns to his face. It's reassuring, even if it's far from his usual geniality.

"This isn't saying that we'd be wholly different creatures if history went down differently. Powers are powers and magic is magic, no matter how the earth turns and who's here to observe it. But there were times, thousands of years ago, when none of our forces were considered *special*, per se."

Maximus's forehead scrunches. "So, everyone on earth was mystical in some way?"

"Hmmm, not exactly. There were plenty of normals, though not at the same ratio as there is today. Every typical human probably had three or four *a*typical neighbors, friends, and even family members. Anyone care to stab at what the current ratio is?"

"Not especially," Kell mutters.

"Smart answer," Doug returns. "It's daunting, and there happens to be a few theories why. The most obvious is recorded in human history itself."

I nod though don't wish to be doing so. "Basic mortal fear." I also don't want to be saying that part, but rotten weeds have to be exposed to the sunlight just as ugly history has to be remembered along with its nobility.

"Another excellent observation. And, regrettably, accurate. As the human race grasped more science and invention, they also enjoyed their new feelings of control and power because of it all. In many ways, rightfully so. The mortals' openness to new ideas and implementations has developed their realm into the largest of them all. But, for the first time in history, that cosmic real estate is shrinking. All the innovations are starting to block humans in. Filling them with grand delusions and insane fantasies."

"Not disagreeing," I say. "But still wondering how it all even started. And why?"

Doug is nodding before I'm done, already expecting my query. "Imagine you're alive a few million years ago, say, and you're living in a cave and eating raw rabbit for dinner every night."

Kell shudders. "You asked the question, sister. *You* go for this one."

"Suddenly your friend shows you how to make fire with flint and some sticks," he continues. "The miracle of fire is no longer a mystery to you. In the grand scheme of the universe, that hasn't stopped fire from actually being a miracle in its own right. But now you start to look at your *other* friend... The one you've always revered because they can create fire with a snap of their fingers—a little differently. Why were they bestowed with this ability and not you? And why don't they just create fires like everyone else? You start to resent them."

"And perhaps worse," Maximus murmurs.

"Exactly. You question having to bow to them when they walk by. You question how they came by their ability at all. Then you make up nefarious stories about that, and those stories feed into darker fears. You share those stories with the other normals in your village, and soon you're *all* afraid. And that dogma starts to trickle to new generations."

"And that's the energy that's empowered Hecate's grimoire?" Kell asks.

"Part of it." The doctor cocks his head. "The other parts are spun from more complex superstitions, as well as the general direction of the human race as a whole."

"General direction?" I echo. "Headed for where?"

"The last two centuries alone are that best compass," he asserts. "Humans have learned so much. They can now split atoms, eradicate diseases, send vast information on palm-sized devices, and program robots to cross minefields. There are even serious conversations about colonizing other planets."

"Yet all those minefields still exist," Maximus concludes. "And the race to space is still all about who can build the prettier rocket. Humankind has never come so far yet been more polarized. Or more proud of it."

Doug barely moves and doesn't have to. His features broadcast his total agreement. "Because they've never been more afraid."

"A truth for sure." Kell frowns and rolls her head. "But *the* truth? Yes, everyone's afraid, but not necessarily of *us*. Demons and vampires are now the stars of poster art, streaming hits, and fan fiction. Gods and witches are being romanticized and exchanged like playing cards. All the creatures people used to hide from at night are just—"

"Being called by different names." Doug rearranges his expressive brows as if getting ready to turn that into a question but doesn't. His tone remains an adamant drill. "Instead of fiends, hags, bogeymen, and Lucifers, people are ducking and hiding from anyone who wears odd clothes, looks like a deviant, or speaks a language that sounds suspicious. *Different* has become the new *sinister*. It doesn't need the night to scare people. Not anymore."

Kell coincides a harsh breath with the end of his statement. "Which makes stuff scarier for us too."

Doug scowls her way. "As it should, scamp. As it should."

Despite the ominous direction of our exchange, Kell looks ready to throw down in response to the endearment he used during our childhood checkups. I yearn to join her, returning to simpler times and lighter concerns. But deeper instincts are already speaking, enforcing the feeling that we don't have that kind of time to burn tonight.

"I appreciate your honesty, Doctor. *We* appreciate it." I add the last while again reaching for Maximus's hand. "Now I guess it's time for us to figure a few things out."

"And quickly," Doug says, his syllables even sterner. "But, I'd most strongly recommend, quietly."

His last qualifier punches past the point of nunchaku. It's a katana now, breaching the air like a dangerous whisper. His features are just as ominous, set so rigidly that I'm riveted.

"How quietly?" Maximus issues the inquiry with the same gravity. Even without my abilities, he's aware of the same subtext.

Doug's lips twist. "You remember the day Jaden tried that stunt on his skateboard and landed on his face instead? And how paranoid your mother was about it leaking to anyone because he was up for that new TV series?"

Kell scoffs. "You think we'll ever forget?"

"Well, quieter than that," he returns. "And yes, I'd even seal off the dome of silence from the grandparents-to-be."

Maximus takes a stiff breath. "My mother has no trouble keeping secrets."

"But *their* mother is close friends with a chunk of the underworld high council," Doug states. "And while Veronica can be a triple-locked safety box of intel when she wants to be, how long do you think she'll be committed to silence about her first grandchild, a one-of-a-kind blend of demon, demigod, mortal, *and* magic?"

My stomach wrenches up into my throat. It's not a new feeling by any stretch, but it feels eight hundred times more intense outside the safety of Maximus's apartment and the security of our little confidence. Outside the space of those who already know what Hecate is planning.

Does Dr. Doug know too?

If so, what have we risked by coming here in the first place and entrusting *him* with my new…situation?

There's only one way to find out.

"Is there a big reason for being concerned about that?" I ask, freaking about riding the line between being casually intrigued and outright paranoid. "I mean, aside from the obvious?"

The physician tosses a double take. "Isn't the obvious enough?" His caramel eyes get unexpectedly warm while his posture keeps tracking toward frigid. "Once the powers that be are in full knowledge of your announcement, it'll spread through the underworld faster than a *Daily Spill* hot break."

My stomach lurches. Its flows of color, until now so steady and even, are now frantic flashes. "As far as the bottom circle? Even to…the castle?"

"Oh, especially there." He clears his throat, already knowing I can feel the pogo sticks his nerves are suddenly favoring. "I'm sorry, scamp. No way, no how do I enjoy being the Debbie Downer for your visit. But I'm also not going to be the reason you're not prepared."

"For what?" Kell doesn't waste a second to get it out. It's not the same for Doug's pause, stretching several more seconds than the comfort zone for us all.

"For the chaos." Though now that he's started, he rushes into the rest. "The mayhem that's going to ensue once Hades, then every deity in every realm, learns what kind of a creature is about to open its eyes on this world."

His last word is nothing but a long, terrified screech.

Not his. It's the one from inside my mind, peeling back layers of my spirit. Again, not because I *don't* know all this. Because now I'm forced to hear it as reality, a truth I can no longer stuff away into the corners of my brain.

I have to face it in full.

I have to accept it as the reality, however surreal, of every decision I'll make in my life again. My very marrow confirms it. But most of all, every fiber of my heart does. I already love this child with parts of my heart that I never knew existed. Expanses of elements beyond my mere feelings, a part of me beyond just the flesh we share. It's visceral and elemental and spiritual. But most of all, miraculous.

Poetry I can't be reciting right now. As soon as Doug continues his explication.

"Claiming you, and that hybrid gem inside you, is going to be the most valuable prize on everyone's list," he asserts. "Both of you will be their key to controlling a majority of the realms. And because of that, to conquering them. With the mortals so fractured, they'll be effortless to split apart and subdue. Any detractors will be easily hypnotized by your offspring, who'll be well-schooled in how to speak the words they all want to hear. After that, Poseidon will have no choice but to surrender the seas. Or, more likely, he'll form an alliance with the new ruler through marriage. He has plenty of sirens, of all genders, to offer—"

"Stop." I croak it past all the screams, still exercising their torque around my throat. "Please. Stop."

Though I know he's not specifically painting my child into that scenario, he's not ruling out the possibility either.

But there's *no way* will that happen. No way will my beautiful son—nor especially my daughter—grow up the same way I did. Painted into a cosmic corner. Knowing that the only path out of it is by submitting to a spouse they never chose. A lot they never asked for.

It's too much. Just like the love I never imagined, my fears churn into pain I never fathomed. Panic I never could have conceived.

Tears blur my vision as I drop my gaze to my white-knuckled grip around Maximus's fingers. To the mush of his answering clutch to me.

But only my oscular view is muddy.

In my mind and spirit, the way is blindingly clear.

I lift that brilliance up to Maximus, blinking to clear my eyes from the oncoming floods. But they spill down my cheeks as our stares lock, the flow increasing as I latch on to his captivating cobalts—and the unblinking purpose in them. Intention that matches my own. Determination that powers new words to my lips.

"We have to get back to the grimoire. And then I've got to figure out a new place for us to hide."

Though Maximus's quick nod is exactly what I need, Kell's rough scoff isn't. My sister is ready for my whip of a glare, waiting with one bounced brow to go along with her sardonic grimace.

"Hide?" she drawls. "Because that worked when you were stowed beyond the Styx...and then in an unmapped witch ashram...*why*?"

My stomach is back to flashing like a stressed disco

strobe. Doesn't stop me from pushing off the table, stomping to the exam room door, and yanking it open like I'm the dance club bouncer preparing to evict a wasted sailor. But instead of Kell, I rush Maximus and myself out the portal.

"So we're supposed to throw in the towel and let the whole pantheon have at us?" I bark over my shoulder anyway. "Because between us, these walls, and this disgusting hospital tile, I'm not okay with that."

Doug, who's bringing up the rear of our line, stops hard enough to make his shoes squeak. "Hey. I just replaced this tile."

In the meantime, Kell rushes up to match my pace. "You think *I* want to see the sapling chopped up for everyone's fire? But I also don't believe in wasting time on doomed plans."

I stalk across the waiting room. "I don't think *failure* is a word the grimoire likes either."

"The grimoire that was created by Hecate. Who is a goddess created by Zeus. Who is, last time I checked, the baby daddy of *your* baby daddy and able to find him no matter where he goes," she counters. "So now that we know it, let's work together and brainstorm something better than a hide-and-seek reboot."

I don't want to tell her that she's possibly right. Not yet.

Instead, I turn to where an escalator is located beyond a pair of flawlessly polished glass doors.

"Doesn't this mall have a few maternity stores?" I venture, already anticipating my sister's predictable derailment.

Kell's low moan ricochets off the glass walls. "That's a

damn dirty move, mama. But this time, and only this time, the judges are allowing it. Ferragamo texted to say they got the new peep-toe booties in my size. I swear I can hear them calling my name."

"Your partner in crime is here, scamp." Doug grins. "Never met an inch of Italian leather I didn't like."

I look at Maximus, a step down from me on the escalator but still several inches above my sightline, while swinging our joined hands. "Guess you're stuck with window-shopping for elephant dresses with me, Professor. That is, if you'll lend me your jacket to hide our little glowstick?"

A surge of a good mood hits me, waiting for his response. There's so much good literature to mine for windows and elephants that I'm excited for what fun quote he'll pick.

My hopes are scuttled as soon as the space between his brows knits into deep canyons. And his gaze, like a river through those canyons, gains Prussian shadows—as he fixates on something far down the way, past the modular silver furniture and shiny bustling stores.

No. Not something.

Some*one*. A someone I recognize too.

"Mom?"

His query hardly carries any sound, and I already know why. Because Nancy Kane isn't alone.

She's with someone else. A figure I also recognize but am instantly uneasy about doing so.

CHAPTER 11

MAXIMUS

"MOM."

I wait until Kara and I are much closer, about ten feet away, before stating it again. This time, not as a question. This time, imbued with the force of what I'm really feeling.

Shock.

Confusion.

Ire.

Stuff that would probably already be escalated to more if I weren't so worried about hauling Kara's arm out of her socket with my run-walk across the mall's polished concourse. Though I know my fierce beauty can take it, I'm not a dog driven solely by my balls and tongue.

Not like other beasts who are leaving their trail across all this white tile.

"Maximus?" Mom grates, slamming a hand to the base of her throat. But only one, because her other is fitted against the broad palm of the male by her side. The one now soaking in my glare like a Jedi staring down a red saber. Calm to the point of maddening. "And Kara. Hello there, sweetie. So nice to see you again."

Liar.

How does she think any of this is *nice*? For any of us?

Okay, maybe Mom *is* actually enjoying herself. Grudgingly, I take in her dewy face and fancy attire. She's in a form-fitting dress that flares slightly at her knees, with strappy shoes in the same shade of gold. Her pretty features are framed by hair that's been carefully, possibly professionally, styled.

Damn it.

I almost seethe it out loud.

My mother is glowing, and it's likely due to the tranquil asshat next to her.

"What are you kids doing here?"

Aha. Though there's only a trace of antagonism in Zeus's murmur, I'll celebrate it. Aggravation loves company, even if it's in the form of my father's elegant smirk and matching attire. The guy's tie is an exact duplicate of Mom's shoes, while his ivory three-piece suit coordinates with her clutch purse.

"I was about to ask you the same thing," I declare past clenched teeth.

"We're…ermmm…just grabbing a quick drink," Mom blurts with a breezy laugh. At least I think that's what she's going for. All of her syllables wobble as if Kara and I have come up on her and Z in their underwear.

In his dreams.

Only, by the way Mom ropes her hand around his elbow and hangs on like glue on a kid's valentine, maybe her dreams too.

I barely stifle another growl. Maybe it's time to refocus on the girlish gleam in my mother's wide stare. Even the little smile teasing the corners of her mouth.

"In the mall?" I finally manage an awkward laugh. "Come on. It's a valid point, right?" I usually bow to Jesse about all things high-end and boozy, but even I can look around and see nothing but a couple of casual coffee places and a gourmet boba stand.

"Actually, it's nonsense," Z states evenly. "We just stopped here, trying to decide between the winery or the whisky tasting room."

"Which both sound amazing."

As Mom gushes it, Z cants his head toward her. He smiles, looking past the point of smitten, before fingering one of her curls and tucking it behind her ear.

"Whatever strikes your fancy, *agapi mou.*"

This time, my larynx doesn't stay cool about suppressing my snarl. It's not a complete eruption, but enough to ensure my father snaps his head around and up. This time he's more Geralt of Rivia than Gandhi on a good day, with his flashing eyes and a curled lip. And once again, I withhold from the mental confetti and fireworks. But barely. It shouldn't feel so good to be making him forget his tender words for Mom, but it does. Maybe he'll look deep enough to see it in my answering glower.

"We need to have a few words, son." He jogs his head toward an alcove near a wall-sized abstract painting. "In private."

"Great plan. After you." While I sweep out one hand, I squeeze Kara's with the other. "Be right back," I husk, pressing a pair of reassuring kisses into her furrowed brow.

On the way toward my father's side, I silently vow not to be the direct cause of her furrows after this. At least for the next nine months—or however long this is all going to take.

Also during my walk, I gaze up at a huge modern painting consuming the wall—and make yet another inward promise. This one's for me alone. My brain isn't going to keep emulating this furious explosion of paint across a house-sized canvas. I won't keep doing this to myself, or to Kara. We both deserve bet—

The affirmation is severed between one stride and the next.

I'm no longer making resonant bootsteps on pristine white flooring. My feet are sinking into moss-covered ground that stretches between columns at the exact same placement as the support pillars for the mall. But they're not gleaming acrylic poles with LED lighting. They're formed of Grecian stone, similar to the look of Labyrinth's architecture.

Though this definitely isn't Labyrinth.

The beach club vibes are replaced by the most verdant forest I can imagine. Where Honey Bacchus's realm was an elegant establishment that sprawled sideways, this is a multi-layered tower that pushes upward, similar to the mall's architecture. The plants and trees encircling the bottom floor, where Z and I stand, are a shade of dark juniper.

Six floors up, the hues graduate to something more like a Palm Springs golf course. Along the way, there are hanging flowers in shades of pink, orange, and purple that seem to glow from the inside out. The same color theme is present in all the dining tables, each set for two. Every table occupies an intimate bower of its own. A few are positioned around an interior lagoon fed by a waterfall that's twice my height.

The place is, in a word, breathtaking.

Though, right now, I'm not losing a molecule of oxygen over it.

Because I also notice that every private bower has a curtain across its backside. And I'm ready to bet that those curtains aren't a polite way of hiding the servers' stations.

At once, I round off to confront Daddy Dearest. "Is this your prelude to getting me tanked again, Pops? Because I promise not even the good stuff behind *this* bar will make me forget what moves you're pulling with Mom."

Z glides a hand down his tie. "Fairly certain even you wouldn't be able to handle the ambrosia in this place, my boy."

"Which is *what* place, exactly?"

He casually sweeps his hand. "Welcome to Oread."

I take another look around. I don't want to be so impressed by the place, but am. "Named after the mountain nymphs, I presume."

He nods. "One of whom, Nomia, is married to our own Medea." He indicates toward the female behind the bar, who studies me with a fierce bright-green gaze. Her eyes match many of the streaks in her hair, which are varying shades of spring forest colors.

"Medea," I echo, dipping a short bow. "Nice to meet…" I trail off and step back. "I don't think she likes me."

"Oh, she likes you a lot," he drawls. "She's just trying to determine how fast it'll take you to pass out from her concoctions." He jogs his chin with a commanding flair. "I'm afraid he won't be staying around long enough for the fun, Mistress."

While Medea takes the time to grumble in return, I throw a curious glance around the rest of the bar, which boasts a column of swirling clouds in place of Labyrinth's fire tube. The atmospheric spire is reminiscent of the tornado from *The Wizard of Oz*, with actual items swirling in its vortex. But instead of trees and cows and a cackling witch, it's all fresh fruit. Before Z and I turn away, Medea leans back with lithe arms to grab an apple and a pineapple from the swirl. Without faltering, she throws them down and chops them up with the speed of a cooking-show contestant. During the whole process, her keen gaze never falters.

"All right," I say at last, watching the willowy woman scoop the fruit chunks into a blender. "So why are we here?"

"Two birds, one stone," my father explains. "I need to make sure the staff has prepared my table to my specifications. Good enough time to also deal with the burr under your saddle."

The *burr*?

My mind spits it out, but my throat is suddenly incapable

of sound. Not even a worthy snarl. But since he's started things rolling with the yippee-kay-yay bit, I welcome some new fantasies of drawing a Winchester on him.

Instead, for the sole purpose of being the good son my mom raised, I compel myself to use my words.

"Your table. Because you're not just taking Mom out for *quick drinks*, are you?"

There. Those are words. I just draw the line about agreeing to be civil with them.

Zeus doesn't say anything. He doesn't have to. It all makes sense now. The Sonny and Cher outfit game. The starry-eyed gaze locks. And, in Mom's case, all the gawky date night small talk.

"Your mother deserves a nice night out," he says past tight lips. "She's been working nonstop since Hades turned this city upside down."

"A point I'll easily concede."

"And you want a medal for it?" He flags Medea with a finger, and the bartender twists her multihued hair up into some kind of fast but fancy bun. At once, she's switched from bartender to hostess mode.

As she takes another second to stow her apron and circle toward the bar's flip-up exit, Z angles a little more toward me.

"So listen. I'm only trying to—"

"Don't." At last, I can no longer keep my growl trapped in. "I know exactly what you're trying."

"Okay. Well. That's actually good." He jumps a brow entirely too easily. "In that case, you must also be aware of how happy it's making your mother."

"You mean up to the part where you break her apart again?"

His stare becomes an icy storm at midnight. "*She* wielded the hammer, damn it. *She* smashed us apart."

"Because you gave her no choice!" I finish it with a harsh hiss, aware of Medea's approach. "Because Hera and her harridans were turning the *dream life* you created into a fucking nightmare—for us *both*."

"She could have come to me!"

"And you'd have done...what? Marched into your wife's boudoir and called her out? Razed the room with a few lightning bolts? Ordered her to stop harassing your mortal side dish and her bastard son? Expected Hera to actually listen and obey?"

"Yes." As soon as the word spews from him, lightning-like sparks erupt around his head. The restaurant's boughs and leaves, stretching at least half a mile above us, tremble as if expecting a violent cloudburst. "*Yes*, damn it. I'm her sovereign husband. Her consecrated king. Hera *will* be loyal, dutiful, and tractable to my hand!"

"Wow." I rock back, folding my arms. "Well, *that's* pretty...swell. And, I'd say, the perfect vibe for winning over Mom, who's been looking after herself, her son, and wards full of patients for the last twenty years."

My remark brings him up to a froth. He's breathing like a bull to the point that I expect sheets of rain, even in here, any second.

"Your mother and Hera are nothing alike."

"So miracles do exist in Olympus." I resettle my weight into a solid brace. "But if that's supposed to make me feel better about you in the Gatsby get-up and the Romeo eyes…"

His fume fades as fast as it struck. He takes his own turn at cocking a hip and dipping his hands into his front pockets. "I don't expect you to understand. Only to know that I looked so long and hard for Nancy for a reason." He fills his chest with air. "I do love her, Maximus. More than I've loved anyone in my existence. And I promise you, with every striation of every cell in my being, that I'll take care of her no matter what."

I tilt my head, intensifying my scrutiny on him. He doesn't flinch. Even his hands leave his pockets, dropping next to his thighs with tight determination. This energy… I've not felt it since the first moment he set foot in my apartment and initially laid eyes on me. He's stripped off the royal urbanity. An emperor with no clothes. He *wants* me to see him like this, vividly exposed. Brutally honest.

"I see you mean that," I finally utter.

"Thank you."

His shoulders relax. Poor guy. He really thinks he's done here.

"But I already doubt how you'll back it up."

Sure enough, new tension shoots up his spine. But his voice continues as a calm flow. "She doesn't just deserve the beauty of tonight. She should start enjoying the rest of her existence. So, I'm going to build her a new home in Olympus. This time, it's going to be a palace. Every feature she wants and more. I've had the location reserved for a while now. It's in a valley that even Hera doesn't know about. Your mother will lack for nothing there, Maximus. She can do all the things she wants to. Reading, gardening, painting…"

"No."

Before half a second passes, I long to take it back. Not the word but its severity—and the bullet of panic driving it in the first place.

In reply, Z makes the restaurant tremble again.

Even Medea, with her proud posture, looks ready to do the same while quietly gesturing toward a table in the corner with lighted votives and a bouquet of the rare green orchids that are Mom's favorite.

He thanks the graceful attendant in a quiet tone. His rebuttal to me is equally toned down, but only in volume. His indignance is dark and savage in his throat.

"No? That's it, hmmm?"

I jog my chin but harden my stare. His intent is all too clear—to push every one of my buttons as possible—but I won't make it that easy. He's my father, but he's never been my *dad*. Not a shred of that history is here to mess up my mind.

"You heard what I said. Two simple letters. *N* and *O*."

His features tighten. So do his fists. "So…*no*, you don't want your mother to have the life she's richly earned? The home she's worked so hard for? Or *no*, you don't want her to be fully happy and fulfilled? To never lack for anything, ever again?"

He's looking more like Gatsby to me by the second. At the same rate, I'm feeling more like a bullet in the chamber, newly knocked by a firing pin.

"Do you really think I don't want any of that for her? *All* of that?"

"Then what, exactly, is your problem?" he charges. "You're staring worse than the damn gorgons, when I've just declared I want to take your mother away from her hovel and make her my adored *agapi* until the afterlife takes her."

I suck down a hard breath, accessing my ultimate self-control to ignore how he knows about Mom's *hovel*. That's before my attempt to address the intimate endearments he keeps insisting on.

Somehow, in some way, I return his unblinking surveillance—even as he pushes in closer to me.

"You hearing me?" He's near enough to clasp his hands over my shoulders. "I want to give her paradise, Maximus. I swear it to you on my balls."

At any other time, under any other circumstances, I'd likely give that declaration more credence. The All-father putting *both* his balls on the line…that's some meaningful stuff, as my fifty-plus half-sisters and brothers would likely help testify. But here and now, all I can offer the man is a tighter regard than before.

"Yeah?" I finally return. "And what if paradise isn't there any longer? You have a contingency plan for *that*?"

Z cocks his head. Lifts half a brash smirk off the upper end of his mouth. It freaks me out, reminding me too much of a mafia boss in a cross-assessment with an underling. I'm nothing like that to him, and I know that, but the uneasiness is persistent.

"What are you getting at, son? Tell me. I command it."

At once, my muscles flinch in protest. They're serving my mind, which yearns to tell him where he can put his *command* and every vain assumption behind it. But timing is an essential life skill, especially when doling the sting of humility.

"Olympus...isn't safe."

His tawny brows push toward each other. "Bullshit. Who fed you that nonsense? Was it Hades? Certainly not Poseidon..." Just as angrily, they jump back up. "No. I'll bet it was Regina Nikian. I should've told Ares to yank her home sooner. Couple of decades of gossip magazines and reality TV, and even the most loyal soldier will hatch all sorts of insane schemes."

"No," I protest. "You're looking in the obvious crevices." As if manifested from the purpose of helping my point, a multicolored spider creeps clear of a seemingly small fissure in the stone wall near my head. But when I hold my hand out, the creature climbs out and fills my palm. "The most dangerous foes hide in the friendliest places."

"What?" he spits out. "Feed me *facts*, boy, not poetry. And put that beast down!"

I lower my hand to feed the spider into one of the fern banks along the grass. "Hecate," I state, straightening and confronting the rebellious expression I've fully expected. "Yes, *that* Hecate," I go on. "Your ally hasn't been feeling the supportive vibes lately. Best I can guess, she hasn't been feeling them for quite a while. Your adventures away from the palace, along with Hera's retaliatory antics, have been a drain on the whole pantheon, as well as the lesser deities."

His head jerks as if I've punched him.

Here comes the humility.

"My adventures? Do they mean the days and months and *years* I put in to ensure harmony among the realms?"

I hike my own brows, my only defense against spewing with a laugh. "Do *you* mean to really use the just-business-trips line with one of your bastard kids?"

He spins away in a silent fume. For the next few minutes, I'm playing the waiting game while watching the violent rise and fall of his hunched back.

"All right. What's her plan?" he finally mutters. "I'll have all of it, right now."

I bristle but smooth it out with an actual chuckle. It has to be better than my first instinct, to smack my father in his pretentious face.

"Okay, sure. Let me get right on that. I think I have all her strategic plans in my back pocket here..."

"I'm sorry." He pivots back around with a morose head shake. "You deserved none of that. I don't do well with broadsides."

"Don't know anyone who does." I see the ante of his apology, which likely didn't come easily, and raise it by a quiet reassurance. The kindness is a necessity considering what has to come as my follow-up. "And I wish I could help you with more details, but we know very little right now.

Only that terms like *war* and *sacrifice* are being woven into conversations that reference battle strategies and rearranging shadow constellations."

"Who? The Iremia *ministras*?" His stance stiffens. "They'd never."

"They already have," I counter. "In order to hasten the moment that Kara and I met each other."

There's a sound from beneath his breath, shooting like a profanity but in a strange combination of languages, before he switches to something intelligible.

"They've played with cosmic fire. Tempted spectral dangers even I cannot control."

A lot of air gets hauled into my lungs. I expel it before drawing more, but the extra oxygen doesn't help me with my response. Not this time. Not at this massive crossroads. Even with my pulse pounding through my ears, I know that this time is the occasion to listen to my father. His rasp has just told me so. This isn't his first time hearing a piece of news like this. Or being this freaked about it.

When the king of the gods is drained of all his color in ten seconds, a guy is wise to pay attention.

And maybe, in his small way, to offer some help.

"Well, we're pretty certain why they dared it."

"Sure. Obviously." He's so terse about the comeback, I already know he doesn't see the whole picture. "Kara is the ace Hecate needs up her sleeve. The hybrid who assures that hell and its dwellers will take the witches' side in this thing. Hades and his high council will have no other choice."

Another long intake of breath. "Close but not exactly,"

I say during the exhalation.

His gaze flares. His lips fall apart. At last, the total truth is sinking in.

Weirdly, my own breath comes steadier. Watching the turbulence of his comprehension brings an odd comfort. A fellowship we haven't had, even after the disastrous field trip to Labyrinth. Probably because I was never certain—and still aren't—that Z hadn't accepted some private payout from Hades to get me there and ensure I was too plowed to resist the hell god's stabs into my mind and memories. Especially the ones about Kara.

Bitterness I force myself to release right now. An anger I don't even want to hold on to as my father levels his gaze and beholds me with new intensity. With an energy I've never experienced from him before. All right, maybe the ferocity *was* already present, but I refused to see it. Refused to let *him* see past my walls of disappointment and abandonment.

I have to be better than that.

I have to start right now.

I'm not going to repeat this empty distance with my own kid.

Somehow, Zeus reads that across the fresh expression on my face. But even more, he's *hearing* it.

"Maximus," he rasps. "Are you and Kara… Is she…"

Before he can finish, I wave him into silence with a harshly swept hand. The action helps to propel me past him, toward the lagoon. More specifically, the waterfall that tumbles into it.

Because in the sparkling sheets of water, I see her.

Kara.

Spinning from side to side like a kick-ass action heroine, even with her small form buried under my coat—until I catch the alarmed ignition in her eyes. The tense pressure across her forehead. The frantic words that she repeats with her lush lips.

No. Just one word.

Maximus.

"Shit."

I almost tromp into the waves of the lagoon, needing to get to her. Flashing back, too quickly and clearly, to those passages in the underworld when I saw her just like this and worse. When she was begging me to come to her and I couldn't. I struggled and fought and cursed, but hell—and its ruler—were against me. Against us.

"Maximus. *Son*. Answer me, damn it. Is Kara—"

"We have to get out of here," I snarl. "You have to get me back to her. *Now*."

CHAPTER 12

BEFORE I CAN PROCESS that Maximus and Z are back from—well, wherever Zeus phased them out to—my demigod is by my side and hauling me in like I'm about to fall over a cliff.

I nearly fall into him instead, inhaling his musky vanilla and soaking up his protective concern. The moment isn't productive, with just a few seconds left to give him my rasped warning, but I greedily take it anyway. And just as quickly compel myself to give it up.

But not for long. I push away by barely a step before he's tugging on me again, his face as urgent as his hold.

"What is it?"

I shake my head, hoping he comprehends my look of feigned confusion. "I'm not sure—"

"*Kara.* I saw you calling for me. What's wrong?"

He doesn't get it yet. I grit out a smile, making it clear that the expression is nowhere near my eyes. "Everything that we can't let on, okay?"

I want to sob with relief when he finally comprehends, intuiting that the flirty toss of my head is more a directional cue. His scrutiny, following the invisible arrow I've supplied, flies across the concourse. The second the corners of his eyes constrict, I disguise fresh instructions behind a horribly fake laugh.

"*Don't* let her know you see her."

Her being the shopkeeper at a little store that looks like every designer brand signed a licensing deal with Iremia.

Standing there, opposite of her usual boho flow style, is Hecate.

I'm relieved to see Maximus recognize her as fast as I did. At once, he sees past her magenta skirt suit, trendy eyeglasses, and braided-back hair. From the spot where those two braids meet at her nape, her hair is loose but flattened, dropping to her waist like a dark-blond blade. Fitting metaphor, since I'm wondering if shock can sever a person.

Shock…and incredulity.

Is that store even real? Or has the goddess manifested it to spy on us? If the latter, did she really think the CEO regalia would fool us for long? And what happened to her agreement about giving us some breathing room?

"Okay. Lady Macbeth's back before her cue. But why?"

As usual, Maximus distills the point better than me. Also as usual, he pivots with grace that tempts my imagination to redraw him as a mighty knight in the faraway court he's just invoked. But there's no time for those fantasies. Not a single extra second.

"The twiglet and I have been stressing over the same point." As soon as I stealthily flip one side of his jacket, exposing how my belly now aspires to be a brake light during rush hour, his gaze bulges. He steps in, working with me to ensure the glow is completely hidden.

"Did anyone notice?" He whips his gaze around, like I was a minute ago. "My mom—"

"Didn't see anything. I made sure of it. Actually, I'm thankful for it. Having to keep everything buttoned down for her was probably why I didn't turn into the mall's new light show."

"But she suspects something," he murmurs, again fixing his regard on Nancy Kane. "I can see that already."

I place a hand on his forearm. It's like a branch petrified from tension. "I told her I had a stuffed mushroom at the fundraiser and it didn't agree with me. It's not far from the truth."

His blues, so worried and intense, drop back to my face. "All the more reason to get you out of here. Can you text Kell? Tell her we need to leave?"

"She's probably waist-deep in shoe boxes right now. Even if she heard her phone, she'd ignore it."

"Then can she find her own ride home? Or can we ask the doctor to give her a lift?"

I want to tell him both options are fine—Kell's nose is a reliable front line of defense, and Doug has helped every Valari out of worse binds than this one—but something else scratches at the edges of my intuition.

No. Not scratching.

Creeping.

A weirdness I can't figure out. An energy from someone, newly arrived in the building, that throws my senses on a frazzled fence. I'm not afraid, but I'm definitely not ready to hum along to the lullaby-like tune from the pianist in the courtyard below.

I wrap a protective hand against my middle. The other stays solidly clutched on Maximus.

As soon as Kell rises into view, carried by the escalator from below—

Without a single shopping bag on her arm.

More concerningly, so is the retail diva glimmer behind her grin.

Most alarming of all, so is her shopping buddy.

Dr. Doug isn't even bringing up a distant but good-natured rear. But Kell hasn't returned by herself. I get that much from her forced smile before even tapping into her wonky energy.

What. Is. Going. On?

"Funny thing happened on the way to Ferragamo," she grouses for my ears alone. There's no time for a return quip since her companion is already moving into both our personal spaces, complete with a cloud of perfume and a nervous Chihuahua under one arm.

"Mother," I manage to mutter. "It's…uh…you."

Veronica chuckles hard enough to make the dog sneeze. At least I hope that's the case. The tiny animal is exhibiting huge interest in my stomach.

"Last time I checked I was, darling."

"What are you doing here? The fundraiser… Aren't you one of the co-chairs?"

Kell jogs a brow. "Told you she'd ask exactly what I did."

"Then good thing my answer hasn't changed," our mother replies. "The drivers talk, you know. When mine found out that yours had been instructed to come here, I was terrified Kell's leg had gotten worse."

"So you left a major society event to find out?"

Mother doesn't flinch about my incredulity. An earnest reckoning takes over her face. I even feel it from her spirit.

"I said *terrifying*, didn't I?" she snaps softly. "And in case you haven't noticed, I'm trying…to get better at all this. Being your mom in the ways that matter, instead of the obvious stuff."

Kell's high-pitched chuff is a great representation for both of us. Fortunately, Veronica gets the teasing purity right away. Even she has to know, in some small way, that to most mothers, the obvious stuff *is* the important stuff. Things like stressing about their kid's health to the point that they leave a major Hollywood party to track their daughter down.

Which would, right now, be the coolest—except she's got the wrong daughter, the wrong health plight, and the *really* wrong perception that she can be of help with any of it. At least not yet.

So how much of that do we give away to her? If any at all?

I dart a glance at Kell, pleading for direction. She's ready to do more than that.

"Okay. We appreciate it," she offers, extending a hand

toward Mother. "But I'm fine, as you can see."

Veronica nods, conceding that point—but not all of her mission. "So, you girls decided to leave the fundraiser before the photo ops were finished, with your brother flying the whole Valari banner during the bowling game, to do exactly what?" She taps a foot. "Don't think this coy twins thing is going to take you far either. Doug might be wrapped in his little Ferragamo frenzy right now, but you know he'll eventually talk to me. The inevitable doesn't have to be your enemy."

"Why do I feel like I should know what movie that's from?"

I'm as surprised as my mother and sister when Maximus's mother accents her interruption with an easygoing laugh. Anyone within ten feet of this conversation, empath tendencies or not, is likely aware that none of us are thinking *easy* right now. But the woman's smile stays open and deferential.

"Or perhaps the line is an original?" she says, nodding toward Veronica. "Wouldn't doubt that. Kara's a smart and beautiful girl. I have no doubt her mother is the same way."

Veronica tilts her head the same direction, though her expression isn't jaunty. "Excuse me. And *you* are?"

"Oh, goodness. Where are my manners? Hi." She extends a hand. "I'm Nancy Kane. It's lovely to meet you, although it seems I'm doomed by a ships-in-the-night thing on getting acquainted with all you busy Valaris."

Her attempt at humor is lost on my mother—no surprise, since it coincides with Zeus's fresh appearance at Nancy's side.

"Well. It seems the mall *is* the place for all the cool kids—and pooches—tonight. Nice to see you again, Veronica. And you too, little one."

I'm astonished to see the sour twist of my mother's expression become more melty—and even more surprised when her socially testy Chihuahua nudges Z's hand for a repeat ear scratch.

"A pleasure as well, All-father," she says with a cordial nod, seemingly copied by the dog. I think it's Calliope this time, who's prettier but pickier than Crius. It's not the largest thing to think about right now, especially as we all look on while Z wraps an arm around Nancy's waist.

I trade a quick look with Kell, who's clearly sharing my Mother's paranoid reaction to the move. But after a couple of seconds, our stress vanishes. Z's affection is like an approval seal across Nancy's forehead, softening Veronica's stare to an outright smile.

"Your majesty, if we've interrupted anything... important...please don't let us—"

"No, no," Z cuts in, lifting what's supposed to be a casual smile. But nobody here, especially and obviously my mother, is believing it. "Of course not. As a matter of fact, this might be advantageous timing." He circles around to reach for Maximus, drawing him—and me, by way of my latch on Maximus—close. "Isn't that right, son?"

For a long second, I'm too dumbstruck by the sight of my man next to his parents to comprehend anything else. *Wow.* With the towering stance, tawny hair, and arresting blue gaze, it's clear Maximus got a huge chunk of his father's

DNA. But the noble bone structure under it all, along with the kind ridges at the corners of his eyes and mouth, are all Nancy.

The recognitions make my head spin. My throat go dry. This obvious evidence of what he and I are about to do—bringing a living, sentient being into this world—hits me harder than the roof caving in.

Thankfully, as soon as Nancy speaks again, the rough moment fades.

"I was just thinking the same thing, Z."

But the woman's kind tone and bright smile don't dull the jab of her inference. Her good intentions are weak persuasion against the memory of Dr. Doug's warning.

Until we figure out a way to balance peace between the realms, Twiglet Kane and I aren't anywhere close to safe.

Not that Nancy is getting that exact point yet. Instead, she pivots toward her son with a cute but challenging wink. "Well, Maximus? Are we calling this right? Might this be an auspicious moment to have your loved ones near? Perhaps for a very special…announcement?"

Somehow, Maximus manages a neutral veneer, and I avoid swathing a hand to my middle. But our efforts are wasted. The point bashes Veronica like a punch.

And doesn't stop there.

Like the world's biggest bad penny, Hecate suddenly pops up on our perimeter again—at least forty feet closer. And this time, there's a new piece of spare change next to her.

I jerk around and back, not happy about the unnerving jump scare.

Who is she?

Not another Iremia *ministra*, as I would assume at first glance. But I don't know her at all. Her spirit is too cautious and guarded, even after my gentle prods. The resistance is an unnerving contradiction to her outward beauty, with her huge eyes, long nose, and full lips balanced into an arresting overall beauty. Her titian hair, in a half-up style, is as long and curly as Hecate's. At the ends, the intense crimson blends into various shades of obsidian.

But none as dark as the depths of her pupils.

Those eyes that settle on me, intense and unblinking, and don't flinch even after my mother visibly startles. I look her way for a second, hoping to probe for a small hint about our guest's identity, but Veronica jerks her head with violent emphasis.

Not now.

It's impossible to keep her stress from compounding my own, especially when the new girl does a glance-exchange thing of her own with Hecate and I still detect just thin threads of their energies. Nothing substantial to go on, even as the goddess fully faces us with her portrait-worthy serenity. That smile, so smooth and pretty, that's practically coercive with its comfort. But I know better now. I have no choice.

"Well met, then!" Hecate brings her hands together with a tiny smack. "Our timing seems to be perfect now. An announcement? Of the special kind?"

"No." Maximus slashes a hand up, matching the ferocity of his interjection. "Nobody said anything close to that.

Mom, I love you, but you're rolling toward a conclusion—"

"In the same direction *I* am?"

Veronica's blurt gets a fast scoff from Kell. "Not sure Maximus's mom is playing that coy about my leg, Mother."

"Who says I'm referring to your leg anymore, dear?"

Kell's breath snags. Through her supreme effort, no one hears it. But oh, how I feel it. Every new shard of her agitation. And alarm. And the snark she's already preparing as her default reaction. As if Mother isn't going to see through that like one of the mall's spotless windowpanes.

"Wait. You think that just because we bugged from the fundraiser—"

"You mean one of the most important industry parties of the week? The *month*?"

"Whatever." Kell's huff is glaringly forced. "You instantly assume that our excuse is—what's the word again—auspicious? Even *sus*picious?"

Veronica wheels around with fluid grace. Crosses her arms with matching aplomb. "All right, then. What *would* you have us assume, after being assured it's not a medical or fashion emergency? And seeing how nobody's even cried their makeup off…"

"Valid points." Nancy adds a chiding frown at her son. "Don't pretend this confuses you, mister. I know fancy parties aren't your thing, but neither is skipping out on a chance to help people. Unless you're hiding the big wagon somewhere close by?"

As a groan and a blush take over Maximus's face, I drench Nancy's with a curious stare. "The big *what*?"

That's all she needs to keep going. "Many years ago, some kids in our building found a wood shop cart in an alley. Maximus was in high school by that time and working regularly with Reg and Sarah at the store after school, but he always found time to give them rides in that old thing. Goodness, how they loved it." The wistful tint in her tone matches her newly adoring smile. "You've always had such a magical way with children."

"Interesting. Kara's the same." Veronica brings on my turn to groan, though I manage to clamp down the sound as she goes on. "She never turned down a chance to help with her brother and sister. So many maternal ways, even when she was young."

"Maternal."

The echo doesn't belong to Nancy. Or even to Hecate. Our mystery girl is the one offering the new observation, in a voice as fervent as her stare but confectionary as her beauty. She steps around, hands out as if she's used to fluffier attire than her pencil skirt and secretary jacket, and regards me with a tilted expression.

"Hmmm. Yes. *Maternal* is most accurate, I think."

I pull in a sharp breath, yearning to answer her with an intent glower.

Who are you, and why do I care what you think?

But fate spits out its own retort in the form of the fresh energy taking over Nancy and Veronica.

They agree with her.

Ugh, ugh, ugh.

I funnel my answering glower into a new glance at Kell.

Help. Help. Help!

Thankfully, she's in motion after the first hail. "All right, all right." Her hands flatten across the air as soon as she works her way in front of Mother. "You're right. We left the Pendry in haste and on purpose. It was all my idea, okay? But it came from lots of love in my heart."

"Why?" Veronica demands. "Love for whom?"

"These two, I would imagine."

The beautiful stranger is at it with more unwelcome input, as I struggle to convey past my thudding throat and muddy equilibrium.

"Sometimes people need to be pushed in the right direction, especially if big, scary decisions are involved." Kell beams a confident grin around the circle. "And I'm a *very* good pusher."

Just like that, my heart's balloon of sisterly gratitude is nearing a pinprick.

"Kell," I warn.

"Kell," Maximus growls.

"Kell?" Nancy rasps.

"*Kara?*" Veronica blurts, already inching closer. "Big, scary decisions? Of what kind?"

My sister rocks back on both heels.

"I insisted we come to the mall because these two need to look at rings. I mean, you can't start planning a wedding without rings, right?"

Now I'm twisting the balloon—and exploding it as fast as I can. I use the figurative rubber remnant to hypothetically wring her neck.

CHAPTER 13

MAXIMUS

WITHIN SECONDS, KARA'S NAILING her sister with a glare so intense, I can practically hear its message in my own head.

Are you out of your mind?

I step around as Kell thickens her answering scowl, hoping to be a human smokescreen for them—at least as far as Mom and Veronica are concerned.

And, of course, Zeus.

Who, the next moment, ensures that *no one* forgets he's here—by snapping his fingers hard enough to whisk us all back to Oread.

"Well, well, well." It's no surprise that Hecate speaks first. "The day gets more interesting."

"In ten words or less," remarks her mysterious new companion.

I wheel around to stab a look at my father. He's standing in the same spot we occupied a few minutes ago, knowing and serene. The sight makes me pull some of Kara's agitation into my energy.

"Z." I hike my stance to match his. "What is it now?"

If his answer is anything besides the word *necessary*, I'll be officially hunting for an exit.

A plan that's scuttled as soon as my mother's delighted laugh floats into the air.

"Zeus? Oh, my goodness. This is all by *your* design?"

"Well, I had some help," he explains with the face cream smoothness of a pretty game show host. "I mean, just a little."

"You're being modest," Mom protests.

Bullshit, my brain retorts.

"It has so many of your touches," she says. "All the little things that make the difference."

Sometimes I really hate it when she's right. But now that I track her gaze and view things anew, I have to grudgingly agree. There's a lot I've missed—perhaps that I chose to. But I admire it all now. Elements like the Greek embroidery on the napkins, the laurel wreath carved into the bottom of the reflecting pool, and the subtle smells of thyme and jasmine in the air. It's all a pretty classy love letter to Greece.

But not just that.

Not tonight.

I also see that those ornate napkins are held by rings embedded with cartouches. The orchids on their table are embellished with lush papyrus. Along with the Greek Island scents, there's the savory tinge of falafel and kebab.

Wow. How did I not see all this before?

Oread might be a massive homage to Greece, but tonight it's getting a sizable visit from Egypt.

The land in which the two of them fell in love.

No wonder he's so confident about Mom accepting his invitation to run away with him again.

I'm revving a long glare to tell him my own answer is still a giant *get lost*, but it never materializes. Not when the man only has eyes for one person in the room. Not when he turns to her with so much adoration, it does something strange to my anger. Something that feels like a slushie in the sun.

"The difference here is you, my *agapi mou*."

And now I'm in danger of becoming nothing but sugar water, watching how the king of all the gods chooses instead to be the disciple. How he stares at Mom like he'd turn this place into a full shrine for her if she asked. How that leads to uncertainties about how I've seen him all along.

Has real love been the reason why Z has searched so long for Mom and me? Has he really been trying, in his own odd way, to reconnect and make up for lost time? Mom and I had to leave Olympus so fast. What if that ugly surprise left a twenty-year hole inside him?

A wound I could never understand…until the second I embraced the reality of becoming a father myself.

I'm so consumed by the epiphany that I don't notice Kara grabbing her sister's elbow.

"I'm so sorry for the interruption." She turns to all of us with a determined look. "But Kell and I need to visit the ladies' room. *Now*."

Mom and Veronica give identical nods of understanding. Z, already knowing not to argue when that many females are in such wordless solidarity, points toward a spot past the curtained tables.

"It's just through…there…"

It's doubtful the sisters hear him past the first syllable. Because Kara's dragged Kell into the elevator and pushed a button with more force than a gamer going up against a boss.

Rather than wait for the lift to come back down, I rush toward the stairs that climb right next to the shaft. Since they're a free-floating artistic touch to the place, it's easy to follow the pair to Oread's top floor.

The three of us arrive within seconds of each other. Good thing, since Kara stomps out of the elevator with more words clearly ready to go.

"Damn it, Kell!" She doesn't wait for her sister to turn around. "You really went there? With a serious face?"

Her sister pauses before executing a flawless turn atop the large, light-up leaf embedded in the floor. "So what *did* you want me to do there, darling? Let Twiglet Kane's grandparents simply figure out the whole story, with Hecate standing by for the full scoop? Guess I really could've gone there, right? Is *that* your point?"

Kara's already past the landing, starting to pace across an area that's likely populated with tables on nights when Z doesn't deign to buy out the place.

"You could've thought of something. You were on the ball enough to come up with the engagement announcement."

Kell narrows her eyes. "Which wasn't going to happen at some point or another?"

"That's not the point."

"You're right. It's not. You should be suffocating me with a hug of pure gratitude right now. *That's* the point."

"Even as Veronica and Nancy are downstairs penciling in wedding dates?"

Kell lets that one drop to silence while tension permeates the air. As the wet-leaves-on-fire energy grows, Kara wheels around and glares. A truculent V takes root between Kell's eyebrows. She steps back and sinks into a gold wicker teardrop chair that's suspended from the slanted ceiling.

"Hey there, Professor Kane," she drawls at last. "Perhaps you'll do better in the making-my-sister-see-sense department?"

Kara huffs. "*Sense* and *recklessness* only go together in rock songs."

"So do *glowing* and *baby*." Kell pushes out of her chair just as swiftly. "You guys were all but painted into a corner, darling. I simply blew open the perfect exit window for you."

Kara drops her head between her hands and rubs her temples. "Holy…shit. What are we going to do?"

"What are you talking about?" Kell snaps. "This is a perfect solution, okay? From a lot of angles than the obvious."

"*Perfect?* Not exactly what sprang to my mind first. Or even second."

"As I can clearly smell." Kell wrinkles her nose to

match her forehead. "But look around. Who do you *not* see, still circling their little wagons around your campfire?" She pushes back the edges of my jacket, still hanging around Kara like an oversized poncho, to poke at her sister's stomach. "Veronica Valari and Nancy Kane. That's who. And if we pick a poofy enough wedding gown for you, we can probably get away with pushing the big day to December. That gives you nearly three months of breathing space, for the most part—which is also, hopefully, enough time to outline a workable plan of dissolving Hecate's grand scheme."

"The big day." Kara echoes it in a rickety mutter while defeat takes over her posture. "A poofy gown. Oh, God. I already don't like it."

"Because you're already forgetting the *breathing space* part." Kell tugs at the jacket's lapels until Kara jerks her head back up. "Hey. Listen to me. All you need to do is tell Veronica and Nancy that you trust their judgment about stuff and that they should do whatever they feel is best—"

"Is that supposed to make me feel better?"

"From a strategic standpoint, yes. From a major cringe standpoint, not so much."

"Yeah, definitely not feeling any better," Kara mutters.

"I know." Kell's tone softens, now as benign and knowing as her touch. The kind of sentience that only a sibling can possess, after years of conversations the world will never be privy to. Not even me. "I really do know, honey," she adds. "But let's try to manifest a silver lining. Since this isn't going down exactly like Veronica dreamboarded it, maybe she'll change up a few things. Lay off on the pageantry a little bit."

Kara's sharp laugh causes Kell to startle. "Oh, sure. Because that's absolutely going to happen," she quips. "I mean, with a demigod at the end of the aisle instead of an incubus, that changes everything. No need for a speck of grandeur now."

I've been maintaining a respectful distance but now cut into the boundary by clearing my throat. "So…I'm the big, gaudy parade float in the middle of the room? Is that it?"

"No." Kara rushes toward me with urgent steps, amber light flashing from beneath her shirt. "*No*, my love. That's not it at all." Her hands press both sides of my face. "And even if it were, I'd hop on for every minute of the parade route."

Our stolen moment of a tender kiss is pierced by Kell's long groan. "Bordering on TMI, sister. Maybe a few steps past the border."

She ignores the commentary, curling her fingers deeper into my beard. "I love you." And then pulls my lips back down to hers. "And I want to spend my life with you. The next life too. All of eternity, if the cosmos allows."

Though I cherish the kiss as much as its predecessor, I'm the one to inch away first. My intention is to ensure our gazes lock, but I wuss out and fix on the tip of her nose instead. "But you don't want to marry me."

Kara twists her lips. Hard. I know because I'm looking right at them. I imagine Kell's are configured similarly, if her harsh huff is any clue.

"And that is completely my cue to find a way out of here." She slides around behind Kara. "*Any* way out of here. But preferably by way of popping back through the Ferragamo store…"

The elevator doors aren't done closing on Kell before I have her sister in a tighter hold, where she's obligated to look nowhere but up at me. I'm waiting for the impact of her wide but tremulous browns, taking me in with tiny sprints of uncertainty.

"Maximus…"

"Don't." I press a gentle hand to her face. "Let's just move on, okay? You don't have to explain anything."

More truthfully, I don't want her to. She's ready to, as conveyed by the focus in her stare and the urgency in her touch, but her confession will mean I've got to give up mine. That until three weeks ago, I was the one who assumed I'd always be on *her* side of this discussion. The one who'd seen, through so many years of my life, what kind of toll got paid in the aftermath of deep emotional commitment. All the nights when Mom sobbed herself to sleep, thinking I wasn't still up reading under my covers. All the days we'd be enjoying a walk to the store or park, and she'd drift off to a memory that sent rogue tears down her cheeks. All the times I wanted to hug that pain away from her soul but knew even my brute power wasn't enough.

All the times I vowed to never let anyone have that kind of power over me. To never surrender myself that fully. To never make a vow intended until the day one of us died. Which was technically the same thing, right?

Wrong.

I've been so wrong.

But the joy of that concession also brings its pain. An agony I willingly endure as Kara lifts her gaze fully back to mine.

"Please," she rasps. "I need to say it." She seems grateful for the long pause before my small nod, consenting her confession. "I love you, Maximus. With everything I am and everything I will ever be."

I arch both brows. "But?"

"But...marriage...and weddings...those weren't ever quixotic words for me. Not growing up, at least. They were always talked about like transactions. Something I'd have to endure. Nothing different than getting my wisdom teeth pulled or going on a press junket for a new product endorsement. It wasn't until I was thirteen, at a birthday party for one of Kell's dance club friends, when I first realized that white lace and promises were supposed to be good things, not sentences."

"Thirteen?" Though my tone is soft, my stare has intensified. I stretch my fingertips into the edge of her hairline. "My God. You were practically an old maid."

"To a bunch of jaded girls from West LA, I was. They decided to show some goopy romantic saga at the party—which apparently, they'd all seen a hundred times before. The movie wasn't half over before they were all passing joints and playing some kind of kissing game with each other. But I couldn't keep my eyes off the screen, especially during the big, emotional wedding scene."

I narrow my gaze. "The movie was that awful?"

She rears back. "It was that *beautiful*. Oh, come on. You

know what I'm talking about, right? Tell me at least one of your girlfriends has forced you to sit through one of those."

"What girlfriends?" I deliver a sound kiss to her disbelieving pout. "Let's just say you can be my first. I've read many of the books they're based on, so that has to count."

I hope for an equally breezy comeback, but the melancholy memory only persists in her eyes. "They all teased me when I couldn't stop crying during the scene," she murmurs. "But I couldn't help myself. I didn't even want to stop. It was…a revelation. An incredible but confusing one. I didn't understand how something I'd perceived as so ugly was actually so wrenching. So wonderful. So jaw-droppingly beautiful."

I hear every word she's saying, but my expression clings to solemnity after her first statement. "They made fun of you? For *crying*?"

She drops a hand to my chest and lightly bats at me. "Adolescent girls giggle about everything from phallic-shaped clouds to soda commercials. You should know this, Professor. Some of them are determined to stay frozen at that age, even in college."

I give up a reluctant grunt. "That's barely an excuse, even on their behalf. But Kell was there too, right? Didn't she defend your honor?"

"Who do you think kept me in a decent tissue supply?" I return. "Though to this day, I suspect selfish motivations. She may be the queen of sneaking feelings past others, but not her own sister. My big, weepy ball was plenty lubricated by what *she* was holding back from those twits."

She smiles through that last part, but it's not without a few fresh tears. I look at them carefully as they absorb tiny prisms, gravity pulling them down until I catch them with broad strokes of my thumbs. Not to erase them away. To treat them like the precious stars they are. The badges of the struggles she's endured, the hardships she's survived.

To much of the world, she and Kell are princesses in a castle on a Hollywood hill. But they're not close enough to see the castle has cracks and enemies are lurking at the ramparts. Even in the form of jealous twelve-year-old girls.

"Well, none of the twits get invitations to the wedding," I whisper, kissing the tip of her nose. "And if you want a day just like the one in the movie, then—"

She pushes fingertips against my mouth with a rough-edged laugh. "What I want…what *we* want…doesn't matter. Your mom will find that out quickly enough too. Nothing will be more important about this wedding than every optic, designed for every camera angle from every sponsor, all conveying exactly the messaging my mother desires. Our biggest responsibilities of the day will be showing up, hitting our marks, and speaking our vows. And likely very little else."

During her rundown, I say little. React even less. There's no need to feed her fuel or put up an argument. Kara knows Veronica much better than I do. For that matter, more than most of the world. She doesn't *want* to be making these assertions about her own mother, as I can see from the contortions across her face, but fighting her own assertions is an even scarier prospect for her right now.

"Oh, my God," she finally adds, backhanding her forehead. "I'm sorry. I'm rambling. And believe me, nobody wants to be wrong about this more than *me*. If Mother really told us that nothing matters more about our wedding day than our own happiness…"

When she extends a long sigh into more silence, I drop my hands around hers.

"What?" I utter. "If that *were* the case, you'd do what, Kara?"

Her head jolts all the way up. She searches my gaze with her own, again with those furtive little sprints of her big browns, until her whole body jerks in the same unpredictable way.

"You're…serious," she states.

"As Charon on the Styx."

"Not funny."

"Wasn't the intention. I've met Charon, remember?"

Her fingers twist mine tighter. "I'll never forget. *Ever.*"

When she looks ready to lose it again, enforced by the dark hell memories that are my own stupid fault, I squeeze her hands in a new way. The rhythmic compressions are a prelude to my roguish grin.

"And now you're skirting the subject. Come on, out with it. What would you do if our wedding day was all ours to control?"

She rocks back on her feet. Not very far, perhaps a few inches, until she starts a back-and-forth kind of swish. It's adorable, but even more so when she arches up to capture my lips on a couple of those girlish pass-throughs.

"Hmmm." One playful smack. "You mean something that doesn't involve a beach and a yurt?" Another kiss, longer and mushier. "And a dog named Bubba, of course."

"Well." On her third sweep up, I pull her in close. "Can't forget Bubba."

She presses up and in, sealing our lips tighter. But I'm glad when she keeps the tongue contact to the barest of touches. Longer waltzes with her tonsils would have my cock screaming commands about getting her prone in the space we seem to have to ourselves tonight.

A conclusion I've grasped with scarily lucky timing.

Kara and I aren't nearly finished with our lip lock before a loud tone sounds from the elevator landing. As we break contact and look up together, one of the leaf-shaped lights in the floor comes to life. Embedded beneath its clear cover are the words *Car Approaching*.

Sure enough, only a few moments pass before the elevator doors slide open.

I expect Kell, stepping out to declare she has no idea how to get out of this secret realm and has Ferragmos impatiently waiting.

Instead, a slightly familiar figure moves past the doors. By slightly, I mean that I've seen her but don't know her. Not even a name.

She's the striking redhead who appeared when Hecate decided to join our klatch back in the mall. From the time the two of them took it upon themselves to just hang out with us, her arrival was a curious occasion—even to Mom and Veronica, who treated her with manners but glanced secret looks at her that were drenched in curiosity.

The same interest with which I regard her now. Not so passively.

"Hello. May I help you…ermmm…miss?"

She casually tosses her long, corkscrewed curls. The black tips on the heavy ringlets are a perfect match for her impenetrable stare. The rest of her face, while strikingly stunning in an ethereal way, is just as unforgiving about revealing her purpose. Trying to peer even half an inch into her is impossible.

A stranger…in more than one sense.

"Not *miss*, all right?" she snips out. "*Please*, not *miss*."

"All right." I revert to a little sheepishness simply from the music beneath her voice. The confidence, couched in vocal harmony, that has me going as still as Kara. "So…"

"You can call me Maiden. Or even Kore." Our visitor pauses after a couple of steps, suddenly seeming like a cautious fairy in some mythical wood. "But most…call me Persephone."

Kara gasps. "Oh *my*."

I'm able to recover my composure more quickly. "What are you doing here, Persephone? And what do you want from us?"

"Only to talk," she replies, full of the same mellow-but-don't-believe-all-of-it vibe that Hecate first gave off to me. "And hopefully, to make friends." That part, she flings directly at Kara. "But even more hopefully, to congratulate you on your nuptials. And to beg that your wedding takes place as soon as possible. At any conceivable cost."

CHAPTER 14

Kara

IF IT'S POSSIBLE, PERSEPHONE'S more striking in Oread's muted light than she was in the mall's flesh-colored floods. But her desperation is distracting from the effect. It takes over her large, intense eyes and rapidly fidgeting fingertips. Clearly the woman's existence, with spending half the year talking to plants and the other wandering around Hades's dismal citadel, has taken its toll on her social skills.

I try to ease her discomfort by lifting a friendly smile. "Well, there's the conversation starter I didn't expect."

"Not a conversation," she flings back at once. "I'm so sorry, but *that* I don't have time for. Hecate thinks I'm in the bathroom taking care of female things. And there's still too much information to get out here." She grabs the bottom of her crisp business blouse, working the hem like fresh dough. "So very much I have to say. Too much, too much."

"Persephone?" Maximus is gentler now. He probably sees what I already have: that the goddess, who's technically one of his many stepsisters, is as stressed about this as we are. "What is it? And who, exactly, do you need to tell?"

"Well...you. And you." She ticks a nod at Maximus and then one at me. "Isn't that obvious?"

"You know what they say about assumptions."

My second attempt at humor harvests me another frown that teeters on dismissive. "After all, you're the golden ones," she rattles off instead. "The new *it* couple. The news on everyone's lips. I mean *everyone*, in *every* realm. I suppose that makes Mother Hecate very right about things. Hmmm. I wonder what Mother Demeter thinks about all that?"

"Wait." Maximus stretches out a hand as if trying to calm a skittish kitten. "Hecate—*Mother* Hecate—she was right about *what*?"

His sharp emphasis brings the goddess's head up. Her eyes bore into him, just as wide and fierce as before, but those blue and onyx depths seem different now. At their corners, little tremors form. The vibrations take over the edges of her lips as well. It's as if Maximus's stress has given her permission to offload some of hers, but now she doesn't know what to do with the relief.

"About...having to help her keep an eye on you. She said it last night when she came and retrieved me from Olympus. I'm not due in Dis for another ten days, but she said *she* needed me early. That it was a job she couldn't even entrust to one of the Iremia diamonds."

Unlike the rest of her revelations, all of that practically pours out of her as one garbled sentence. Halfway through, she scoots her gaze away. By the time she's done, Maximus and I are watching her cut a tense path to the light-up leaf and then back. A couple of times, the elevator detects her approach and opens with that cheery but annoying chime.

"Okay. So," Maximus finally utters. "You…and Hecate…have been basically following us all day?"

A hesitant giggle tumbles off the goddess's lips. "Not while you were at the big Beverly Hills mansion, of course. You Valaris have all those nosey neighbors."

I grimace. "Truth."

"So give us a little credit, Professor."

My frown changes. I bristle by a little, not enjoying her invocation of his title. It's different than when Kell or Jaden uses it, almost as an endearment. Maximus is now, semi-officially, part of the family. Additionally, I'm still not certain this petite *goddess* is who she claims to be. Any cosplayer worth their salt could deck themselves out to resemble Persephone this closely, especially if Hecate loaned her magic to help along the cosmetic process.

I hate thinking that way, especially if this girl is the real thing and expected at the hell king's castle soon, but I'm not living in a Hollywood bubble anymore. Not everyone has my wellbeing at the top of their list. My own horrible stay in Dis, though a fraction of what Persephone is in for, was enough of a lesson for that.

And maybe I'm just grabbing any reason to dodge her main message now.

Which, thankfully, she doesn't seem eager to get back to either. "We *were* at the gala, though," she says, breaking into a surprising smile. "Did you see us? We were in disguise as servers. Can you believe that? I got to take a drink to Timothée Chalamet!"

Just like that, my own smile resurfaces. The moment reminds me of an occasion where Jaden and I got to do the same thing, of sorts. As a prize for a charity auction, we were hired as snack servers at the birthday party for some movie executive's kid. We were teenagers at the time and didn't know any better. Two kids vomited on me while Jaden made out in the closet with the group's babysitter. If, at the time, someone had told me I'd look back on the memory with a grin...

So many things a person will write off as impossible.

So many jokes that life is waiting to play on us.

No greater proof do I need than this very moment.

Standing here with the queen of the underworld, trying to forget that she's all but mandated me to get married before the year is through. In return, only thinking that I want to ask her what Timothée Chalamet was wearing tonight.

Thankfully, Maximus is here to bail me out. "How did you know we left the party?" he asks, his tone as quiet and valid as his purpose.

A shrug from Persephone, along with an irritated frown. "Hel-lo. We were standing right there. You just didn't notice because you'd been *trapped*"—she gives her emphasized word some hard air quotes—"in the Pendry's elevator for so long, and Kell had your attention while Hermes was taking care of the video footage that would've had everyone talking about you for *other* reasons."

I cock my head. My frown isn't as irked as hers, but it's just as deep. "Hermes?"

The goddess nods. "Known to you, at least, as Namazzi Wood."

Maximus snorts. "The mild-mannered night manager?"

"Another illusion you were supposed to believe," she supplies with pinup-girl swagger. "Hermes isn't Hecate's counterpart for empty reasons."

"He's a shapeshifter too," Maximus supplies.

"Summoned to keep me in line, I suppose." Just as swiftly, the poster girl vanishes from her mien. Like a douse of ink wash, she's again struggling to breaststroke through edgy insecurity. "I get jumpy when the time nears to return…you know…to *him*."

The last rasps of her confession are like gravitational magnets on my legs. I move toward her whether I want to or not. I try telling myself that I *do* want to, but the subject matter has other ideas for my nerves. For the very fibers of my psyche.

Just having to talk about this again…about *him* again… is torture. But for the shivering woman in front of me now, even as I take her hands in mine, I endure it.

"I *do* know," I tell her. "You know I do. If I could take away the burden of all this from you, I would."

"No."

Her response is as adamant as the way she jerks away. Though the sorrow persists on her face, there's a fresh stab of stiffness up her spine.

"No," she repeats, more emphatically than before. "You can't take it away. Even if you could, you wouldn't. And you won't." She sets her head higher. "This is so important, I dared to sneak away from Hecate and come looking for you two. Now you have to hold up *your* end." Her gaze sweeps out, boldly scooping up Maximus in its fresh ferocity. "Both of you."

Behind me, Maximus scrapes the air with his contemplative rustle. "By getting married," he concludes, to be answered by a slight repose from the goddess. Not a complete mitigation, but enough that I fully notice. But she shores herself up enough that her jaw is stiffer. There's more conviction in her scrutiny.

"Your wedding is the key," she states. "The event that must save us all."

"Us all," Maximus echoes. "As in who?"

"Us *all*." She huffs, openly frustrated again. "Do you want me to be plainer? Every creature that exists in every realm that you can conceive. Perhaps a few you aren't aware of. That none of us are."

As she speaks, I pivot around toward Maximus once more. He closes his eyes and drops his sockets against his braced fingers. They're among his signs—the ones I know so well by now—that he's struggling to access his self-control. The stuff that, until three weeks ago, was the main tableau of his character. The key point of his pride. Now, thanks to the nonstop chaos I've brought into his world, he's struggling to find it because of a woman barely half his size. And he's doing it willingly.

Just like that, my love for him grows yet again. To heights I can barely measure anymore.

"That's a lot of creatures, Miss Persephone."

"Why else do you think I'm here, Professor?"

She's more resolved than ever. I acknowledge it with a dip of my head while circling back around and stepping forward.

"Few other reasons make sense. I'll hand you that," I offer. "But I'm still wondering...why?"

Persephone's a handful of inches shorter than me, necessitating another defined jog of her chin before our stares fully meet. When they do, I'm more convinced of her resolve. Her irises are streaked with more inky shades than before. Colors that make me feel...miserable. Sorrowful.

"Hecate means to declare war on Zeus. On all of Olympus."

I accept that with no outward change, which openly stuns her. Though I'm relieved to look at a feeling other than her desperation, I'm glad when Maximus doesn't let her extend it too long.

"We know," he says, filling the unsettled silence. "Not with actual proof, though a couple of days of lurking in the Iremia shadows was worth its weight in overheard rumblings."

Persephone swallows as if trying to get down some gravel. "So you heard it from *her* own lips? From Mother Hecate?"

"In so many words?" he returns. "Yes."

Her shoulders drop. Her features crumple. She recovers herself by pushing a harsh chuff up her throat and resetting her jaw.

"I suppose I was hoping for a negation. But I should

have assumed from what she's already inferred…" She jerks her head as if attempting to shake off a nightmare "My word. She's really considering it."

"More than considering." Though Maximus remains where he is, he walks over as if she's been wounded and needs help. I'm tempted to join him. The poor woman hunches over as if ready to steel her hands on her knees. "But… why is that such awful news?" he asks her in a gentle tone. "She's probably already told you that she's got Hades over several proverbial barrels. If push comes to shove, he'll be obligated to align with her. Pressing the hell hoards into service will create a daunting army. If that tips the scales toward Hecate's victory, you'll be queen of a very sizable realm. Likely able to enjoy new freedoms, as well."

"Freedoms?" She rears back up, nearly spitting the retort. "To do what? In what world that will be left?"

Her posture stiffens with every new question she hurls, making her resemble a warrior with a pair of invisible spears.

"If this war occurs, the realm that will die first and be destroyed the worst will be the one that all three of us love the most. The humans will be exterminated. Nothing more than collateral damage. Their grand cities and beautiful homes will be razed, and then the land beneath will be burned. *My* land, Professor. The springtime fields that I have protected and loved through every eon. The reason I endure so many months being ogled and imprisoned by the lord of hell."

The increasing cracks in her voice, warning of tears to come, have me lunging forward. But she slashes her arm at me, a brutal order to stay back as she pins her glittering glare into Maximus.

"*Why* do you assume I want to be that varlet's queen for another second of my existence? Why do you accuse me of caring more about his crown on my head and his chains on my soul more than the fields I bring to life after such an ordeal? The young flowers who greet me with nothing in their spirits but joy and color? Not wanting anything from me. Only wanting to give everything they have to the world. Even to humans who hardly recognize their precious power anymore…"

Gravity loses another half step to me. It's only a few inches but enough time for one of my hands to travel to my middle, pulled by instincts beyond my control.

"I understand. I really do." My rasp matches the shiver in her voice. I don't try to hide it. I don't want to. "More than you think. Persephone—"

"If you understand, then you have to help." She dashes her stare to mine, imparting some relief with the new shades of blue that break through. Though they're as blunt as sharpened steel, it's better than her hopeless black. "You don't want to. I see that, and I know that. I knew that from the second your sister stepped in and dropped the announcement out on the promenade."

"Hey. It's not that we don't *want* to," I persist. "We love each other, Persephone." I step back and scoop a hand beneath one of Maximus's. "And we want to be together forev—"

"Save it. I'm fully aware of all that. I'm referring to Kell's true motivation. The bigger secret you're hiding, which I truly do not care to know in full. That's between you two and the ultimate maker. What I only need to know now is that you're really going through with the *wedding*. That this is really going to happen. And that it will be as big a deal as what your mothers have started discussing."

Even from my vantage point, I can see Maximus's free fingertips stretching and tensing.

"Why?" he demands. "What's this got to do with anything, especially Hecate's war plans?"

She pivots back in his direction. The lighting catches the top of her head, turning it into fire that illustrates her tenacity.

"You mean what it has to do with stopping the clash altogether?"

I'm thankful for his instant and pronounced grunt. The one he saves for occasions when nothing makes sense. Also a trait that's likely gotten overused in the last three weeks.

But I'm not arguing with him. Because I thoroughly agree with him.

"I'm sorry. I don't think we're following."

Not by even half an inch—which makes me pray that she won't pick now for a huff or an eye roll. Her manners might be a little old school, but some quirks are timeless. Relief rushes in as soon as she resettles her stance, as if expecting exactly what I've declared.

"If your wedding *is* an occasion for the realms, then every notable from the realms will be expected to attend."

A new kind of hum from Maximus, which brings

another downpour of comfort. When he follows the sound with a chuff that's almost a laugh, I feel my own lips curling upward.

"And when they're all in one place, we can turn the reception tables into negotiation tables."

As soon as he states it, Persephone beats me to the big smile. "Sometimes, one cannot hope for peace. But one *can* facilitate understanding."

"Which comes from communication," Maximus supplies.

"Which, at this point, nobody wishes to attempt."

By *nobody*, I already sense the goddess is targeting Hecate but not stopping there. If the high witch was the only roadblock to all this, we wouldn't be having this conversation.

This exchange, as bizarre as it seemed at the start, is making more sense to me by the second.

"So, you're referring to most of the Pantheon?" I query.

"*Most?*" She scoffs. "No. They're *all* acting like badger cubs with a stick. Snarling and snapping over pieces of nothing. And not just them. It's the functionaries, cupbearers, concubines, emissaries, oracles, and minions too."

Now I'm fairly sure she *is* referring to Hecate. But like Maximus, I stow possible responses. It's also clear that she's not had a listening ear for a while. Poor Persephone, used to being everyone else's helpmate, is now a frantically furious ball of wildly pacing energy.

"Nobody takes the time to *listen* to each other anymore. If they don't agree with a single comma or apostrophe in another diatribe, they don't just—what's that term nowadays? Burn the scroll?"

"Scroll by?" I offer. "Though yours makes more sense."

She stops pacing. But that only means she's back to funneling her energy differently. As she turns back toward us, her fingers are twisting and her gaze is darting. Once more, the centers of her eyes are nearly black.

"Please." It's only a rasp, but it's obvious how hard the word is for her. Though she bears an unwanted crown for half the year, she's still a queen for all that time, asking and wanting for nothing. "You have to make this happen. You two are the only hope for all the realms."

CHAPTER 15

Maximus

F OR THE BETTER PART of a minute…silence.

And then another minute.

To the point that I actually start wishing for more of Persephone's persistent twitching. I can't believe it, but her consuming stillness is even more unnerving. She's as dedicated to it as the rest of the message she's carried here. I almost envision her in head-to-toe armor, like some medieval soldier delivering an urgent quest to a king.

Except that in this mission, *she's* the hero—who's already shouldering that grand aim. Taking it upon herself, at no small risk from many fronts, to enlist us in her cause. But is her bravery coming at the cost of her sanity? She can't be serious…or expect us to think so.

As weird as the stillness is, I take another moment to recollect my thoughts. There has to be a political way of saying all that.

"Oh!"

But Persephone's the one to shatter her own lull, startling as if something's flown under her stiff suit and bitten her.

"I'm sorry," she blurts, back to her blinking and fidgeting. "Hecate is looking for me. She can't suspect a thing. None of them can. Do you understand?"

"Of course." There's thicker emotion in Kara's voice, matching her urgent steps. She moves as if the goddess's panic is a physical coercion, and maybe it is. She's not even thinking about the flaps of my coat, which open enough to bleed out some baby glow. "Of course we understand. We promise to keep your secret."

Persephone leans forward, sliding her white-knuckled grip up to Kara's elbows. She keeps Kara close, forcing a lock of their stares from only inches apart. She's not blinking anymore. Neither is my beautiful demon, who starts to realize what a slip she's just committed.

"You keep mine," the goddess utters, every syllable distinct, "and *I'll* keep *yours*."

Before I can discern if that's a stone-cold threat or a parting promise, the goddess sweeps around and departs. My steps are nearly in time with hers, as I sprint forward until I'm gathering Kara close. But even then, I don't yank my eyes from Persephone. She's back in the elevator now, meaning she'll turn around and give away some kind of clue...

But as the doors close, she keeps her back to us. There's nothing to note except her determined posture and all ten of her tapered fingers now held steadily at her sides.

But in the last second before the doors fit together, one telling observation.

She's still tapping one foot at an impossibly rapid rhythm.

The edges of my mouth lift with grim energy. The simplest explanation is usually the right one, meaning the petite goddess is nervous about her return to Hecate's side. But if I let conjecture take over, there's more, which is where I start after pressing a consoling kiss to Kara's temple.

"Hey. Don't stress, okay? She needs us more than the other way around, at least for now."

"For now." There's not a note of solace in her raspy reiteration. "Until we're not able to hide the sprout anymore."

I tuck her close, fitting her head beneath my chin. "By then, we'll have a better plan. And a *much* better place to hide. I don't know where or how, but we'll find it. I promise you, Kara."

"But…" She sighs long and hard into my chest. "What if we don't?"

I kick back something between a grumble and a growl, flowing the vibrations into her hair. "Hey. Aren't *I* the token fatalist in this tale?"

"There's a difference. This is realism." She loosens our clutch by more inches than I like, though it's a new chance to behold her full face in its gorgeous intensity. "We've been over this, my love. No place in any of the realms is going to be a haven for us, once all the badgers learn there's something better than a stick to fight over."

I hate the edge of tears around her soft sarcasm, which stings the backs of my own eyes. But we take longer than we can afford to savor the small moment: our ability to seek and find a sliver of light in this quicksand of dimness.

I cup a hand to her cheek. She does the same, scraping her sweet small fingers into my beard. I tuck in my head and slide my mouth along her palm. My gaze never leaves hers—and in the seconds that follow, I'm extremely glad about it.

Extra waves of energy start to shimmer from her eyes. Oscillations of pure fire. Those temperatures climb with her slow, hooded blinks. When her lips part, every blood cell of my human half responds to the sizzling siren call.

Screw it. Every cell of my Olympian half, as well.

I sweep my lips away from her hand and crush them right onto her mouth. I mash them there until she obeys my urgent prompt, opening the rest of her heat to me.

Without hesitation, I delve in. Without remorse, I stroke every inch of her tongue.

Without fear, I lower my hands around her backside.

Before I can squeeze her with enough command, she's leaping up and locking her legs around my hips. I flex my arms, urging her higher. Tighter. Solid enough so I can sweep through a pivot and march toward the darker alcoves of this unused level of the restaurant.

Upon this more detailed inspection, I learn this area is set up more like the interior of Labyrinth, with expansive sofas upholstered in plush fabrics. The colors, dark and verdant, contrast with the vibrant greens that define this level of the atrium. The walls are covered in different panels of marble that are cut to resemble clouds. The whole illusion is that of a hidden garden in a celestial forest.

It's perfect.

I lean over, settling Kara onto a sectional in a far corner. As she leans back, her shiny, dark hair fans against the cushions. Her eyes take on the same texture. They watch my every move like a night sky keeping watch over a growing tsunami…which is definitely how I'm beginning to feel.

I need her.

With all the marrow in my bones, the fibers in my muscles, and the roars of my spirit.

But not for the lusty drive-by that she's clearly expecting. I even move to communicate that, grabbing her wrist as she reaches for the zipper on her slacks.

"No. Not like that," I command with quiet force. "You deserve more. Both of you do."

I'm unsure how she's going to accept that, but I've also forgotten that the woman can see into so much of my heart. That her own spirit has reached across the depths of the Styx and the shadows of dreams to join with it. That even now, when I can't imagine loving her with any more passion, she smiles as if telling me that of course I can…and will. Perhaps very soon.

The wait is going to decimate me. But what an incredible way to be annihilated.

But I'm determined to turn her to dust first. In every way I can.

Starting now.

As soon as I re-form my fingers, meshing them between hers, while guiding her hand upward. I settle her touch across the open inches between the lapels of my jacket, once more using my stare to capture hers in full.

"Open it up." My voice is a grate, but my rising desires are sure to transform it soon. I let the spell take over, pushing more words up my throat. "Then your own jacket and blouse too."

Her fingers tremble. She glances up at me with a knitted brow.

"Do it, Kara. I want to see."

I need *to see.*

The tremors move up, taking hold of her lips. But in all the best ways. Her small smile is my new addiction. Better yet is the confidence that makes her hands deft and swift, taking hold of the fabric layers that are shielding her light. Her *life.*

This miracle that we've formed together.

Glowing even bolder and brighter from the spaces below her breasts.

The sight isn't new, but my feelings about it are. The amazement and wonder that I longed to indulge in the doctor's office but held back out of concern for being her strength instead...they're all here again, only a dozen times more vibrant and explicit. Slicing me so much deeper, as if intent on rearranging all my vitals. Such a direct contrast to how I lay a hand across the gentle sweep of skin that covers Kara's stomach.

As my palm travels left then right, the colors fade into

each other in much the same way they did earlier. The whole spectrum is there, violet and blue melding into emerald and amber, as if our little tree is already trying to bloom in full. Every new shade brings a fresh flow of awe to my soul, as if the cosmos has poured pure starshine through my being. I can't think of any moment in my life feeling any better…

Until I lift my head and look at Kara.

Her tears have collected into full pools in her eyes. In every drop that clings to her lower lashes, I see the same kind of flames that take over her pupils when she's overcome with lust or fury. In this form they're like snow globes, with frosty trees and sleighs usurped by bright ribbons of amber, sienna, and saffron.

For a long moment, I gladly give up my air. What is it to me anyway? Something that gives me life? I understand it all now.

I didn't have a life before her.

I had things to do, nobly labeled as purpose and worthiness. I had fancy titles and experiences and awards. And yes, I had people I cared for, and still do.

But nothing like this. Nothing like the magnitude I attempt to convey now, my jaw and tongue struggling for words that refuse to come. Feelings that mere syllables can't encompass.

"Kara."

I have to settle for phrasing her name as my worship. A whisper I can only hope to inject with the reverence it deserves.

"*Kara…*"

"Ssshhh."

Only now, with the treasuring touch she runs across my cheek, do I comprehend how heavy my own tears have grown. I taste the few that reach the corners of my mouth. I free them from her fingertips by taking those tender pads with quiet, adoring kisses.

"It's all right," she utters past shaky breaths. "I know, my love. I *know*."

I don't believe her. I should, but I don't. How can she fathom all of this? If it's threatening to break me apart with its glory, how hasn't it already shattered *her* like a crystal vase?

I shove away that image by dropping my head and throwing it from side to side. "No," I grate out. "You can't... because *I* can't... *Fuck*." I dig a hand across the top of my head. "How can I say—"

"You don't." Her head is rolling in a slow shake, as well. "You just don't. And that's okay."

"Then what do—"

"You show me."

Her hand, still glistening with some of my tears, again drops to her waistband. With her other, she reaches for the button on mine. In the same coordinated moment, she twists them open. We're both a step further toward freedom. The deliverance that will take us right back to bondage—with each other. Around and inside each other.

"Show me, Maximus. Please."

And I thought my impatience was a living hell before.

With a rough groan, I rear up enough to rebalance

myself. From there, it's short work to get Kara out of her silk pants and barely-there panties. While the glow from her belly has mellowed, the gleam between her legs is like the brightest beam of dawn. It entrances my gaze in matching measure. When will this woman cease to enthrall me?

I already know—and love—that answer.

Never.

Though I don't need an ounce of proof, she supplies it anyway. Her overall shiver is an exercise in hypnosis, riveting my stare toward the glistening triangle that's quickly become my obsession. When she adds to the measure by subtly rolling her hips, the thunder from my throat transforms into a harsh moan.

"Woman." I close my eyes again. It's necessity. Her bare beauty is going to turn my cock into a dagger, destroying the zipper that strains my crotch. "Just when I think you can't lock my heart up any tighter…"

She allows me the trail-off, sending me a sweet uplift of a smile. "Not just your heart I'm interested in, Mr. Kane."

A comeback brims to my brain, filled with pride about how much I love my last name on her lips, but she nearly fell into a panic attack after Kell mentioned wedding rings. There's a lot for us to go over before I propose in the way she truly deserves.

But now *isn't* the time for that discussion.

Now isn't the time for talking at all.

Not with my hands ripping at my fly, hurrying to free the beast from beneath. Especially not as I jerk down my briefs and finally free the bastard.

After one stroke of my fist, I join my vicious rasp to Kara's breathy sigh. With the drops from my cockhead as lubricant, I'm beyond the point of ready. Still, I pause to catch Kara's gaze again. Her adoration is thick in her eyes. Her lips tremble. Her thighs flex along the outsides of mine. The pulse at the base of her neck throbs at her dark-gold skin.

I yearn for the moment to last forever.

I can't wait for it to be over.

"How much do you want, little demon?"

She hooks her heels around my buttocks. With one hitch, she's already guiding my crown between her lips.

"Oh, Professor." Her voice is sultry but playful. "You know better than to ask the class irrelevant questions."

Another yank of her powerful legs. Fine time for me to forget how powerful the little female really is. But it's at the forefront of my mind now, as I push another inch deeper.

Another inch.

One more.

And then I'm lunging completely into her.

My God. So tight. So hot. A heaven spun completely of her. Another moment I long to extend and finish within the same stuttering breath.

Still, I manage to tease back, "Is *that* what this is, then? Class time?"

She nuzzles my neck as I angle over her, obeying the call of her body to mine. "Only if you impose a stiff bell curve."

I chuckle. "Well, that depends too."

"On what?"

"The things you'll do to earn an *A*."

The air in her own throat hits a snag. I swear, when I'm lying on my deathbed, the sound will echo through my senses as one of the best of my life.

"I take great pride in my GPA, Professor. Don't you know I'll do anything not to wreck it?"

And there it is. The best aspect of this woman. The intellect and its nonstop wit that made me notice her in the first place. That made me return to her for more after our first forbidden touch. The contact that brought the currents, so wild and monumental, that I was helpless to resist her ever again. Not that I knew that right away. I was an idiot, thinking avoidance would bring transience.

I'm not an idiot now. Though I can't attest for how she'll describe my smitten smile beamed down at her stunning face as I clench my thighs and stab into her with deeper purpose.

"Anything?" I murmur back. "Even letting *me* wreck *you*?"

CHAPTER 16

Kara

"PROMISE?"

The quip has already cleared my lips when Maximus clarifies the one detail I seemed to have missed.

He wasn't asking an actual question.

So instead, my cute remark is a semi-scream. It rises up and out as he drives hard and deep. I rock my head back and let out another as his swollen stalk pushes at me, stretching me. His rolling thrusts are erotic taunts, rubbing parts of me with merciless rhythm. Tender parts. Quivering parts.

The parts that throb faster and faster, rushing to catch up with his powerful tempo, until every throb of his gets an answering torque of mine.

Until he's groaning into my neck and climaxing into my core. Until I'm clenching and fluttering and flying with him. Until we're sweating and kissing and groaning together, as our bodies speak what will never reach the boundaries of words. A love that shatters those frameworks like the blinding lightning it is. A storm I never thought I'd know—or if I did, would only have one dance in. Rain like this, full and clean and drenching, was never meant to be enjoyed by an incubus's bride.

This man wants to ensure that'll never happen. Maximus wants to make me *his* bride. But how have I reacted? Like a mash-up of Eric Cartman and the girl who turned into a blueberry in *Willy Wonka & the Chocolate Factory*. I'm even tempted to let that energy ride as he gradually eases back on his force, making it easier to moon like I've really turned into a big piece of the juicy fruit.

I have to shatter his illusion.

"Maximus."

My soft but vital tone is the switch to his brake pedal.

His hips still. His face reverts to a scowl.

"Uh-oh," he mutters. "Did we suddenly jump to finals week while I was wrecking you, Miss Valari?"

"Which, for the record, I *did* enjoy," I ensure with an impish smile.

"But?"

I take a long second to run fingertips over his breathtaking features. That high, firm rectangle of a forehead. The noble brows slashed against its base, hunching over his mesmerizing blues.

Mesmerizing—and unblinking.

The rest of him is equally still. My body has a tight grip on his, but he's braced soundly on his thighs, poised and powerful. Pausing his whole being…waiting on me.

I pull in a deep breath. On the exhalation, I force words out.

"But you don't have to do this. *We* don't have to. That doesn't mean I don't want to…" The protest is a frantic tumble on my lips. "But if you need time to consider all of this, you have it. I'll tell Mother we decided to go short on the courtship and long on the engagement. She'll just have to d—"

The word clutches in my mouth as he presses a thumb to my lips. Or is it the vexed glitter in his eyes that's turned me speechless?

"At the risk of pure redundancy, little demon…do *you* need more time to consider?"

When I pull in breath to properly protest, he taps his thumb at my mouth in gentle reprimand.

"Don't blurt what you think I want to hear, Kara. Everything you've already said… I listened. And I get it."

Now he rubs that big rough pad from one corner of my lips to the other. At the same time, he undulates his hips just enough to tell me he isn't softening anytime soon. In more ways than the obvious.

"Our love is bigger than rings and ceremonies and cake, okay?"

I burst with a teasing gasp. "Wait, now. No hating on cake."

"Never." With my outcry shooing away his thumb, the way is clear for him to peck my lips. "There are just easier ways to get it."

"You mean instead of signing on to tolerate my family for the rest of your days?"

Several troughs appear across his forehead. "Is *that* the real scratch on this record? You do know I rib Kell and

Jaden because I like them so much, right? And if you have to question where I stand about Gio—"

"I'm not referring to any of them, and you know it."

I fight to keep my emotions out of what his reaction will be, but his chest-deep chuckle is nowhere on my expectations list. When my stunned stare likely betrays as much, the maddeningly magnificent man just gives me a longer laugh and a more purposeful push of his groin. Before I can comprehend it's there, a high sigh bursts out of me. My brain blanks.

What, exactly, were we talking about again?

"Sweetheart, your mother loves me."

I groan. This time, not in pleasure. Oh, yeah. *That* was the subject.

"All right, all right," I mutter past a new smirk. "I mean, she hasn't said so, in so many words, but…"

"She loves me." It's wrapped in a sultry snarl now, which he delivers down the column of my neck. The dip doesn't stop him from another suggestive slide of other body parts. "And I'll always love and take care of her too, as much as my own mom. I promise you, Kara."

I squirm a little, his heartfelt pledge throwing me into emotions that I swore away when bringing up this subject. But now they're squeezing in, melting my heart and moving my soul—but luckily, shifting my body too. My discomfort almost comes off as impatience. I seize that angle, nervously yanking at his beard.

"Are we really going to keep talking about our mothers?"

A sandpaper sound reverberates from him. A new wave

of vibrations answers from every corner of my body. As soon as Maximus slides his hips down again, I shove up with answering passion.

And it's all even better than before. Oh, dear God, so much better.

I lift my head enough to lock eyes with my lover—my *fiancé*—once more, embraced by the matching sentiment in his soul. And lust in his blood. And pledge in his heart, to pleasure me like this forever.

Suddenly, forever doesn't seem like long enough.

An hour later, we're back to being respectably dressed despite our wickedly satisfied grins. As we link hands after summoning the elevator, the area beneath my navel becomes an embarrassing and demanding rumble.

"Somebody's hangry," Maximus quips.

I fling my free hand up, palm out. "Hey. This twiglet is your offspring too, Mister Kane."

"And how much did either of you eat at the fundraiser?"

His query is mostly rhetorical. I had as much to eat at the Pendry as he did, which was essentially two bitesize hors d'oeuvres and a swig of sparkling water.

"Sounds like somebody needs a trip to Cole's French Dip," I say with a bigger smirk.

"Sounds like you're speaking my language." Maximus smacks his lips to mine just before the elevator arrives. "Now let's hope this lift does too."

"Should we click our heels three times and make a wish?"

Whether Oread's elevator really heard me or not, we'll never know. But I deem the conveyance a friend when its doors reopen and we're down to the mall's valet parking stand again, with the car and driver waiting for us. Immediately, I'm unsure whether to wait on Kell. My conflicted frown becomes a warm smile once I get out my phone to text her, only to find her message already waiting.

Found a ride home. Fancy wheels are for you and Baby Daddy. Tell Maximus to take advantage of the super stretch!

I fight the urge to spurt a new laugh. Doing so will only alert Maximus, who'll demand I read the message aloud. Instead, I plaster on a smile and dip a playful curtsy as my dashing date beats the driver in opening the vehicle's door.

"Your carriage, beautiful."

"It would be my honor to join you, Lord Kane."

As he grasps my fingertips with his, he lifts a searching stare around the marbled porte cochere. "Is Kell still selling her soul at the Ferragamo shrine?"

"Not sure. But she's checked in. She'll be all right."

That I can state without a splinter of uncertainty. Even if both my sister's legs had her limping around, she'd be doing it at the height of grace The press hasn't nicknamed her *The Vanguard Valari* without good reason. Whether she's simply ordered another car, run into old friends, or met a new person with which, in her words, to canoodle, she'll land on her feet with more polish than a pantheress.

When we arrive at Cole's, the place is shockingly sparse

for this hour on a Friday night. We're also surprised by the staff's eager smiles—in downtown LA, practiced diffidence is an artform as much as it is in New York. But instead of enjoying the friendliness, I fight a wave of sadness.

"Business must be really bad since the quakes." I sneak a hand beneath my borrowed coat to rub at the morose indigo hue taking over my belly. Despite the dark color, I sigh in relief. It's the first shade to come back since our earlier lovemaking. I've been worried that the jump into Z's alternate realm might have done something to the sprout. Admittedly, it's likely the initiation into a lifetime of stresses, but I'm grateful it's smaller for now. "So maybe we'd better order big and tip bigger," I add to my first comment, to be answered by my man's gruff chortle.

"Ah. Good plan." He winks as if he can actually hear the new snarl from my stomach over the alt rock hit that's blaring from the kitchen. "I mean, even if we don't plan to eat it *all.*"

"I'm sure a few of their to-go boxes are clamoring for a new home."

In the end, we've inhaled two plates of garlic tots, a large French dip, and half a grilled cheese sandwich with soup. By the time we leave and head for Maximus's place, I'm glad for the chance to walk off a little of my sex and food coma. But only by a fraction. My sleep-deprived brain is looking forward to hitting the pillow as fast as possible since I already anticipate some early morning texts from Veronica. Our wardrobe choices for the EmStars will likely have to be reconfigured because of the engagement announcement.

For now, as we turn onto the street in front of his building, I hold steady at basic counting-the-blessings mode.

Since there's not even a lone photographer lingering out here despite the balmy breeze in the palm and fig trees, logic leads to a calming conclusion. Mother has chosen to go the traditional route for the freshest Valari scoop, supplying our engagement news to select media outlets first. Or perhaps— hope of all hopes—she's being super strategic and waiting to collect a few more juicy details from Maximus and me.

If so, that gives us several hours of tomorrow to be transparent hermits in our downtown retreat. I smile a little, daring to look forward to more sunshine and coffee on the balcony.

But first things first.

As we leave the elevator and approach his front door, every pore of my skin is elated about a naked bask between his silky sheets. Less than twenty more steps, and it'll be reality. But the fantasy has dug in so well, I stumble a little across his foyer.

"Hey." Maximus pivots and cups my elbows before I fall all the way over. "Easy there, sleepy one."

"You mean sleep*walking* one?" I take advantage of getting to sag into him. "Just point the way to the bed, please."

"How about one better?" He squats low and hooks his arms beneath my back and knees. I'm sighing at once, tucking my forehead against his neck.

"I hereby worship you for the rest of my days," I mumble.

"Impossible. I'm already checked in at *your* temple." He uses a foot to scoot out a chair from the table. "Sit tight," he instructs. "Just going to grab us some waters from the fridge."

"Mmm–hmmm," I return dreamily, though a narrow needle pricks the back of my brain. As long as I'm right here, I might as well check on—

"The grimoire."

The words hurt as they burst up my throat and past my lips, natural effects of sheer panic. But I force myself to pull in a deep breath, ignoring the wild new array of light that starts flashing from my midsection.

"It's okay, Sprout," I whisper. "It's going to be fine. I'm sure there's a logical reason for this."

This being the fact that no amount of my prodding, sliding, and searching is yielding the book at my fingertips, lodged in the tight space where it should be. Nor does a visual sweep of the table's underbelly, along with the floor underneath.

I sit back up, now flattening a hand to my sternum in a fight to calm my sprinting heartbeat.

"Kara?" Maximus slams the water bottles to the counter after clearing the kitchen archway. "What's—"

"The grimoire." Though I pray my repetition is less desperate, it's a lost cause. "Did you do something with it?"

"I don't follow," he utters. "I know where you put it, which means someone would have to upend this place to find it. Much better than the sock drawer or under the mattress."

I gulp hard. Blink back tears. For what reason, I have no idea. "Apparently not."

A rough huff makes it up his own gullet. "Huh?"

"It's not there, Maximus. I think…the grimoire's been stolen."

CHAPTER 17

Maximus

"**Y**OU'RE SURE YOU'VE LOOKED EVERYWHERE?"

Jesse's query, mild enough, daggers my exhausted brain. It's only nine a.m., and my three hours of sleep have to stretch for a long while more, so I'm bumping around in my kitchen on a desperate search for something to put into the coffee maker.

"If you can seriously find a corner we didn't check yet, have at it."

I let my dry tone stand for itself since I've succeeded in locating half a bag of Sarah's ground Arabica. Shockingly, it still smells decent. Even more surprising, there aren't any cobwebs in the carafe. I sigh heavily, wishing providence was feeling as magnanimous in other ways.

"Valid point." My friend maneuvers his wheelchair in a smooth three-sixty to behold the piles that evoke dystopian havoc across the apartment. Everything from clothes and hand weights to books and vinyl records are evidence that I'm more nostalgic than I pretend *not* to be. Shit, there's even a jar of the marbles I used to collect, as well as a Roman centurion costume from some Halloween rave that he talked me into attending a few years ago.

"Tearing the place apart was the only way I kept Kara from freaking out completely," I say while jabbing the machine's start button. "I think she forced her head to the pillow only because of anticipating Veronica's early summons this morning. Between perusing my baby picture album and the high school yearbooks, she finally passed out."

"Thank God for small miracles." He shakes his head. "I'll never live down that bad haircut from junior year."

"The cut or the DIY purple highlights?" I snark out the last part while rounding the corner to respond to a knock on the door. My instincts are already snapping to attention, pre-emptive expectations for another bad surprise in what's felt like a year of them, but I breathe back the anxiety. Lately, the worst blows are from guests who don't bother with the door.

"We're streaking *what* purple? Or should I ask?"

I blink at the slight leather-and-denim clad figure on my welcome mat.

"Reg." While I withhold the overt question mark from my tone, it's probably apparent in my gawk. "Are you okay? What's—"

"Take it down a peg," she reassures. "I'm merely here at your father's request."

"Request?" I sneer. Zeus no more requested this of her

196

than a sultan asking a lutist for a tune. Refusing was never her option.

"Don't be daft." She smacks my shoulder while letting herself in. "You know damn well why he materialized this morning as if he owned the bookshop. Middle of the erotica section, to be exact."

"Shit." My grimace comes hard and fast. "I'm sorry."

"Be more sorry that you proposed and didn't even tell us," she retaliates. "Bloody hell. Not even a glance at the ring."

"Ring?" Jesse grabs his armrests and stiffens his spine. "Kane! What the living f—"

"*Chill.*" I swing up a stiff hand. "There's no ring."

"But you plighted to her, yes?" says Reg.

"Plighted to…?" Jesse's gaze bugs. "You *proposed*? Way to bury the lede, asshole."

"No," I snap. "I mean, yes. But no."

Their narrowed stares bore into me.

"We *are* engaged…so to speak…"

"So to speak?" Jesse's at another full huff. "How? Because I hear you *speaking*, man, but nothing's making sense."

"Does anything, when the Valaris are involved?"

I try proving the point by committing to another scoff, though Regina's scrutiny is in fine form too. Between that and Jesse's ongoing glare, I'm toast.

"Kell…kind of blurted it," I confess.

Jesse's energy instantly goes sideways. Not enough for Reg to notice, but just enough for me to. "*Kell?* How?"

"Her intention was completely noble," I defend. "But

the circumstances were nuts. We were at the Beverly Center and found ourselves crashing a date between my mom and Z. A minute later, Veronica was there with a Chihuahua under one arm and a whole fiesta in her eyes—"

"Hold up," Jesse cuts in again. "This was last night? Weren't you and Kara at the Earthquake Relief thing at the Pendry? How did you end up at that mall?"

I drag a hand through my hair. "Long answer or longer answer?"

"Neither," Reg injects. "Just get to the proposal. Well, the *non*proposal. Though now that I know the All-father was there, the cups are starting to fit the saucers."

"Don't pour the tea yet," I mutter. "There's still the part where Hecate showed up too."

"Shit," Jesse grouses.

"Ah. Lovely," Reg croons with a sardonic smirk. "No wonder Zeus was a bit impatient about scooting me up here. If *she* knows—"

"Not just her," I cut in.

"Holy crap." Jesse sags back in his chair. "Were you live streaming or something? The crowd got bigger?"

"Only by one." Though I supply him with an answer, I maintain my scrutiny on Reg. "Persephone was with her."

She joins my buddy in knocking back fast. She hits the edge of the kitchen counter so violently, the beads on her braids clatter. "For crying out *loud*."

I almost imitate the move at the burst of Jesse's grunt, coinciding with his dig into his chair's side pocket for his plastic hand flinger. But instead of his usual restless flicking, the man weaves the flexible rubber between his fingers.

"Loud but still logical," he adds to Reg's remark. "So, I assume she's suspect number one in the case of the missing grimoire?"

The casual edges of Regina's stance are officially erased. "Grimoire?" she snaps. "What grimoire? Not the long or longer answer, young man. The *complete* one."

"Damn." Jesse has the grace to color a little. "I guess Kell isn't the only one for unintentional spills this weekend." He adds an apologetic flinch. "Sorry, man. I figured she knew. I mean, if Zeus—"

"Also doesn't know," Reg retorts. "Or he definitely would have told me, if my presumptions are correct regarding this grimoire…which has gone missing. Or should I say *stolen*?"

I shore up my stance. I owe her that and more. She's a former decorated guard of Olympus. A warrior who gave up all that glory just to safeguard my sorry ass for twenty years. Still, I purposely click back to cagey for my reply.

"Depends. What *are* those presumptions? And are you willing to help us figure this out?"

For a soldier so small, Reg's sigh is more of a huge exhalation. But she adds nothing to it before shucking her leather jacket. Beneath, she's wearing a black T-shirt with a ripped-out neck. It's got a half-faded design of a girl drummer with her kit and some words below.

Just Throw the Sticks

It feels scarily appropriate.

Especially when Reg folds her arms, knives me with a

determined glare, and speaks again.

"Maybe you'd better just start at the beginning."

I didn't expect her to be giddily awestruck by my story. But her ongoing glower has me worried.

Strike both. Regina's visually daggering me now, not just glowering. And I'm close to leaving *worried* behind for something more like *sweating with stress*.

Thankfully, sweating doesn't make a sound. If that were the case, I'd probably miss her taut mutter into the room's strained silence.

"All right, then. Just so I know I've got this lined all the way up…" She pushes her head forward like I've got her on a bridle. The tension across her features is cinched just as painfully. "The king of *hell* popped into a party you were at with Kara and took her before your eyes, prompting you to go to her grandfather for help?" Her nostrils flare when I do nothing but extend my quiet tension. "And having a trained Olympian warrior who could have helped you out… That never once occurred to you in the process?"

I press my hands into prayer mode. Push them to the tight seam of my lips. "Reg—"

"*Maximus*." She sniffs harder, going for indignation-puffed lungs. "You think books and coffee have turned me into parchment? I still have several spears, boy, and can easily drive any one of them into an enemy's heart."

"Before they get one into yours?" Goodbye, prayer fingers. Hello, incensed challenge.

"You calling me a fossil?"

"I'm calling you critical. And not just to Sarah, Mom, and me."

"*Ehhh.*" After rocking back again, she jacks her head back. "I don't think the reading club regulars and the downtown mission crowd are a sound point."

Her snort gets a run for its money when Jesse jerks forward. "Time for thinking bigger picture, soldier."

"A whole lot bigger," I add.

She drops her head and sweeps narrowed eyes at us. "Which means what?" Just as fast, her pupils dilate and her jaw pops. "Ohhh, *bollocks*. After you got back…the earthquakes…"

"Weren't random." It's stating what she clearly already knows, but it feels good anyway.

"It was Hades?" Her mahogany lips take on a full purse. "The wanker got a bit cuckoo when someone took away his interesting shiny-pretty, eh?"

"In a few fun words, yes," Jesse quips.

"But we're not that far from the autumnal equinox! He had only a couple of weeks at most before Persephone's return!"

Now my friend yo-yos his rubber toy. "Ever try telling an oligarch they've got to wait two minutes for a glass of water, let alone two weeks for their queen?"

"But the quakes stopped," Reg states, once more flicking her glance between Jesse and me. "Do I want to know *that* part of the story? How'd you get him to stop faffing over all of it?"

A defined breath makes its way into my lungs. At the same time, I trade a purposeful look with Jesse.

He jogs his brows, encouraging me to go ahead with my next words.

"All right. Check your battery life and open a new file," I tell her. "Notes will be necessary."

"I'm ready." She steps over and settles a hip against an arm of the couch. "I take it the lecture topic is *Hecate*?"

"From beginning to end," Jesse mutters.

She only shrugs at that, which helps me sort through the insane twists of the last week. Right now, because I still can't help my impatience about getting together some kind of a plan, I hand pick only the essentials. Hades's horrifying appearance atop the Valari mansion's pool. Hecate pulling off the miracle we needed, yanking Kara from a second stint in the hell king's clutches. Her cryptic summons for us to join her at the Iremia compound, somehow cloaked from the human world in the middle of Topanga Canyon. The haven we couldn't believe we'd found there, on the banks of a eucalyptus-lined creek. And finally, the awful truth we discovered instead. The secrets of Hecate's ultimate plan.

"A war."

Reg's reiterating croak is a harder ordeal than all the words I've just had to form. As I expected, this was the part she didn't see coming. It brings new movement across her face. Rapid flickers betraying harsh thoughts. Lines of worry for friends who are likely still stationed in Olympus. Furrows of fear for the toll this conflict will take on the realm she now knows and cares for. Clenches of anger at the goddess who cares nothing about any of it.

"Has she gone utterly dingbats?"

I clench my jaw. "To her? No. Not dingy. More like despondent. It's obvious when she's privately speaking about the issue. As if she'd like to show everyone the bruises from banging her head against the wall. Centuries of looking on while Z, Hera, and the rest of them quibble…"

Reg bristles. "It's not always quibbling."

"But it's not always diplomatic disagreement," I counter. "Right?"

Her answer doesn't tumble out in words. But the way she rears back, as if I've uncovered a jar of bees, hands over my validation like a thousand stings. I don't want to be right about this. Any of it.

"So war *is* her intention. But so far, not her execution. How are we going to separate the two? Permanently?"

Her challenge already has Jesse popping forward, swinging his plastic hand like a dagger on a rope dart.

"A few humble musings? We've got to get the grimoire back first. But if Hecate's gone to ground, or even back to Iremia—"

Reg whips around. "Hecate doesn't have it."

"What?" I demand. "But—"

"I'll stake every inch of my armor on that."

"How are you that sure?"

"Because of what *he* just assumed." Reg swings her head toward Jesse. "And what many others in the same mindset would. But why? You think Hecate has something to gain by getting that book?"

Ridges form in Jesse's brow. "Does she have something to lose, then?"

"The grimoire bears her name," she states. "It's a book of *her* conjurations, which means she already knows them backward and forward. It's like a VIP access pass when you're already the star of the show."

"But there's got to be a chance she'd still want the pass."

"Only if she has someone lined up who can capitalize on it. Someone with extraordinary ability."

I haul in a huge breath past the new pound of my heartbeat. "Someone like Kara."

Reg angles her head with shrewd consideration. "Writing's huge on that wall, as they like to say. I reckon she showed up to the Valari compound *tout de suite* after learning what Kara had done with the grimoire less than an hour after finding it." She meets my gaze with direct purpose. "Clearly, the grimoire speaks to your woman in significant and magnificent ways. Hecate knows that without a doubt. So why would she want to break up the dream team, especially if she's certain that Kara will gear up for the Iremia Squadron when the battle trumpets sound?"

"Shit." Jesse's energy changes so fast, the toy hand stalls and smacks down on his head. "That's making a large amount of sense."

I claw a hand through my beard. "All right. Let's assume that's so. But it only narrows our search by one suspect—if finding the grimoire is still a priority."

Reg folds her arms. Twists her lips until they reach contortion status. "Not a priority. A necessity."

"Why?"

"Kara's bond with the book is strong but not exclusive. If I'm aware of this, with my limited knowledge about the underworld, then others are too. *Plenty* of them. And, as we speak, they're likely hatching sure-fire plans to escalate the VIP pass value for that nifty tome."

"How?"

Jesse ensures I don't have to blurt another query. That's a very good thing, granting me the head time to snag an answer on my own.

"Humans."

My brain is slammed by a new vision of Dr. Doug, along with everything he revealed to us in his exam room.

Beings like us…we're awesome and amazing because we've been allowed to be…through the dominion that the humans have handed to us…

"It's the humans," I repeat. "More specifically, the ones that'll be gathered in one place in Hollywood tonight."

"Okay…" Jesse extends the word in time to his wary scrutiny. "Do I dare ask for those details? Because, dude, if you even mention *Soilent Green*…"

Reg cuts in on him with a bark so sharp, it borders on laughter. "Oh, my. Professor North, we need to get you out more."

Another well-timed pause, allowing my full conclusion to solidify. "The grimoire will become more powerful if the thieves get their hooks into humans."

Jesse snorts. "So, no *Soilent Green*. We're just skipping straight to the Donner Party."

"*Psychological* grips," I clarify. "The intense energy that can only be supplied by a lot of ambitious souls."

Between one blink and the next, my best friend's face ignites with realization. "Like the kind of crowd that attends a major Hollywood awards presentation."

Reg steps forward again, her pace determined and her shoulders steeled. The grit on her warrior's features makes me wonder if she's going to manifest a pair of sticks simply to throw them.

Instead, she forms words. They're phrased as a question, though I already know that part's a flimsy formality.

"How do I get added to your security detail for tonight?"

CHAPTER 18

Kara

"**D**ARLING, ENOUGH WITH THE modesty. I've seen you naked before."

Mother's line is like a whip for laughter from Kell and me. But I cut my giggle short, wondering if we're overdoing it with the double dose of reaction. After all, Veronica isn't lying. Style consults and fashion fittings have been as normal to all three of us as sunrises and sunsets. No time nor tolerance for timidity. Even now, as she leans against Kell's bedpost during the chastisement, Mother's long satin dressing robe slinks open and exposes half of her barely covered chest.

"Most of the gowns they pulled for me are the Victorian-inspired thing," I say with practiced ease, because I *did* rehearse the line after totally anticipating hers. I smooth one hand over the corset covering my stomach, the other down my full-length satin slip. "This just makes it easier for changes."

The excuse does make sense—this time. I haven't dared to think far enough ahead about the next fitting. By then, maybe Sprout will listen if I ask for a temporary Off button on the glow. Even better, Maximus and I will have found the perfect cabin in Siberia to hide out in. Perhaps a tent in the Sahara. Or a treehouse on some unnamed island in the South Pacific. Now there's my favorite proposal on the list—second only to our yurt and Bubba near the waves, of course.

"*Kara.*"

I jerk my head up, shaking it free of fantasies about pineapple breakfasts and treehouse sex. "Sorry. Hmmm?"

Veronica closes her robe with a peeved tug while stepping over to me. With her other hand, she pushes stray tendrils away from my cheek. "Where has your head been today?"

"You have to ask?" Kell drawls while hitching up her full skirt and stepping onto the box in front of her three-way mirror. "After I had to fetch her from Maximus's bed for the second day in a row?"

Mother groans. "*Please* change the subject." As if needing physical distance from the conversation too, she turns and crosses for the kitchenette in the room's other corner. Now there's an order that'll get my eager compliance.

"You should go with that one." I gesture toward my sister's sparkling gown. "I mean it. That royal purple is a great color, and the gold details at the neckline bring out the similar ones in your eyes. Also, the frothy train gives you permission to go daring with makeup."

As I anticipate, she smirks in pleasure. "Never a gutsy shadow palette I didn't like."

"Your sister's right," Mother adds, assessing from her same position while pulling a jade face roller out of the mini fridge.

"Fine by me," Kell murmurs. "Color's good, and I can wear the new gold cage heels with it." Nobody's surprised by her pile of boxes from yesterday's retail binge, including a gorgeous pair of strappy sandals that will indeed look incredible with the dress.

"Good. Great. Now we've just got to figure out what the bride-to-be will wear...besides Miriam the Librarian's underwear ensemble."

An authentic laugh bubbles from me, and I don't bother to edit it. "You know that's pretty much a compliment, right?"

Veronica doesn't free a hint of a smile, rolling her forehead with dedicated drive. "Try the dark-crimson one next. With the black appliques on the bodice and the overskirt that looks like flower petals."

I make a face. "It's so..."

"I know, I know." She twirls the roller head like a type A drum major. "But with the engagement announcement releasing in an hour, you'll be all over the socials. If they call you in at the last second to present an award, you need something that makes a statement."

I sigh. "They're not going to—"

"Humor me."

I tell myself it's only ten minutes out of my life—until I know it isn't.

The second I step onto the box in front of the three-way, I can see the whites of my mother's eyes from across the room. Worse, Kell's face pops with the same look.

And, damn it, so does mine.

The worst thing about looking like a Versailles wedding cake? When the cake looks…shockingly nice.

"Wow."

And there's the very best thing. When one's fiancé arrives in the room and turns one syllable into sorcery. Especially that syllable.

"Oh, my God," Kell rebukes. "You'd better be glad we're all currently decent, mister."

"Sure…okay." His responding mumble, matching the fixated gaze that I lock to via the mirror, relays that Kell could've declared a tsunami watch for the coast and gotten his same response.

Thankfully, the only storms to heed are the ones in his irises. Flagrantly, I keep tracking them with my own. Shamelessly, I expose the flames that flicker at the edges of my vision.

"Oh, shit. And the damned all wept," Kell mutters.

"No, no, no," Mother dictates. "Weeping is forbidden until tomorrow. My eyelashes are already on for tonight." Her equally forceful steps cause distinct rustles behind Maximus. "Come now, Kell. We're smart enough to know when four's a crowd."

"In my own room?"

"Which just means you've had more practice making graceful exits." One more distinctive rustle—a good thing, since it mutes my small chuckle—as Veronica pops twice on tiptoe to air-smooch my tall demigod. "Hello, Maximus. You look lovely." She pats at his neatly styled ponytail. "I trust the tux alteration meeting went well?"

I suppress another giggle as he flounders like a five-year-old at church. "Uhhh, everything fits," he finally utters, squirming again when Mother appears to wait for more. "So…yeah."

"Excellent." She pats his cheek. "See you both tonight, then. I'll text with any last-minute changes to the itinerary." With the same hand, she points back at me. "Kara, don't take that off. I'll send up the seamstress right away for the last-minute adjustments."

"Adjustments to what?" Maximus growls as soon as the door clicks shut behind her. "Sweet little demon, that dress was made for you."

I sigh. "If one's into looking like a target for Jack the Ripper, I suppose."

He approaches, yanking me off the raised box with such force that I'm airborne for a few seconds, clutched hard against his big body.

"Just let the bastard try." His possessive rumble sends delicious shivers through my form, and that's before his lips totally claim mine. When he's done, I'm physically unable to answer for the better part of a minute. There's definitely advantages to being a breathless and swoony mess in Victorian garb.

"Well…only if he's capable of time travel," I rasp at last. His taut grunt is a hotter-than-hot reply.

"At this point? Wouldn't rule it out."

"You probably wouldn't be alone."

He pulls up by an inch. Scans my face. I'm not kidding so much this time, and he nods to acknowledge it. The moment is sobering for us both, like a pause in a cavern with no discernible way out. We can't map the way back to where we once were, but we have no idea where we're headed. It's one terrified step after the next. But thank God we're taking them together.

I want to put all of that into words, but his tense vibrations have me thinking twice. He calms by a few degrees when I slip a hand up the middle of his chest, pressing assuring fingers atop the heavy beats between his pecs.

"Did you have a chance to connect with Jesse?" I murmur for his ears alone. "Was he able to help with theories about the grimoire?"

It's an awesome surprise to watch some warmth move into his features. Here come the crinkles I adore at the corners of his eyes, as well as hints of a smirk on his lips. Still, I tilt a dubious scowl for his full view.

"Oh, no. Should I be excited or scared about this?"

"Full disclosure?" And he's chess-match serious again. "Healthy doses of both."

I push my brows together. "So, what'd he say? He had some ideas, then?"

"He did after Regina got to the apartment."

Just as fast, my gaze flares. "Reg showed up? Why?"

He has a new half grin, though the temperature is definitely cooler. "Why do you think?"

Just when I thought my eye sockets couldn't accommodate a wider gape. "She was acting on orders? Were they from *Z*? Do you think he suspects…about the baby?"

He shakes his head with adamant force. "His concern is solely about Hecate's next move. At the moment, you and I are his strongest conduit for that."

"But we can't be the only ones."

"Of course not. But he's not fatuous. He knows an easy information pipeline when he's got it. Reg is the obvious appointee for security duty on the *asset*."

His air quotes on the word send clenches down to my belly. I swear that I can feel our twiglet shifting as well, beating at me with instinctive tumult.

"So what did you tell Reg? Everything?" My second question is filled with rhetorical hope. The grimoire isn't mine, but it's impossible to shut down this possessive connection to the book. The mystical threads that reached out since the moment I put my hands on its precious leather cover. Hecate must know that too. She had to have felt it even back at Iremia.

But if she had a problem with that knowledge, she could have sent someone to take the book right then. Surely she already knew it didn't come with us to the compound out in the canyon and was likely stowed back at Maximus's place. During any of the hours she'd made sure that Maximus and I were lost in each other in our little cottage, she had ample opportunities to go back for it. More directly, she could've simply magicked it out of the apartment last night when standing only six feet away from it. The grimoire was there at that point, and after she left, I checked for it myself.

There's something else going on here. Something that even the magic goddess isn't aware of. It might have nothing—or everything—to do with her grand plot. But orchestrated by whom? And why?

I'm rescued from that confusing scourge by a closer embrace from Maximus. Better yet, from the firm and reassuring words he offers. "Jesse and I laid the whole story on Reg. We're glad we did, all things considered."

"All things?" I echo, returning to a new frown. "Like what?"

He pushes out a heavy breath. "Her soldier's sovereignty, I guess. She was a little bent that I went to Gio for help on the helldive stuff instead of her."

"Which she got over quickly, right? Once you explained that we might need her more now?"

"*Now* being the operative word." He accepts the small lean of my head as the commitment for a bigger explanation. "Reg is positive that Hecate isn't our thief. She's also ruled out all the Iremia diamonds."

With a tug of teeth at my lip, I offer a nod. "I was starting to push at the same conclusion. Sometimes the obvious *is* too glaring. Not to mention illogical."

One side of Maximus's hold is a tighter possession at my waist. With the other, he brushes a tender thumb across my cheek. Something flares in his eyes, answered by a sharp call from my instincts. Every note of it screams at me to leap off the block and drag him down the hall to my room. But

I'm certain Veronica is lingering nearby, one ear primed for the snick of the opening door.

"There is *that*," he murmurs, still looking torn between his inner scholar and caveman. "One of the several points Reg clarified before she got to the interesting part."

My focus spikes. "Does she already know who did it?"

"She has some solid theories about suspects," he says. "As well as the kind of co-conspirators they'd need to take full advantage of the book's powers. Coincidentally, a nice crowd of them is scheduled to be gathering in one place tonight."

Forget the focus. Comprehension barrels in on *me* now, slamming so hard that I choke. "At the EmStars?" I don't wait for him to reply. "Oh, God. Of *course* at the EmStars. Those dots connect better than all the rest of it."

I shake my head, stunned that I haven't already followed those basic circles—at least before Jesse, Reg, and him. More than the three of them, I've logged thousands of observation hours at the Hollywood get-ahead game. The spotlight lust. The glamor masquerade. More than anything, the desperate excuses for grabbing at more.

If someone was on the cusp of snagging that big brass ring—or whatever they perceived as such—they'd willingly sign their soul over to the devil. Or one of his minions. Or a witchy-leaning friend. Or some other otherworldly ally we haven't fathomed yet. A supernatural support team that we have to find…

Before it's too late.

"So where did you leave it?" I prompt. "With Reg? Is

she going to contact someone? LAPD? The FBI? CIA?"

Maybe another agency in that alphabet soup. Or all of them. We need every scrap of help we can get right now.

But after three seconds' worth of Maximus's continued stare, I know those scraps aren't coming. Not a single one.

"What'd there be to tell them?" he proposes. "That we lost *one* book that we hid in a locked apartment? That nothing else was taken or damaged, and we're both okay too, *but* they've got to drop every other case on their desks because the cosmic realms are about to make World War Three seem like a sweet movie effect?"

I flatten my hands along the planes of his shoulders. My own sag before I can help it.

"So, what's the plan?" My prompt is a dismal grate. "*Is* there a plan?"

I'm unable to control the tears beneath the last of it. I drop my head, recognizing they've surfaced out of guilt. I should have been more responsible about the grimoire. Maybe—probably—insisted that we lock it in a bank, bury it in a bag of rice, or tuck it into a locker at the train station.

But the self-flogging only accomplishes one of two things. Attests that I've consumed more cheesy crime than I want to admit or proves that I'm too freaking tired for my own good. Or anyone else's.

Once more, Maximus strips away the burden of having to decide.

"Ssshhh. *Hey.*" His mouth is strong but soft against my temple. His hand is big and reassuring at the back of my head. "There's a plan, okay? We're not helpless here. *You're* not helpless."

I dip a nod against his wide, warm chest. "Okay." Then burrow closer into the haven of his embrace, savoring its perfect safety with my whole heart. At my center, there's a growing warmth. Twiglet also knows when Daddy's giving all the best nuzzles. "So, what are we going to do? What do you need *me* to do?"

"I just got Reg signed on with your family's regular security detail. Since I vouched for her, and she leveled the two biggest guys in a spontaneous combat challenge, they're letting her start tonight."

"The two biggest—" My own snagged breath is my interruption. "Do you mean Tor and Duncan? Reg is half their size!"

"And apparently has kept up with her Olympian training," he returns. "So, she's on the roster for tonight, but we fed the guys enough vague details that they know to give her some space. Without you there, I didn't know if your team is wholly human, demon, or a mix of both."

"Tor and Duncan are demons, but we're never sure about the rest. They regularly rotate team members just to play it safe."

"Good." He ducks in to press his forehead to mine. "Because if they don't do exactly that tonight, I'll feed their balls to your mom's Chihuahuas."

I pull back an inch. "But what can *I* do to help?"

"For now? Exactly what Veronica wants you to do. I know that's the last thing you want to hear, but the better you are at dazzling everyone on that media line or even up on stage, the more room Reg will have to slip around behind the scenes and watch people when they don't think they're *being* watched."

My nerves jangle. I drop my hands and fidget at the sparkling lace on my full skirt. "You're right. I don't like it one damn bit. But I do understand." A heavy breath leaves me. "Sacrifices for the cause, right?"

A smile makes its way across his noble lips. It climbs into his eyes, which turn into cerulean magic spells all their own.

"Thank you, beautiful. Your professor commander is thankful."

He emphasizes the husked words by putting those incredible lips to a heart-stopping purpose. All his kisses are full experiences for me, but this one is sweet and sensual and gentle and intense, all in the same span of enchanting seconds. His passion makes me dizzy. His devotion makes me woozy. I sway dreamily against him.

"If you have any more orders, sir, now is absolutely the time to issue them."

His grin is wider and more wonderful than before. "Actually, there *is* one."

"Name it," I whisper. "Whatever in the world you need."

He sweeps those stunning lips down the bridge of my nose. The rasps from his beard turn me into a mass of hypnotized tingles.

"I *need* for you to not look at me like this tonight. Because if you do, I'll be *needing* a lot of *other* things from you."

I let my head fall back, openly offering him more of my neck—and anything else he sees—to nibble. "And that's a bad thing...why?"

Another wave of sparkling frissons from the continued quests of his lips and tongue. He taunts me in this state, refusing to respond until he's reached the bottom curve of my left ear. "Regina asked us to provide a decent distraction, not an indecent side show. We won't do her any good if we're kicked off the carpet before getting in the door."

I grab my turn at a rough growl. "Fine. I'll be good."

He busses the sensitive skin between my ear and nape. "Your professor commander is again grateful."

"Which he'll prove later tonight, right? By letting me be...bad?"

He abandons his silken caresses for an intentional dig of his teeth. The brief nip of pain pushes a gasp from my lips. Turns my fingers into gouges at his shoulders.

"Oh, sweet demon... Now *that's* a promise."

CHAPTER 19

MAXIMUS

GOD HELP ME.

I didn't think Kara could get more gorgeous in that Victorian revival ensemble, but as I turn to help her out of our town car at the start of the EmStar Awards entrance carpet, I silently call myself twelve kinds of a fool. The tirade gets finished with just three words aloud.

"God. Help. Me."

Because some prayers really need to be heard.

Though if I'm the only one muttering it in the next three hundred feet, I'll paint myself six shades of shocked. They'll all be variants of the hues now defining *her*. The lush gold cosmetics that accent her huge eyes. The crimson on the graceful ribbons of her lips, matched to her gown's underskirt. The more fiery shade of the dress's petal-shaped top layers, defined by beads that resemble tiny yellow flowers. There are more of the custom beads across the pointed toes of her shoes and secured in the ornate curls of her hair.

No wonder everyone calls her Hollywood royalty.

No wonder *everyone* seems to be jostling for a good angle of their lens on her, crowding against the media barricades like bees to their queen.

For once, their behavior makes sense. If I were on their side of the stanchions, I'd be making like one of the large Lakers statues in front of the arena across the street, bounding my way up front as fast as possible. Anything to get into this enchantress's view lines.

Instead, I'm the lucky blockhead who gathers her arm under mine and beholds her dazzling smile beneath the glaring lights that lead to the theater across LA Live's wide front courtyard. I'm the one who gets to stroll with her up the lush red path, reveling in holding her closer as flashbulbs explode, only to do it again another eight to ten feet.

Stroll. Stop. Smile. Laugh. Repeat.

Like date night, I guess…only with five thousand close friends. Take it easy about that part, and the game can be kind of fun.

The game.

I welcome the designation, which makes it easier to see the frenzy for what it really is. For a good majority of the people in this realm—in this *city*—pictures of Kara and me are nothing but ten seconds of their time while riding a train to work or standing in line at the grocery store. After that, more important things are on their minds. Stuff I know about firsthand. Jobs. Bills. Families. Everyone just wants to make it to the next day. This world is nothing but a separate, silly game marked by shouted phrases that seem set to *repeat* mode.

"Kara!"

"Maximus!"

"Over here. Over here!"

"Kara!"

"Maximus!"

Marco.

Polo.

Fish out of water!

I almost laugh. It all meshes into the same rhythms, demanding similar rote moves.

Until, between one flashbulb flurry and the next, it isn't.

My goldfish bowl, such a thick barrier between this and reality, gains a crack.

A scary one.

I blink to make sure I'm not imagining the sight at the back of the media crush…

I'm not.

But I don't dare expose my disquiet to anyone, least of all the ravishing female fitted into the crook of my arm. Kara's too busy doing exactly what I've asked of her—charming every reporter in this crowd nearly out of their skins—to heed the multi-braided head toward the back of the crowd.

Regina.

Who, at the immediate moment, is moving much too quickly for a mere recon sweep.

I know it without a shadow of a doubt. Even in her last-second tuxedo rental and at this early point of the night's revelry, my warrioress friend has sighted a possible target. I only hope, with every synapse in my mind and spirit, that it's the quarry she came here for.

That *we* came here for.

If she'd only give me some kind of sign...

The swift snap of her head, with sights arrowed at me, wasn't what I expected. But I'll happily take it.

Or will I?

With her braids pulled back and coiled in a bun, I can read my friend's whole expression. The experience brings another unexpected—and unpleasant—punch.

Reg's gritted teeth are exposed, white and angry. The new jut of her head hurls yet another new message at me.

She's wasting the effort. I'm not picking up a thing. What the hell does she need?

I start shaking my head, feigning wonder at this whole spectacle, in hopes that she'll comprehend...

Except it turns into the moment that *I* do.

When she gestures with her head again, including Kara in that frantic dart. At once, she flashes the look back at me. A look that, in some ancient TV sitcoms, would be a stand-in for expressions like *hanky-panky* and *getting it on*.

She's got to be joking.

I suppress the sentiment as best I can, though I'm positive my wow-so-glad-to-just-be-here look has vanished. In its place, I'm probably broadcasting something between flashbulb exhaustion and constipation.

Neither of those fly with Reg.

She's holding steady with the original instruction in

her eyes. The Olympian soldier version of the message that's going to detonate in thirty seconds whether I like it or not.

But there's the rub.

I don't *not* like it.

If anything, this is the best damn mission I've had to execute so far in this wild saga—as I prove without another second of hesitation. As I commit to with full passion, not giving Kara the chance for half a yelp of protest, as I sweep down and crush those gorgeous lips beneath mine.

Not because her yelps aren't important to me. In this crucial moment, they've just got to be voiced in different ways. Everything in my senses joins my mouth in sending the message to her, even twisting the contact until we're mashing tips of tongues and edges of teeth, to the euphoria of every media member lining this carpet.

As the crowd erupts like a hoard of headbangers during an encore, I slide both hands to the middle of her back. In the same motion, with our lips still sealed, I lean into a lunge and drop her into a dramatic dip.

And here comes the roar for the second encore.

A din that should have me jerking back up and gauging how many more steps until we're done with this gauntlet. More importantly, ensuring that I've given Reg a window of opportunity to gain on her quest.

But in this moment, a better victory already claims me. A bolder freedom.

My open declaration for Kara. For us.

It shouldn't feel so easy, but it is. In the glare of these lights, on the plane of this carpet, comes a brave new variety of…intimacy. The theory strikes me as completely crazy, but not after I see it confirmed by the keen sparks in her stare.

Because we don't have to worry about hiding anything, we can reveal everything. And God help me yet again, I never want it to end. Such an incredible, beautiful bubble…

Which, like all bubbles, is doomed to pop.

We could pick worse than Veronica to be our inevitable pin bearer. As she pauses a few feet away, having closed the gap between her photo stop and ours, she curls a coy hand against her chest as if she's actually hiding a hat pin. Or, knowing her, a switchblade. I almost lift a hand to warn the reporter she's now addressing, but that's before I observe the guy's smooth laugh.

That's also before noticing that he's not a guy at all, but a glittery mop disguised as one.

Ellery Gentry.

I'm too late to kiss Kara back as a new diversion. She's already locked a glaring bead on the diva in dickbag clothing who's enraptured by Veronica's answer to a query he snuck in while Kara and I were still enjoying bubble time.

"Well, as was detailed in the announcement, Maximus's proposal was impulsive and unexpected—our professor *is* wildly romantic that way—so of course there's not a ring yet. But these two will be rectifying that soon. We're even looking at some lovely collaboration designs from major names in the jewelry world."

"My, my, my," Gentry croons back. Then, as if he's already in on the answer, "Any idea when that auspicious shopping trip will occur?"

"Soon, of course. But you'll be personally notified of the occasion. You have my word, Ellery."

Sometimes I've envisioned self-control like air conditioning. Depending on outside forces, I have to turn it up or down as needed. Weirdly, Veronica's words feel like a heat wave. No. Not just that. I'm holding Gentry, and his smug smirk of reaction, just as responsible. I crank harder on the dial when he pulls in a lot of air, clearly not finished with his moment in the Veronica Valari sunglow.

"And the big day itself? Should we be red circling anything yet? Ordering a stylist to go any special direction for nuptial togs?" He waggles his pink-streaked brows in our direction. "Adding NSFW stickers to our live streams?"

And now I'm frantically hunting for the *glacier* setting on the air conditioning.

A squandered quest, only understood when Kara steps closer to me.

Damn. How can the woman be rocking blow torches in her gaze but practically dripping icicles from her fingertips? So much poise that she's mesmerizing. Control to the point that a man—or woman—wouldn't dare make her lose it.

Thankfully, the effect's not lost on Gentry. The journalist—an honor since I'm feeling weirdly generous now—doesn't look happy about acknowledging Kara's upper hand. Granted, the hand is pretty firmly coming for *him.*

Well, damn.

The sudden comprehension has me rubbing one side of the beard next to my renewed smile. So that's the deal behind the slick putz and his nettles for Kara. He's not piqued at her. He's *afraid* of her.

As he probably should be.

Thankfully, it doesn't seem to be fresh news for my regal, graceful woman. She's exhilarating but agonizing to watch. I can't lend any support outside of just standing here, and it makes me twitch. This carpet isn't my classroom. I can't order Gentry away on the simple basis that his ego might blow the top of his head off any second.

"You say you need some stickers, Mr. Gentry?" From one end of the query to the next, her voice changes from stiff silk into hammered leather. "Because I'd be happy to customize a few for you alone." The words are further molded by her snarl and polished by the kilns in her eyes.

Despite the dramatic delivery, I doubt anyone but Gentry and I are aware of it all. Even the closest production assistants see nothing but her wide, charming smile and her intense attention to Gentry.

"That won't be necessary."

But unless Gentry has a solid grasp of ventriloquy, the objection isn't his. His lips aren't moving by the barest of millimeters. His voice, while as smooth as pretentiousness can guarantee, was never as confident as this. Never so low that even a gender identifier has been stricken as a clue.

Then who the hell...

"Go on. Tell him, Kara. Take it back, darling. *Now.*"

As soon as I figure it out, I wheel around and brace my stance. But not fast enough. Veronica's already here, holding her daughter in place from behind. The only thing that shakes her talons is Kara's violent gulp, vibrating along her collarbone.

But once more, nobody but Gentry and I seem to see the friction. Weird? I'll concede as much. But enough to call out in front of a hundred camera lenses, when I'm the guy hiding Olympian DNA and a glowing infant in my fiancée's stomach? Not going to happen, especially when my woman is forced into playing nice with Gentry.

Forced being one of the most sickening understatements of my life.

A second later, *sickening* joining that list.

Does Veronica care that she's tearing her daughter's skin? That she's marring her own offspring in the name of making nice with a "close family friend"?

But right now, there's not a damn thing I can do about it. If I so much as cross my eyes wrong at him, I'll be branded an even bigger outsider. The stalker overprotector instead of the gallant fiancé. If I'm guessing right, Gentry's probably saved a few new nicknames for the purpose.

Professor Prick.

Kane the Insane.

Mad Maximus.

"Yeah, okay, asshole. You win...this time."

I grit it out for my ears alone—or so I think. It's too late for remembering I've fallen in love with a wildly gifted empath who's also learned how to levitate things. It's also too late to predict what would happen if she funneled both gifts on me.

Much, much too late. Because it's happening before I

can think about it. Or do anything about it.

As in, struggling to keep my balance as my whole form is lifted up by a good two inches. Then working to act like it's totally normal that I'm being pulled backward, between a break in the curtains that line the back of the carpet walk. By the time a couple of seconds have passed and I can breathe again, I look around in time to watch Kara flinging similar powers to gain significant distance from her mother.

"*Uhhh.*"

It's the only sound my throat can take back from my shocked senses, erupting in time with my pedaling feet— which are still two feet in the air and grappling at mostly air. At best, my purchase on the ground is limited to fleeting toe taps.

I finally make it back to the curtain and am able to steal a few glances between the velvet panels. I see enough to determine that the crowd is eating up the spectacle like a vegan ice cream sundae. Thanks to the puckish tilt on Kara's lips, everyone thinks her rebellious little act, presumably to get me alone, is an elaborate effects stunt. Even Ellery Gentry is applauding the plot twist, especially as Kara floats herself to the same curtain partition she sent me through.

Unbelievably, my woman has turned around every scowl in the crowd—except the obvious one. There's no way I'm *not* noticing it, particularly since Veronica doubles down on the anger once her daughter's intention is clear.

"Kara!" The seethe doubles once she rushes offstage as well. "What do you think you're doing?"

As Kara whirls, the thick layers of her dress billow and

sweep. The effect is graceful enough for an animated princess film, though no way is my woman committing to the cause.

"What do you think *you're* doing?"

Veronica hardly alters her raging gape. "*What* is going on? How...are you...doing th—"

Kell stomps over from another break in the curtains. "Holy shit." Obviously, she witnessed enough of her sister's surprise to double back from her spot in the photo order.

On her heels is Jaden, dressed in a tux that's as edgy as his eyeliner. Completing the vibe is his taut expression.

"Oh, K-demon..."

"*Demon?*" Veronica snaps. "You certain of that, darling? Don't be tactful on *my* account, everyone. Come on, now. Fill me in. Is it K-witchy now? Or something more fun? Sorceress Supreme? High Priestess of the Powerful Arts?"

Kara pivots and growls. "Does that even matter right now?"

"You think it doesn't?" The woman spins, looking just as ready to throw a real punch. "Do you really, thoroughly, think it doesn't? All of you keeping such a huge secret from me?"

"You think it *does*? When you're keeping an equally gigantic one from Maximus and me?"

"Huh?" It spills out before I can think twice. But I'm already too slow on the snap.

Gigantic one...from Maximus and me...

Really, *really* late.

CHAPTER 20

A WILD CRAVING HITS me at full force. The temptation to laugh.

This doesn't make me totally insane. The oxymoron of the moment has to be visible to someone else. Surely it is to Kell and Jaden, who both can't have left their logic behind. They have to see it too.

The fact that my professor fiancé—so brilliant he can recite anyone from Chaucer to Tolstoy and back—is still so oblivious about what Mother is trying to orchestrate here.

Or perhaps already has.

The more I rotate my mind around that angle, the clearer it all gets. Why she decided to stroll over and milk the moment Maximus kissed me. Why she was instantly chummy with Gentry, even commenting about our wedding rings and date considerations. Finally, why she's so incensed about me steering things another direction, in very much my own way.

Most of all, why her ire hasn't diminished since then.

Because she's not actually peeved about the information we kept from her. Not wounded, confused, or sad either.

She's riled about my interference with *her* biggest, newest plans. The master game board she's already starting to map, using our "royal wedding" as collateral, until she achieves the grandest prize of all: global media domination. After all, it's what she does best. Her own superpower contribution to the Valari empire. A service that's guaranteed our status and life of privilege.

So how do I tell her that this time is different? That she's probably pedaling with blinders on? And that once she does see the end, it'll probably be a dead end?

That even if we save the realms from an all-out civil war, they'll never be the same again?

How—why—do I *not* tell her that?

The answer comes from my gut. Too fast and too hard. As I turn from them all and search for someplace to hurl everything from my stomach, my mind resonates with the awful admission.

Because I don't want to accept it for myself.

Not yet. *Oh, God, please. Not yet.*

"Hey."

Maximus offers it as a murmur for my ears only while pressing up behind me. The significance of his presence is exactly what I need, enough to calm the turmoil of my gut. I glance over my shoulder at him, conveying hasty gratitude. If even one reporter catches me vomiting in the bushes a handful of hours after our engagement announcement, the obvious innuendos will be hashtagged and posted before we reach our seats inside.

"You okay?" he asks, rubbing my back.

I lift my head, unsure how to respond. The ground still feels like a funhouse floor. My vision continues to swim. "Define *okay*."

Half a dozen *clonks* sound from the cement behind us. One surety I can make about Veronica Valari: she's predictable in her tells. There's not a single misstep of her red soles against the sidewalk, despite its earthquake-induced cracks and humps.

"Come now, Kara. Melodrama isn't your brand."

My vision sharpens as I snap all the way up and all the way around. "Melodrama. Well, there's a convenient label for the collar, at least."

Her head reels back. "For the... What are you—"

"You heard me." I hook a hand under Maximus's elbow to maintain my balance. "And you understood too. Can't have a leash without the collar, right? And the collar won't stay put if the puppy learns how to slip free from it. So why not some sparkly labels to make it more appealing?"

A new pair of red-soled *clomps*, courtesy of her stiff backward step. "My word. Is that really how you see it? Even now?"

"You mean especially now?" I blurt it as fast as my lips will allow, before her wounded rasp can wind all the way into my heart. Oh, it'll get there eventually, but I vow to be ready this time. To lock down my atriums and ventricles against her calculated show. "Careful, Mother. Woeful and weepy isn't *your* brand."

She rocks back again. Executes a wooden turn. But after that, there's no controlling stomp. She's shuffling now, her shoulders dropped, her aura dripping with defeat.

I open my mouth, fumbling for something to say that isn't direct surrender.

Until she angles back again and beats me to it.

"Darling, I'm not the one who matters right now."

I'm suddenly frozen in place as if my feet are bound in ice blocks. Mother moves as if she's pushing through the same frozen boundaries, her motions jerky and awkward.

But when she steps away from me this time, it's for good. She takes two steps. Four. Eight. Sixteen. Until there's an atmospheric tundra between us, wide and freezing and bitter.

And awful.

I tuck my arms against my sides, but my body can't decide whether to sweat or shiver. It torments me with both at once, on the same unnerving loop. Back and forth, again and again and again, feverish then freezing.

My heart and mind wage a more terrible tumult.

I should still be incensed with Veronica. I have every right to be. But I'm not. I can't even force the fury to come back.

Because it doesn't baffle me anymore.

Because now, suddenly...I get it.

My child is still just a sprout, but I already understand what it feels like to love it beyond reason. To vow I'll do whatever it takes, past all logic or laws, to ensure this creature's safety and joy. Yes, even the things they might hate me for. Things they might misinterpret, misunderstand, or even take for granted.

Things like sucking up to an earthworm masquerading as an entertainment reporter just to make sure their wedding gets the best press spin.

"Oh, God."

I croak it so slow beneath my breath, even Maximus doesn't hear. Only Jaden, still a good thirty feet away, cocks his head while pivoting around. My distress has him already crunching a tight frown, though he doesn't play solitaire with concern for long.

Kell swings around, abandoning her quest for the nearest bar to confirm my SOS has hit the air in more ways than one. Since she's closer, she gets to my side with fewer strides.

"What's going on? You smell like you ate a box of matches then doused them in lime juice."

I close my eyes and clutch my stomach again.

Fortunately, Maximus knows exactly how to interpret it.

"Not the best visual for keeping her on the good side of the porcelain god," he tells her.

"Won't do her any good if I lie." While her comeback is crisp, she clutches my shoulder with tender firmness. "Now that we've established our little safe zone, what's actually happening, darling?"

Safe zone. It's her way of stating that we're past the point of putting on smiles for the cameras. That if I even try to convince her otherwise, the scent references are going to get worse. Regardless, why am I even thinking about finishing the media walk-up?

That answer meshes much too perfectly with the dismal honesty I unveil for her.

"I was a wretch to Mother," I confess in a dismal mumble. "Some things...*a lot* of things...that probably shouldn't have been said."

"I know." She gently tick-tocks her head. "Your vibes were a touch aromatic. But it's not like she wasn't pushing you toward the ledge."

Jaden moves up during her allegation, ready with a concurring nod. "She's not clueless about how all three of us feel about Gentry," he offers with a twist of his lips. "That d-bag is worse than a mosquito bite. The harder you fight, the worse the rash."

"A fact we're all used to by now," I volley. "Which makes my detonation more disastrous."

Kell pushes up a hand. "She was right about one thing. The melodrama does *not* work. Take a breath. She'll figure it out and pull herself together, okay?" But when she takes in my reaction, a pointed look toward a non-distinct side entrance to the theater, she blanches. "Holy shit."

Even Jaden freezes in bewilderment. "Is she going inside with the mob?"

Ironically, the term is a Veronica original, which intensifies our shared shock at watching her shiny updo in the throng of "regular" people making their way inside the theater. Even after she disappears into the building, the three of us refuse to move.

At last Kell mutters, "Okay. What the freak *did* you say to her?"

Before I can gather enough breath for a reply, there's a new frenzy of activity in the area where we've taken cover.

The raucous is so sudden and loud, coming from the narrow access between two catering trucks, that I spin around and prepare to see half a dozen people. But only two figures emerge, engaged in a walk-shuffle-struggle gait. They're both swearing, though not in English.

I'm unsure how to react—and am saved from the decision as soon as Maximus rushes forward. "Reg?"

And even more so as Jaden scuffles backward—once we all focus on the person she's dragging by a pair of handcuffs.

No. Not a person. At least not the way we see it.

A recognition that doesn't astound me as much as my brother's voice, pushing from him despite the petrified glint in his eyes.

"Rerek?"

His bravery inspires me to reach for my own. "Oh… wow."

Kell emits a sardonic huff. "And I thought the craziest sight of the night would be Maximus's and your double tonsillectomy."

Clearly—and thankfully—she's not expecting obligatory laughs. I zoom my attention away from the demon, focusing on Reg.

"What's going on? Where'd you find him?"

And why does he look that way?

My logic, as well as another glance at my brother's

stressed glower, orders me to keep that part under wraps. I'm not sure Jaden is ready to hear—or see—it. Not yet.

But the difference in Rerek now…it's so distinct that I can't *unsee* it. It's another fresh irony, coming from the one who's always strived to ignore the arrogant jerk as much as possible, but it's undeniable. If I had to describe him in a word at this moment, it'd be *desperate*. Even…*needy*.

"Jaden."

The demon justifies both my descriptors as soon as the haggard syllables tumble from his shaking lips. The breaths beneath are haggard. His posture is dragged by defeat. It's so blatant, I can't help but continue my stare. Is this the same urbane blade who channeled Bowie, Jagger, *and* Styles just a week ago? Right now, he's more like a gorgeous-but-sad street rat.

"Jaden," he repeats with twice the destitution. "Please. I came here—"

"We see that," my brother spits.

"Why?" I direct the interjection straight to Reg, again following my instinct. Something tells me her answer is different—and probably more accurate—than the demon's take. "*Why* is he here? What's he doing anywhere *near* here?"

"I reckoned the same thing," the soldier returns. "Which shouldn't have puzzled me as much as it did, I suppose. This one always did love jabbing in business where he didn't belong."

"Oh, dagger me twice." The groan is threaded with enough of Rerek's impudence that it's an actual comfort. "*Now* I remember you. Veronica's little secretary. You used to chase me out of her office with a family crest paperweight."

His broad mouth curves up until Reg tugs on his cuff, making his pained grunt take over.

"Assistant, not secretary," she spits. "And it was a letter opener, not a paperweight. Just so you know, I've always been good with stabby things."

Rerek dips a respectful nod. "Noted."

"Good. So now, perhaps, you'll be a little more open about where you've stashed the grimoire."

Again, I absorb a strange reassurance from the demon's snobby snort. "For the tenth damnable time, I have no idea what you're talking about."

"Ah. Of course you don't." Reg flings a low huff. "Which is why you were chatting up that gang of simpering starlets like you'd introduce them to every casting director in the building? Maybe a bit more than that, hmmm? Telling them that if they hooked up with you, they'd have power and influence beyond their wildest dreams?"

"No." Rerek yanks back so hard, the cuff gouges his wrist. He winces but ignores it. "I solemnly swear, on my own two balls, *no*."

Kell sweeps up a hand and unleashes a wince. "Way more information than we needed, Mr. Horne, but okay."

"Uh-uh. *Not* okay." Jaden recovers a couple of his steps by stomping forward. He's close enough for Rerek to confront the whites of his eyes and the seethe of his teeth. "It's. Not. Okay."

"He's right." Doubly as quick as the rest of us, Rerek acknowledges that Jaden is referring to more than this confrontation. "He's completely right. It's not okay. Nor was it ever okay…to do what I did to you, Jaden. But I knew I couldn't just show up at the mansion and say it, so I thought a public setting might make you feel safer. To see that I mean what I'm saying, and—"

"The same way you *meant it* when you encouraged me to invite Kara to your place for that party?" Jaden growls. "And the same way she was *safe* when your overlord showed up and danced her straight to hell? The same way you kept *me* safe by hexing your house so I couldn't get out? Right. Because my safety is so damn important to you, buddy."

Unbelievably, Rerek's face contorts tighter. "It was wrong. And I came to understand that—"

"When Kara and Maximus came and tore through your force field."

Jaden starts pacing, his chest pumping hard. His fists flex harder. He's dark and tortured and heartbreakingly heroic.

"If they hadn't arrived and done that, tell me what your line would be now," he challenges. "Would you still be locking me behind the steel doors at night? Telling me it's all for my own good? Reassuring me that I don't have anything to worry about because you *love* me?"

"Because I do!" The cuff clatters against the floor as Rerek plummets to his knees. "I love you, Jaden Valari, with every aching fiber of my being. With every fiery electron in my mind. I…I just don't know what to do about it. Or how to prove it to you."

Jaden erupts with a laugh that's unrecognizable to me. It's hard, bitter, and weary—not at all like the brother who's always craving his next hit of G-force fun.

"Well, it's not by stealing a book that's one of my sister's most valuable physical possessions and then using it to rally recruits for your team in a war that—"

"Jaden!"

Kell turns my shout into a joint effort. She joins me to pound forward, our steps a matched pair of determined stomps. But too late, we all realize our brother's already said too much.

"Recruits?" Rerek demands. "For a...*war*?"

"Crap." Jaden swings around, locating the bar that Kell was just seeking out. He looks ready to drop his elbows against it until realizing the bartender isn't on duty yet. "Sorry," he mutters, reaching over and grabbing a bottle of Grey Goose by the neck. "Sorry. *Fuck*. I'm sorry."

No way do I expect Reg to re-enter the conversation with a shrug that comes as a strange relief. "Maybe this is all just tickety-boo, yeah? Now we have a good excuse to kill him."

Scratch the relief. All of it.

Though now I'm stuck at perplexed. For all intents, the Olympian is making a solid point. Rerek might be a key minion for Hades, but he's still a *minion*, little *m*. The hell king wouldn't give his disappearance half the shrug that Reg just offered. And he thought nothing of helping to make *me* disappear...

"That's not a bad idea. At all."

So why am I not nodding heavily at Kell's concurrence? Why am I back to weird relief when seeing Jaden isn't either?

I *am* sure about one thing. The profound calm that soaks into me when Maximus reenters the exchange. His shoulders are set. His movements are steady. He commands our tense circle as if we're a packed lecture hall. Gratitude floods in next to my relief.

"Or…we can choose to trust him."

Until he says that.

"You're kidding," Kell mutters. "Come on, big guy. *Tell us* you're kidding."

"He isn't." Jaden's glassy eyed after his third long swig of vodka but far from plastered. Though I sympathize with his ultimate goal for the night, I'm glad he's not there yet. His enunciation is stoic, clear—and miserable. "Not kidding. He's really right."

Kell huffs. "How much of the pharmacy is in you on top of those geese? Do you *know* what he just—"

"I heard him," Jaden retorts. "And I agree with him." His glance at Rerek is doused in disgust. "I hate it, but I agree with him."

Rerek, looking ready to sing a joyful aria even for that glance, clamps his composure back down. "I'm…not quite certain what's happ—"

"You love me." Jaden slams down the vodka hard enough to make some burst back up across his wrist. He shakes it off while circling smoothly around. "I got that part right, hmmm?"

Rerek's eyes, deep set but doubly huge now, are also shiny with heavy liquid. "Yes, sir. You do."

"Yet you've been stumped about how to prove it, aside

from locking me down in your villa for days and nights on end."

"Jaden—"

"Yes or no, chaos boy. Just yes or no."

Rerek sags his shoulders. Looks ready to follow suit with his head. Instead, he whispers, "Yes. All of the above, okay? Yes."

"Good. Because now you're getting a perfect chance to prove it. We need eyes and ears inside the underworld, especially for details about where Hecate's grimoire has landed. And if, anytime during this process, you decide it's more fun to spill with Hades than us, we'll decide it's fun to let Reg bury her dagger in your carotid. Sound like a plan?"

It's the moment of truth for Rerek Horne.

Reg senses it too, with a visible cinch on the cuff—though her effort won't mean a thing if the chaos demon decides this is an ideal chance to feel more like himself again.

If we're still dealing with the typical Rerek, he'll seize this chance to scoop up every new revelation we've just handed over and leave with it under the cover of a sudden windstorm, earthquake, bomb threat, power outage—perhaps all of the above—before heading straight for an emergency audience with Hades.

But if we get to keep this new Rerek, who professes his readiness to earn my brother's love and trust, maybe Jaden's massive gamble just succeeded.

If not, we might have just made the most dangerous mistake in this game.

I only hope we find out before it's too late.

CHAPTER 21

MAXIMUS

"**H**OW IS SHE?"

Kell punctuates the query with some soft *tings* of her fingernail on the rim of her half-full wineglass.

The chime blends with the rest of the late-night sounds that drift up to my apartment balcony. The rumble of a Metro train. A salsa tempo from a live band up the block. An uptick of wind, rustling the trees and skittering loose newspapers up the street.

Most nights, all of this would be welcome music for my tired senses. Tonight, it's just a background track for the whirlwind that persists in my mind. Taking a seat doesn't help the noise. Neither does a long breath in and a longer one out.

"Exhausted," I finally mutter as an answer. "Can't say that I blame her." While the EmStars festivities themselves went off without a hitch, Veronica was back to her old self after the broadcast, which meant a round of posing for the obligatory family photos at the afterparty. "I don't think my cheeks will be the same for days."

Kell joins a light laugh to her fingernail drum solo. "You get used to it. Well, you *should* get used to it. But to help in the meantime"—she salutes with her glass—"I pilfered a whole bottle of this from the party, and it's eyes-in-the-back-of-your-head good, so have at it with some professorly imbibing."

I wave a thanks-but-no-thanks hand. If anything, the expensive vino will only keep me up longer. Instead, while she's relaxed, I grab a chance for a conversational prod. "So, I *should* get used to it. Any more words of wisdom to share there, from the fast-thinking one who got us here?"

Though I finish with a teasing grin, Kell's reaction is more a squirming wince. "Fast thinking? Or maybe what *was* I thinking?"

And what was *I* thinking, assuming the wine would instantly restore her usual confidence?

"Hey. You did what you had to, given our little mall imbroglio."

She presses fingers to her lips, joking about nearly spewing her newest sip. "You're going to need to spell that, mister professor man, but hold up and let me fish out my thesaurus."

I field her dig with a good-natured laugh. "The point is, it's not like the proposal wasn't already forging hiking trails through my head."

"Understood." Her smile is instant and warm. "And appreciated." She takes another significant sip from her glass while directing an intense stare across the cityscape. "But you certainly didn't need little sis coming through with the bulldozer either."

"Sometimes a bulldozer is what's needed for the job."

"Did you tell that to my sister?"

"Didn't need to," I counter. "Kara knows." I lean forward, propping elbows to my knees. "And in her own way, she's also thankful for how you jumped in. If you hadn't, our mothers would be scheming about a baby shower instead of a bridal shower."

A second laugh flows from her. "Yes, but at least *you* wouldn't be stressing over a bachelorette party."

My growl-groan double punch loosens her up a millimeter more. "Something I *won't* be reminding them about," I grouse. "Though at this point, we might not have to."

She dips her head but hikes her brows. "Because you think they'll simply forget it?"

"Because I think they won't have time."

A quick side-eye over the rim of her glass. "Three months?"

"Three *weeks*, if that. And no, we haven't told Veronica yet. Figured the experience with the steerage entrance into the theater was enough trauma for the woman tonight."

"*Self-induced* trauma." She plunks the wine back on its coaster with a peeved huff. "Don't forget that. You and Kara shouldn't be owning a minute of that stuff."

While I figure out the best way to answer that, she leans against the railing. Why I feel like she's about to brandish a six-shooter in each hand is beyond me.

"Now, back to your info bomb, please? Something

about speeding up the timeline by a way-too-suspicious chunk? Are Kara and the twiglet okay? Is she having weird symptoms? Wombish karate kicks? Braxton Hicks shit?"

"Whoa, *whoa*." Different emphasis, though my guttural laughter is the same. "None of the above, thankfully."

"But enough of something *else* that you two are fast-tracking the wedding?"

I settle deeper into my chair and look out toward the foothills, graceful and dark against the sky as the city shifts into post-midnight mode. My thoughts move in a similar direction. There's not so much neon glare and disco blinkings in my brain right now. Though the general life situation is far from mellow, it feels that way for these few blessed minutes.

"Not a something," I finally clarify. "A some*one*."

Kell's inhalation is abrupt. To most of the world, she's just absorbing and contemplating a new piece of information, but I can practically see my emotions getting sucked away and analyzed by her otherworldly olfactory glands.

After a long ten seconds, she utters, "All right, lay out that tea. A someone who?"

I keep my regard pinned on her. "Last night, after you took off from Oread, Kara and I had another visitor. Persephone."

If she really had six shooters, she'd be dropping them through the floor. At least my reclusive sci-fi writer neighbor would have some new story material.

"*Not* the answer I was expecting," she admits. "Especially because the poor woman has another—what—ten days, give or take, before the new descent into hell?"

"Hecate snatched her away early. Claimed she needed some extra help with some things, and Persephone was apparently the only one she could trust."

Her gaze narrows. "Because her little canyon full of *diamonds* wasn't up for that?"

"She's choosing not to share the grand plan with them all yet. Persephone wasn't too surprised. Frankly, neither were we."

She nods. "A declaration of war isn't exactly the stuff for dinner table chat. Never know when someone will upend the broccoli casserole in protest."

"Oh, man. *Not* the broccoli," I deadpan.

"If not worse." She chuckles it out while casually folding her arms. "But you have to think, if a soldier as loyal as Circe is already tossing back guff about it, more dissension in the ranks is bound to be in store."

I rest my elbows on both the chair's armrests before raising my hands. "Her circus to run, her horses to tame. And definitely not the issue that drove Persephone to seek us out."

She moves her head again, if only for a confirming cock to the side. "Now that you've saved me the trouble of actually asking…"

I close my fingers in, forming a pair of statement fists. "The tension in Olympus… It's more far-reaching than we originally thought. According to Persephone, Hecate's ax is the biggest blade headed for the largest grindstone, but it's not the only one ready for a fight. The friction is pervasive at every level of their realm. Plus—"

"It's not the only realm with the problem."

She doesn't look pleased about being so right. At least her troubled pause supplies a valid excuse for deciding how to best break this all down for her.

"Persephone thinks…our wedding might be an answer to the whole dilemma."

Kell softly scoffs. "Okay, *dilemma* is what you say when you want to wear your dirty jeans or when there's more than three party invites for the same night. What you're talking about here…concurrent, cataclysmic destruction of every realm we know…"

"Thanks for the elucidation," I mutter.

She raises her eyebrows and then slams them back down, echoing my final word with the same mix of approval and sarcasm that Kara would. The effect is a grin I can't hide—up to the moment she responds again.

"So, what did Persephone say after that? About your wedding being the magical fix-it-all for the insanity?"

She listens as I recount the rest of the spring goddess's presentation. The belief that our nuptials will be the must-attend celebration for every entity with an invitation. The plan to transform the event into a giant peace summit. Persephone's belief, so adamant, that it'll work. That is *has* to work.

"And you? And Kara?" she poses after those assertions. "What do you two think? And believe?"

The query makes me gain my feet, as well. I park my elbows on the rail and rub my palms together. An ambulance speeds by below, turning its wake into conspicuous stillness.

"I think…that right now, we don't have a lot of options," I say. "And that if there's a solution for making the future work, we have to seize it." My sights land on the bright glow of the downtown interchange. In this moment, it symbolizes a light I need to be reaching for…believing in. "Because right now, the future isn't just about us."

There's another long silence, which I accept as a good sign. Kell's considering her words. If she disapproved of my assessment, they'd have come faster and harsher.

At last she murmurs, "And Kara? She agrees with you?"

"We've been too tired to hash it out in full. But I hope so." I cant my head, giving her a determined look. "Maybe it'll give her a reason to actually look forward to the wedding."

She kicks up one corner of her mouth. "Instead of holding out hope for something like a rom-com finale?"

I chuff. "Ah. You know that story too?"

"Buddy, I lived that story."

"Well, there *is* that…"

I join her in a fresh round of light laughter but frown as she sobers again. It's not that I didn't expect the change, but her switch-up seems much too fast.

"I'm a little surprised that Kara told you that story," she admits. "Okay, maybe more than a little."

"Eh?" I turn so only one elbow leans on the rail. "Why?"

She lifts her head, now the one to gaze over the streets. "It's not a memory she likes to bring up. I think, in a lot of ways, she thinks it's admitting to some kind of weakness."

"Weakness?" I let my incredulous tone write the essay of words on the tip of my tongue. *Weak* isn't the first or *twentieth* word I'd use for either one of the Valari sisters. "You're not serious."

"On every pair of Ferragamos in my closet." She lifts two fingers of an upstretched hand. "Even the ones I don't yet have room for."

"Thanks, but I still don't get it."

"Because your upbringing was a one-eighty from ours." She nods toward my deeper scowl. "You were taught that your otherworldly side was bad and destructive. That your strength was everything that was going to expose you, destroy you. In Veronica Valari's world, we were told that our demon side set us above everyone else. That humans were enamored by us. Though it was always stressed as a secret, it was because humans had to be *protected* from us, not the other way around. It was like our glamorous superpower."

"Glamorous." I turn the word over while jogging my head back to take in the stars. They're dim because of the noise pollution, but they're still there. Like the truth I'm digging at here. "Seems like a valid plan."

She shoves out a sigh. "Until the moments when it's not."

I bring my head back down. "Like trying to make sense of deep emotions from a human-made movie."

She rocks her head from side to side. "Okay, jury's still out on whether ten miles of tulle and a billion twinkle lights are a triumph or travesty, but solid point otherwise."

I push from the rail and pace thoughtfully. "And separate from the key takeaway here. That Kara remembers that night and all the emotions she felt then, good *and* bad, because it was more than just identifying with something innately human. It was *connecting* to it. Feeling something… for creatures that you'd all been taught were *beneath* you.

Unworthy of you. But that movie, even in its comedic silliness and striving, was worthy of her emotions. She started learning, in some deep and painful ways, that maybe *humans* were worthy of her investment."

Kell is ready for me with a contemplative impression. "Maybe that's why she chose to study classics, as well. She's always been fascinated with the stories of the human condition, even if most are fictional. She works to look deeper, to the grains of truth that inspired them. The bigger picture. How humans can rise above themselves upon so many occasions, as if they envision being transformed into gods just because they imagine it. And even when it doesn't happen, how they try and try again." A small laugh escapes her lips. "It's ridiculous, right? But they never give up."

"Which, in some ways, actually *does* make them gods... Right?" I postulate. "The pride and the hubris can be good things, if pushed toward worthy goals. There's something, I guess, noble about it? To keep pushing, no matter what the odds. To believe that one is born for greatness..."

"Except that gods are already born that way?" she inserts, cocking a wry smirk.

I hurl back a matching look, only without the grin. "You're not getting it."

"Of course I'm getting it." She hitches a shrug. "I'm vain, not vapid. But rather than digging deeper into this existential box, I'm going to opt for indulging my own hubris. It's time to put all of this under a detox mask"—she circles a finger over her face and pulls the glittering shoes off her feet—"and give these doggies a long rest. I advise you do the same. The pace won't let up for you and Kara, especially when you hit Mother with the new wedding date suggestions."

I sense her underlying satisfaction with my pronounced grimace. "Help a guy out? Your prediction of the ultimate reaction?"

"Truthfully?" She's back with the two-fingered scout's honor pose. "I think she's going to be thrilled. This will be a well-timed red bow for the box that's still dented from Arden's point of view, as well as the elite industry folks who were aware he was preparing to propose to Kara."

I rear my head back. "Dented box? You're not referring to being those damaged goods, are you?"

"Of course not." But the adamant reiteration, plus her exaggerated eye roll, tempt me to discredit her. "Don't be silly."

I lift a hand in open surrender, conveying an implied mea culpa and a silent pledge to drop the subject. I can't force the woman into a spill-all about what is or isn't happening between her and Arden. I know that the press is into them but then not. That their stories and posts are fueled by the couple's angry flirting, which then cools. Most importantly, that there actually was an engagement ring, but now no more. Not after Arden hurled the rock into the ocean just to prove a point to Kell.

Which is a lot more than I can claim at this point.

"Hey." Her demand stabs into my meandering musings. "You...*aren't* being silly, right?"

I hold up my other hand, making it clear I'm not angling after her personal business. "Bare-*my*-soul truth?" I say. "I was thinking how shitty I feel that Kara still doesn't have a real ring on her finger."

My soon-to-be sister-in-law truly knows the fine art of droll smirks. "Are you actually stressing about that, after Veronica announced your ring-shopping trip from the red carpet tonight? Your little sojourn will get more click-throughs than the last three presidential debates."

The growl that emerges from me might as well be a profanity. I broadcast the same intent with my glare. "You want to know where all those clicks can go?"

She playfully whacks my shoulder. "And *there's* the brother-in-law I love, adore, and expect to show up!"

While her praise brings a damn nice warmth, it's helped more by something else. An idea that wraps around my mind like conceptual chicken wire. It's that persistent. But it's also that tenaciously good.

"Hmmm," I drawl back. "You love me, huh?"

A small laugh makes her shake. "Said it. Meant it. You're as good as family now anyway."

"Very glad to hear it." I reach out, cupping her shoulders with equal affection. "Because tomorrow, I'm going to ask you to prove it."

Method to my madness: I'm holding her shoulders because I'm expecting a balk. Not only does the woman prove me wrong, but spectacularly so. Instead of reticence, she's suddenly brimming with readiness.

"Ohhh. I detect that Professor Kane is devising an evil but romantic plan for my sister. And is it a plan that little *moi* gets to be a part of?"

I chuckle for a few seconds. "In one very hopeful syllable, Miss Valari... *oui*."

CHAPTER 22

Kara

"I STILL THINK MOTHER is going to kill us for this."

"And *I* still think it's a task she'll gladly cross off her list. Especially after the fun little timeline shrinker that you and Maximus dropped on her yesterday," Kell answers with a simple shrug and elegant grin that'll haunt my dreams for weeks to come.

"Not little and *not* fun," I grouse while trying to readjust the left side of my strapless corset. Something from it is digging into my girl flesh there, emphasizing the *not fun* theme that's dominating this morning. "Still, she wasn't too excited when we threatened to just run away and do the deed in Vegas over Halloween. Oh, wow—" I cut into my own rambling, grabbed by a fresh revelation. "Maybe that's where Maximus disappeared to last night."

Kell's mild mien gives way to a scowl. "And maybe it's time for you to stop fixating. He called *and* texted, right?

Several times? A full Alameda Literature Department brainstorming session? Which, unsurprisingly, probably *did* go all night if President McCarthy's demanding detailed plans for catching up students after the earthquake break."

I fling her a questioning side-eye. "You seem to know a lot about that."

"Because you filled me in this morning."

"I was that coherent?"

A new shrug. "The sun was out, sister."

No better reason for me to embrace a fresh frown. "It was still six a.m., *sister.*"

"Since when have I cared about the clock when it's time to make sure you're being a productive member of society?"

"Truth," I mumble, though it fades into a curious hum as I follow her gaze out a wide bay window, where full cypresses are sentries for a private garden directly overlooking the Pacific in one of Santa Barbara's exclusive enclaves. There's a pod of dolphins leaping out in the waves, explaining her fascination—and enhancing the view that's made the last three hours a little less stressful for me.

Can't say I've reached the same conclusion about Maximus's absence last night. *All* night. Without him wrapped around the sprout and me, my sleep was fitful at best. At the moment, it feels like a decent excuse to toss a deeper frown in Kell's direction.

"I'd have just preferred it if you'd roused me to go lounge down on that beach instead of drowning me in chiffon."

She accepts my nod toward the beach with a light laugh. "Perhaps we can make that a reality once we decide on *the* dress."

"We?" I tug on the corset again, still worried that Twiglet might make an ill-timed appearance. "You mean *you*. Because—"

"Yes, yes," she wearily interrupts. "I know. You'd marry Maximus in a potato sack and be happy about it. But we don't want to be responsible for a Veronica-style coronary, which means you're wearing Madame Verocity, and this is her only free consulting day for the next three months. Since she'll be in Europe until Thanksgiving and then Miami during the holidays, your alterations will likely be handled by a Verocity minion. But for now, we'll get the *big look* handled."

"And let's face it, darling. *Nobody* does the big looks like me."

That perfect purr is the rightful possession of the room's newest arrival, a diva rocking one-inch eyelashes, six-inch stilettos, and a flawless pink smile. Her hourglass figure is exquisitely defined by a short-sleeved sweater set with a wide diamond belt, matched by the jewels on her ears and neck. For all her va-va-voom femineity, she's dragging a fully loaded dress rack like a seasoned teamster unloading a cargo container.

As she does, Kell delivers a pair of playful snaps into the air.

"As usual, Verocity delivers the veracity." She cocks a hip, rolls back on one foot, and joins the famous designer in appraising my lingerie-clad form. "What's our next play with this pretty girl, V?"

Madame comes forward, assessing me. "Well, we've officially ruled out the princess poof, as well as the subdued A-lines. So let's streamline things."

"Not too streamlined," Kell objects. "It's some zazz. Something different. You *know* Veronica."

"Oh, Lord, do I know Veronica." As the designer basks in our joint giggles, she also assesses the massive line of gowns on the big dolly. Most of them are zipped into wide, clear bags. From here, they all look the same. Fortunately, the designer jabs a decisive finger at a couple of low-key receptacles toward the far-left side. "If you go simpler with the overall line, the look will require a statement from another angle. I do think…perhaps a custom-embellished train and veil…might make all the difference in the world."

The whole time she croon-chatters, the woman sweeps a gown out of a bag, gathers it around her forearms, and then lifts it over my head. The shimmering mermaid flare, along with its sparkly sheath dress, tumble effortlessly until I'm fully covered in the front.

The woman only gets to the halfway point of zipping me up before Kell grins like a loon, gasps like a giddy kid, and presses her hands to her cheeks. My own face widens with shock, wondering if she's about to give in to tears as well. I'm unsure whether to keep gawking at her or look away, so I opt for a third option. Blushing like crazy.

"Okay, the saying *is* true," she utters. "You really do know when you put on the right one."

After summoning a huge breath, I dare to take her up

on that and fully raise my head. I tell myself it's no big deal, that Kell isn't going to put me on *block* and *ignore* just for hating the gown that brought her to tears.

Except that it does worse things to me.

Awful word choice. Not *worse*.

In so many ways, despite the sob that burns my throat and the fingers that fly to my lips, it's all so much better. The feeling that I'm not even looking at *me* anymore. The bright soar of realizing that I am. That this beautiful creature, gazing back from atop the high scalloped neckline with iridescent beads, is actually the woman who's going to be Mrs. Maximus Kane. That she's going to be beyond joyous about it.

Most of all, that the professor who took a wild chance on loving little me is going to be just as happy.

Once more, bad word usage.

I don't plan on making Maximus Kane *happy*. I'm going to give the man a lifetime of sheer ecstasy. Of unending passion, exhilaration, completion. Of all the fulfillment and fire he already gives to me.

With effort, I scoot the mush into my mind's margins. Or so I think. It's still a massive chore to push the tears back down as I address Kell. "When you're right, sister, you're really very right."

Kell sniffs and quirks up one edge of her mouth. "But honey, I'm always right."

Madame Verocity, seemingly in her own world while circling me to fluff flounces and pull out the ruffled train, suddenly pops her head up. "Hmmm. Not finished."

She strides to a built-in closet and emerges with a veil so long and gorgeously diaphanous, even Maria von Trapp—the movie version, at least—would bow in envy.

"Aha. *Now* finished. Minus makeup, hair, and jewelry, of course."

"It's perfect." Kell moves behind me, helping the designer to spread out the veil.

"Additionally, we can customize the tiara," Madame states. "As well as the veil, which is actually an interestingly blank canvas." In response to the quizzical glance I join to Kell's, she elaborates, "I have a very talented team of fine fabric embroiderers. They can customize a design here, if you have decided on an overall theme for the occasion?"

"Theme?" Kell nearly stammers. "Not real—"

"Yes," I barge in. "Really. Absolutely."

When Kell flashes me a glare and taps a finger toward the whiteboard calendar on the wall, I stubbornly purse my lips. There will be *some* things in this wedding just for Maximus and me, even if it means photo schedules getting adjusted and late press announcements. Nobody, even Ellery Gentry, will lift a fraction of a protest about it.

Impending realms war or not, this is going to be Maximus's and my *wedding day*. Whether history notes what I'm doing to make it more special for just the two of us is up to the scholars tasked with recording it. They don't concern me.

Only one person fully concerns me.

And between now and our official date, he'll stay that way—come what may.

*✳

"Ermmm…Kell?"

I feel a little guilty about speaking up, since she's the one who just paid for our decadent lunch at the Biltmore Santa Barbara. But not that guilty, considering what I plunked down to Madame Verocity for the wedding gown. The contrition eases even more when I reflect on the veil I detailed with the designer, who lent her avid approval for the custom concept. Part of me even wishes time would fast-forward so I get to see Maximus's reaction too.

But the pangs through my senses aren't solely from wedding fever.

I miss him. Desperately. Stupidly. Painfully.

Though we've only been apart a bit more than twenty-four hours and have exchanged ten times that number in text messages, it's a truth as plain as the big red flower that adorns Kell's floppy driving hat. She plops the thing onto her head while flipping the switch to retract the sunroof on her little sports car—probably to prevent the watchful valet from snapping a surreptitious picture of us.

I've already deployed my wide sunglasses and silky neck scarf for the same reason.

"Yes, m'dear?" she answers to my hail while we clear the last section of the hotel's terracotta driveway and hook a right, instead of a left, onto the drive that ribbons between the resort and Butterfly Beach. "You need something?"

"Yes."

I stab at the volume button to save my eardrums from

the thumping decibels of music she's blasting. I'm as much of an EDM girl as everyone else in Southern California, but not when I've got a serious question to pose. Fate is with me, lending a few moments of greater calm when she slows to check cross traffic at a small intersection.

"Why did you ask the valet for directions to Hendry's Beach?"

"Hmmm. What?"

"You heard me. Why are we going north? LA is a hundred miles the other direction. Don't even go there with *Harry and Meghan are dying to have catch-up margaritas.* I won't believe you."

"Do we have to have a hard itinerary?" she replies as if we've decided to deter from our normal frozen yogurt joint for the simple sake of nostalgia. "Just thought you'd like a little adventure. You always liked it at Hendry's. You remember, right? When Mother used to drag us up here because her favorite masseuse relocated to the spa at the Bacara, and we'd bribe the nanny of the moment to take us to the Boathouse for those decadent burrito breakfast plates?"

I completely kill the EDM and cock my head like a second one has sprung out of hers. "Except that we just had lunch. And, considering Maximus has been up all night think-tanking an accelerated semester plan, I've got a lot of student-type stuff to catch up on. Wait," I bark, a new revelation sharpening my spine. "Don't you too?"

But here's the moment my sister eyeballs the stereo readout and decides she can't live another second without singing along to the new Lizzo song.

I'm ready to throw my hands up but catch myself before wasting time on the futility, especially as she accelerates onto the 101 through the center of town. Rather than attempting another protest that's clearly not going to wash with her, I decide to focus on the dilemma I stand a chance of winning—deciphering why my little sibling, who refuses to acknowledge any *sentimental* bone in her body, is suddenly in the mood to kick off her thousand-dollar strappies and tromp through the sand at Hendry's.

No Mexican food on the planet should be worth that to her.

But half an hour later, as we pull into the parking lot tucked in a small canyon in Arroyo Burro State Park, my sister's grin occupies even more of her face. If possible, it's giddier than how she looked when Madame Verocity zipped me up earlier.

But that's the core of my dilemma. Her dorky smirk shouldn't *be* possible. *What's going on?* Is she just putting on a weird show for paparazzi I'm not yet aware of? Or—an argument making more sense by the minute—has an alien transport touched down from space, taken my sister, and left this mutant in her place?

I glance around with a feigned air of casual perusal. The gentle cliffs and swaying palms are as beautiful and brilliant as I remember, but I'm not enjoying them fully for concern about any surreptitiously lurking lenses in places we still might not know about. Kell and I are evenly matched when it comes to spotting intrepid telephoto glass, but she's still looking off her game in that regard—and others. Why is she still sticking to the Wonderland-worthy smile?

"So." I barely refrain from sardonically stretching it out. "Are we just stopping for a few snaps, or do you want to get out and—"

My breath snags so sharp and hard, my interruption becomes a comical gurgle. I'm not sure Kell's spurt of a laugh makes it easier or harder to recover.

"Sorry," I finally manage to mumble. "There's a truck over there…it looks exactly like Maximus's."

"That so?" She grabs the steering wheel and the middle console to push herself up by a few inches and gaze across the sparsely filled parking lot. "Huh. You're right. But you know how the Santa Barbarans love their outdoor stuff. There have to be a lot of those big boys around here."

During the explanation, I swing my focus back around on her. *Solely* her. Though she'd never openly admit it, my urbane sister has her own ways of giving up important details about where she's going with a conversation. When not one of them surfaces right now, that's also a significant sign. Something in the realm of a glaring neon one that I don't dare ignore.

Or want to.

The admission is like a signed permission slip for everything from my hair follicles to my toe tips. Suddenly, I'm zinging with new awareness. The sun is warmer. The breeze is cleaner. Even the scents on the air, bracing and balmy and sandy, feel like they're hitting me harder than the sister who can probably smell her way up to the botanic garden up in the foothills.

None of it mellows as I get out of Kell's car without a word.

As I leave her behind, letting her indulge an impishly knowing laugh.

As I scribble a mental note to curse *and* thank her for the complicity in this elaborate plot.

I certainly *hope* it's a plot…

Otherwise, I'm going to look like a lovestruck loon in my urgent run out to the sand. At this point, maybe even a miserable maid seeking out her returning sailor from the shore. A stretch of sand that's interrupted only by some people with books on the big rocks and a few more tossing sticks for their dogs in the shallows. The sunshine, golden and persistent, makes everything seem like a dazzling dream.

Especially the figure up on the lifeguard tower platform.

I'm relieved the station isn't staffed on this off-season day, because Maximus is worthy of occupying the elevated spot on his own. I swear, even if he gets on a real throne in Olympus one day, the moment won't suck out my every breath like this incredible moment. The California rays playing over his shirtless, flawless torso. The ocean wind turning his unbound hair into a multilayered banner. Best of all, the mysteries of his mind carving his features into a thoughtful, beautiful silhouette.

The face that will never cease to bind me. Mesmerize me. Draw me closer, step by step, across the sand, until surely my pounding heart is the thing that makes him turn and look.

And smile.

And magnetize me that much closer.

He jumps down from the tower in one lithe move. Hits the sand with magnificent grace.

Then he's there for me. Bold and broad. Tall and focused. Quiet and waiting.

Like he'll always be.

As the conviction dominates my soul, my body is pushed by perfect instinct. I move into his embrace with a sigh that threatens to expel tears along with my breath. Until now, I didn't realize how exhausting it was getting to keep my brave face on for everyone. Now, with the warmth of his pectoral against my cheek and the smell of his sunblock in my senses, life really does feel like a gold-kissed dream.

But it's not the best kiss of the day.

That one belongs to the demigod who tucks his head in and down, finding my lips with the magnificent command of his own. Who, thank God, doesn't stop there. As my tongue responds to the call of his, frantically melting and rolling with his, I sigh once more. No tears this time. Only sundrenched happiness and abiding adoration.

After a glorious few minutes of our well-needed reunion, words finally rise to my brain again.

"Well, good day to you too, Prince Maximus," I take the chance to tease. "Quite a throne room you have here."

He's waiting with a long, intentional growl. "*Professor* is just fine, Miss Valari. You know that."

"Of course. Because you were busy earning it back at Alameda, with the *lesson planning?*"

"And who says that wasn't what was happening?" His half-smirk has my pulse skipping in equal measure. "There are these things called *field trips*, you know…"

"Ahhh," I offer. "Yes. I think I remember a few. Visiting the La Brea tar pits…the zoo…"

I'm stopped from lengthening the list when my secret surprise leans in to take my lips again. As we're clinching and my heartbeat is tripping harder over itself, there's an approving catcall from the parking lot. My sister is beyond proud of herself, and I don't blame her. I don't want to.

The only thing I want right now is more of what my gorgeous professor is offering—and then some. Enough to make up for what he put me through last night. No. More. So much more.

Thankfully, as we pull apart and I stare up into the beloved angles of his face, I already catch the hint that he's aligning plans the same direction.

"Well, Miss Valari, I can guarantee no tar pits for tonight's excursion."

I tilt my head, all too happy about flashing a returning grin full of devilish entendre. "What about the zoo? I've always enjoyed wild animals."

His low chuckle matches the timbre of heat from his aura. "That part's up to you. But if we've got to crack whips to make it happ—"

I cut him off by mashing our mouths harder than before. The man, and his lusciously sinful mind, deserve no less. This surprise adventure is already off to an amazing start.

CHAPTER 23

MAXIMUS

DESPITE THE INITIAL—AND HOLY damn, wonderful—passion of my reunion with Kara, I'm as nervous as a kid at prom during the drive that takes us a little farther north on the coast. Surprising a woman like her... have I blown my whole wad on this idea? After tonight, am I going to be the baby daddy working to live this disaster down even when our child turns thirty?

Kara Valari. Even the syllables of her name are evocative of things like diamond bracelets, gourmet chocolates, and imported lace.

But in less than a month, she's going to be Kara Kane.

And everything in my psyche says that Mrs. Kane was created for a little escape like this. Right now, perhaps she needs it as badly as I do.

I make my mind stick to that belief as I take the exit for El Capitan Beach. But instead of turning toward the state park, we continue up the small surface road. Framed by a variety of local palms and some flowering trees, an even smaller road branches off from it, cutting up toward the hills.

Now that I don't have to worry about other vehicles, I dare a lengthier glance toward my little demon. Inside of ten seconds, it's less difficult to find my confidence. She's already lowered the window on her side of the truck and is leaning her head out like a kid bound for an amusement park.

But following that theme, there are hints of trepidation in her expression too. Maybe she's wondering if this is a similar *gotcha* to the one Kell delivered this morning. Part of me is tempted to ensure her that it's not. I'm even ready with a disclaimer, primed to suggest some backup plans just in case.

In less than a minute, I'm exultant about ejecting them all from my brain. But a thousand times more joyous about witnessing Kara's first reaction to our field trip destination.

"Are you *even* serious?" she gasps out. "It's like…the Garden of Eden. You bribed the staff not to tattle that I'm here, right?"

I grunt my way through an affectionate buss to her neck. "If I've done everything right, we won't see the staff at all."

She's dutiful about obeying my hand signal to stay where she's at. But as I arrive at her side of the car and reach up to help her out, it's clear she hasn't been idle. The gears in her mind are whirring so fast, I can almost hear them.

"So last night…you were here and not at Alameda?" She huffs as soon as I swing a guilty-as-charged side-eye. "But I sent a text to Jesse too, asking him to make sure you guys ordered dinner. He answered me—"

"From his own apartment," I supply. "Or maybe from

one of our building's hallways. I told the guy he was risking his mortality if anything happened to you while I was away. But I had to make sure everything was perfect for this. For you. For us."

She stops swiftly, clutching both my hands so I do the same. Once our gazes meet, she presses a hand to my face.

"Being with you is perfection, Maximus Kane. *This*, right here…moments for us…that's what's perfect."

For a long moment, I'm hopelessly lost in her stare. As excited as I am about what's ahead, the bright satin of her eyes brings a tactile effect as well as an emotional one. I'm so taken. So stricken. So indigent if she's not wrapped around me, mind and soul.

Quickly, I belay the need—though not before it's incessantly knocking on my cock.

Not now.

Well…not yet.

Not if I want to dodge the identification as the Neanderthal who got her here and instantly dragged her into the bushes.

They're pretty cool bushes, if I have to be thinking about something besides burying myself in her lush body. I have myself to thank, I guess, considering the rains I brought to the area have inspired the coastal poppies and primroses into autumnal blooms.

The distraction is a lifeline for my self-control, helping me toward suave surety as I fold a hand atop hers and gently press our clasp to the middle of my sternum.

"Well, Kara Valari," I address to her declaration, daring to coax her body close again. "I can't and won't argue with you about that point. But maybe we can do one better than perfection."

But I already feel like an imposter for suggesting it—because the sight of this woman next to me, with her lips lifted in promise and her face bathed by the sun, I know that I'm already there. The fulfilled promise is in my arms. For me, for always, Kara is better than perfection. And because of it, the one who will make me a better man.

I only hope I'm hitting the goal now.

After fifty more steps up this path, I'll know.

The chapparal and woods give way to a wide expanse of grass. On the other side of it, there's a picnic table with a colorful woven linen on top. There's also a firepit and—

"A yurt."

I stop and examine her face after the words fall from her. I can't tell if she's happy or sad about the declaration, even as her jaw falls all the way open.

"You found...our yurt."

Our yurt. Though that still doesn't tell me much of a thing, it's *some*thing—and it's making me smile. My instincts are leading in a positive direction. I hope they're not wrong.

"It's not directly on the beach, but there's running water and swankier amenities to consider. I'm also afraid Bubba doesn't come with it, but—"

"I love it."

"But the owners here *do* have a cool old hound named Bayard, which I took as a good sign—"

"I love that too," she cuts in again. "And you. Now more than anything."

It occurs that now is likely a good time to shut up.

At the least, to change the subject—though Kara herself launches forward as if ready to do just that. With a laugh, I let her set the pace for our impatient walk-run across the grass, up a pair of steps, and into the round, canvas-walled structure.

"You brought some of my clothes," she exclaims at once. "And fresh toiletries." And then spins around to expose me to the widest pop of her gaze that I can remember.

The last time she was close to this gawk, I had burst in on her in Hades's library with her grandfather at my side. Though Gio Valari isn't here for this occasion, I cling to the wish that she's happier about this unexpected twist.

"*Maximus*. Do we get to stay here?"

Aha. Definitely happier. Which means I'm grinning wider. Probably like a total nutcase by now. We haven't even gotten to the best part of my plan, but I don't care.

"Just for a couple of nights," I qualify. "But it's better than—"

She's avidly interrupting me again. But I'm past the concern about these too, especially when they're kisses like this. Long and wet and wanting, full of tongue and lust and cravings, but at the same time, doorways to more. A heart and soul's worth. Everything I have to give her, even as she rocks back to offer the bold fullness of her dazzling smile.

"It's better than any surprise of my life," she whispers.

Yet just when I expect her to lift her lips to mine again, she uses her grip on my neck as leverage to leap up onto the king bed that occupies a good piece of the circular floor. From her new height, she's back to plunging her mouth down over mine.

And I'm already figuring out ways to make the height difference permanent.

My pulse doubles. My balance falters. Is this what it feels like when *I* move in to kiss *her*? It's helplessness but hopefulness. Anticipation but consummation. Vulnerability that nevertheless constricts my throat into a commanding growl. It doesn't stop me from answering her in a rough rasp of my own.

"Just tell yourself to start expecting the unexpected," I say with purposeful ambiguity and not much more. Internally, I've made the split-second decision to keep tomorrow's surprise activities, which include whale watching and organic applesauce making, a secret. Totally selfish call. It's a shot of pure adrenaline every time I give her a new experience. And soon, we'll be sharing so many new experiences—like all of our child's firsts. The good *and* the bad…

But tonight, it's about nothing except us. And all the ways, bright and brilliant and amazing, that this woman turns all my days into bold, beautiful adventures. Escapades even better than this.

"Which means exactly what, mister?"

"Hmmm. Patience, beautiful." I wrap an arm around her waist and give it a light tug. "All will be revealed soon."

She head-bumps the center of my chest. "Not fair. I endured a whole morning of wedding-dress shopping with my sister for this."

"Endured? That's supposed to be the fun part, right? Or did I miss a memo somewhere about trendiest fun sister dates?"

She yanks back far enough to smack my shoulder. "You know what I mean." But then steps back again, getting free of my affectionate hold. "But you know what you *don't* know?"

I tilt my head with a questioning scowl. "Should I be afraid to ask?"

A few seconds. Less than ten syllables out of my mouth. Yet in that time, the woman's toed off her flats, flung away her flowy blouse, and unhooked her bra. The light-pink thing slips away from her shoulders as she spins around—

And heads for the yurt's open door.

The door that's still wide open to the outdoors.

Our little Eden—in which she now looks determined to be a risqué new Eve.

"What you don't know, Professor..." she calls while pirouetting on the grass, "is that you don't have the lock on *all will be revealed*."

After prying my tongue from the bottom of my throat, I shake the whole structure while covering the three steps to the door. But then the strength leaves my legs, and I'm stuck clutching the doorframe while watching my saucy little striptease unbutton her shorts.

As soon as they fall to her ankles, my tongue takes a new dive to my esophagus. Thankfully, my brain still comes up with some decent comeback words to fill our charged pause.

"Is this going to be a new vocabulary lesson, beautiful? If so, I have suggestions for the list."

She clasps her hands behind her back, clearly knowing what that does for my view of her chest. "You know I'd love to learn some new syntax, Professor. But I seem to have forgotten my essay book and laptop at home."

My teeth clench as splinters dig into my palms. I'm gripping the door support so hard, it's probably about to snap. Paradise has never hurt so good. Or been so breathtaking.

"Maybe you'll have to accept a very firm lecture," I growl.

"Or perhaps you can just demonstrate the terms." She sways a little, teething her bottom lip. "During…a field trip?"

She sing-songs the last of it while starting to prance around the edges of our clearing. My mind bursts with rough words of reprimand, but when I open my mouth, nothing but a laugh flows out.

Why did I think I'd be the only one handing out the surprises here? Less than an hour into our getaway, Kara's blasting away my expectations too. Slicing open my boxes. Unearthing my roots.

But most of all, tempting my inner caveman. Calling out the wild Adam in me.

No. Not him.

Because as I hop the patio rail and push into a sprint toward her, I already know one thing with pounding clarity.

I don't want to get primeval with Eve.

I want the female who got kinky with the snake. The fiery goddess Lilith, often referred to as the mother of demons, who refused to play nice for Adam.

That's the naked creature I stalk, swift but not swift enough, across the grass and into the thick underbrush. That's the fierce fairy who eludes me again, levitating into a leap high over me and back onto the grass. That's the woman who turns, her hair in the wind and her belly glowing with the shades of all the flowers surrounding her...

Making me fall in love with her all over again.

The recognition that gives me power like I've never felt before. And speed to match.

And a grin, now as wicked as hers, after my new charge gets me into her intimate personal space.

But she's only keeping up the smile because she's gauging her next jolt. I already see it, ready to act before she's finished with her furtive glances to each side. Kara gets about two steps to her left before I'm snagging her with my right arm. Then my left.

Her head snaps up. Her eyes are wide. Her breasts a pillow against my pecs at a frantic rhythm. Her nipples, dark and perfect, are as hard as the coral tree seeds that sprinkle the ground around our feet. They betray her to me. She doesn't just feel every fraction of my lust. She shares it.

"First vocabulary word," I rasp, lowering my lips to an inch above hers. "*All locked up.*"

A new clamp of my teeth, as Kara digs fingernails into my beard and drives me into a violent hiss. "That's three words, not one, Mr. Kane. Guess we should be glad you're a literature professor instead of a math whiz."

"*Really don't care,*" I say, punctuating it with a gentle bite along her jawline. "There's three more."

"Well, now you're asking for a trip to study hall."

I chuckle while gathering her thighs around my back. "Field trip liberties."

"Hmmm," she croons into my neck. "That works too. *Oh!*"

Bringing her over to the picnic table was a stroke of genius. My blood roars, wild and hot, as her stunned shriek hits the air. Though the glow at her center has faded, there are other colors that I drink in with growing desire. The golden fires in her eyes. The rosy banners across her cheeks. The tightening red berries of her nipples.

But taking up greater chunks of my focus…

The pretty pinks of the paradise between her legs.

I slide my hands there at last, spreading my fingers along her thighs as I stroke her outer layers with my thumbs. *Shit.* She's already so wet and glistening. There are droplets on her sex like dew on roses.

But is the rest of the flower ready?

I don't waste a lot of time to start seeking the answer. Rolling one of my index fingers in, I press against the edges of her entrance. Then harder. Then deeper.

As soon as her walls accept all of my thrust, a high sigh trickles from her lips.

"*Maximus.*"

I match her exclamation with a low—and increasingly frustrated—groan. Now, of all times, I've turned into a bumbling dork about opening my fly. One-handed has never once been an issue for me.

But one-handed has never included the duties my *other* hand is handling. Especially with a beguiling little seductress who seems determined to help with things.

"*Ohhh!*"

I'm unsure what's sexier: the long moan the woman should consider trademarking or the urgent swivels of her hips, working her tight fissure along my finger. The answer is meaningless. For that matter, so is everything else in the world. If the glamping resort owners decided to traipse through here with a tour group right now, I doubt I could stop the abject greed of my libido, the burning craving of my cock.

"Oh…Maximus…"

"I know, sweet one."

She flashes a delicious smile between long licks at her lips. "That's…*four* words now."

"All right," I force myself to chuckle back. With my erection finally freed, I need every shred of help with the self-control right now. "Why don't I just triple down on that?"

Her forehead scrunches. So enchanting. Too damn gorgeous. "What…do you…mean?"

"I mean…open your legs wider, Kara. Because I'm going to fuck you like we're the only ones in Eden."

That's probably more than twelve words. But once more, a number that doesn't matter.

Nothing is more important than ensuring this woman knows who belongs inside her. For now and always.

CHAPTER 24

Kara

THIS MUST BE WHAT it feels like to be struck by lightning.

Maximus doesn't just lunge into me. He fills me until I'm gasping. Stretches me until I'm screaming. Digs his hands into my hips and pulls on me like the ground has turned to lava and I'm his only lifeline.

And then even my screams aren't possible.

I can only watch him, out of breath and consumed with love, as his body ripples and his head falls back. The sunshine paints his hair with fire, his face with magnificence. He's passion and power and pulsing, primitive need.

Most importantly…he's mine.

The thought is a miracle from a heaven I'll never see. But who cares about getting to silver clouds when they've been gifted with a golden god? A man who's facedt so much for me. The shocks of his past. The fears of his heart. All the crazy leaps of committing to me.

Jumps from cliffs that likely aren't behind us yet. And

that's okay too.

I tell him that by lacing my fingers into his. By matching the violent need of his hold. By widening my body more for him. Opening for him…not just physically. I show him every corner of my soul. All the shadows and insecurities of my own heart.

But he doesn't see that. His stunning blues hold on to so much reticence. He's holding back so much, giving me more thunder than rain. A dark restraint I can no more ignore than the rumbles starting to quiver in the clouds that race our way.

"It's all right," I rasp, tightening my fingers. "We're okay."

He tucks his head back in, conflict sharpening his regal features. "If I hurt—"

"You won't."

"Kara—"

"Damn it, Maximus. It hurts more without you!"

Like glass beneath his thunder, my voice splinters the words. It's pathetic, but I'm past caring. This is about more than the mesh of our sex. Beyond the claim of his cock.

This is a reminder, for us both, of what a force we are when locked in each other. Joined with each other. Entwined like air and fire…

Like heaven and hell.

Finally, he comprehends it all. I see the understanding in his eyes. But when his body keeps rejecting the certainty, I decide an override is necessary.

While sucking in harsh air, I clench in with my thighs. There's no way for Maximus to ignore the pincher thrust against his own legs, but he's only half done with his baffled grunt before I've gone into determined demon mode, pushing up to pitch us both over.

"*Unnnnhhh!*"

Craccck.

Thwommmp.

The timbre of his growl is succeeded swiftly by the actual timber noises: the crash of his spine against the tabletop then the boom of the whole table against the ground.

"Kara. *Fuck.*" It's a ferocious eruption but peppered with a laugh. If the man is set on diminishing my desire, that's not the way to do it. What his inner animal does to my libido...

"Don't stop, little demon."

No laugh this time, and I'm glad for it. Gravity has started doing its duty, working my body deeper onto his. The elements are dedicated to the cause too. As I undulate my hips, rocking my core faster and longer, they heed the command from my lover's psyche and start dumping fat raindrops over us.

Our thrusts get urgent. Around us, the shattered wood planks creak and crack. They give away with more force as Maximus rears up, hooking his arms to my back in a sexual pullup. Shivers claim me as his fingertips become gentle talons, scraping my drenched skin.

"Yes," I hiss into his neck. "Harder, Maximus. Do it. Mark me."

Thank God he's decided to leave the hesitance behind. Without another beat, he's gouging into the flesh that borders my spine. I keen in gratitude before returning the favor, finding brutal purchase in the coiled mountains of his shoulders.

I long to soothe the scratches with the flat of my tongue, but that will have to wait. Our mutual pain is kicking back endorphins to our human halves, ensuring we grab at every erotic delight from each other. Maximus's grunts are hot against my nape. His cock is full against my walls. I move atop him with urgency that's nearly panic.

Chasing it…

Chasing it…

Until the flood breaks loose.

For him, hot and violent. For me, wet and wild.

Completion that pierces me with the same brilliance as the flashes between the thunderheads above…and the sliver of sunshine, peeking from just one corner, sending a rainbow into the center of the grass nearby.

Now I'm convinced.

Maybe Eden *is* a thing.

And if we created it here, maybe our little family can do it again—next time, in a place unfindable by Zeus, Hades, or Hecate.

I make a vow to hold tight to the hope. Next to my love for this man, it might become my strongest ally.

"Never thought I'd be so thankful for a tiny shower stall."

Maximus's mutter prompts me into a new giggle. We've been in the little space long enough to have developed some fierce prune fingers, thanks to his numerous one-liners about dropped soap. By the time I started choking on my laughter, the man decided to pin me against the wall and silence me with a slippery make-out session. One thing led to another, and here we are at wrinkled fingertips.

Still, I lift a few of my raisin nubs and wick stray drops away from his thick eyebrows.

"Clearly, you've never been to some choice European villages," I quip.

He smiles down with his eyes. His lips give a more mellow version of the vibe. "Europe's still one of my dreams. Hey, a single stamp in the passport would be. I've always been working too hard to get away. But now I'll get to see it with a special tour guide."

His declaration is warming and shocking in the same set of seconds. "You've never been outside the country? At all?"

"Does Olympus count?"

There's no smile beneath his words now. How can I blame him? I've already sensed that even the distant memories from his childhood are difficult to confront. No matter how opulent his surroundings, he was still the secret son of Z's side act. Just like my shame about not belonging in heaven, his was directed at being ostracized from his whole realm. I can't begin to fathom such a pain.

"Of course we'll go to Europe," I murmur. "To every place that matters. Paris and Prague, Verona and Florence, London and Seville... All of it."

I keep fighting the urge to sound so wistful, but his new melancholy stirs my own. There's a finish for my statement, but I don't dare lend it volume.

"As soon as my father isn't dogging every one of our steps?"

So Maximus takes care of it instead.

I sigh, realizing one of us probably had to. But I hate the natural drag on my brain, hauling me to the next logical subject. Logical but awful.

"So when do you think he'll stop by around here?"

His expression is dour as he cranks off the water. "Not at all, if he's holding good to his word and learning how to read me better." He leans out and lifts a huge bath sheet off one of the hooks outside the stall. While wrapping me in it with protective pats, he adds, "This time is strictly for us. Damn it, we deserve it."

I curl fingers around the towel's edges, savoring the billowy softness. "I'd ask you to repeat that ten more times, but doubt I'd be conscious during all of them."

He bends down to press tender lips to my forehead. "Get into bed, beautiful. I'll make sure I wake you with enough time to head to dinner."

"Oh. *Head* to dinner? Guess that's a good thing, considering the table."

A low chortle from the center of his chest. "Which I'm going to go and try to explain while you're resting."

"Tell them I'm sorry."

"But you're not."

"Accurate." I giggle softly. "So tell them I'm looking forward to enjoying their restaurant tonight."

"Would if I could." He showers me with another kiss as I drop my head into the pillow. "But they don't have a restaurant."

"Then…where…?"

"Ssshhh. *Rest*."

He's back to yet another full grin. A more devastating version of the one he had earlier, when ensuring all would be revealed. I don't have any more ideas about how to show him up this time, especially with these paradise-grade linens against my bare skin, so I give up a sleepy groan instead.

"Oh, my. You're going to get max score on the next surprise-present points, aren't you, Mr. Kane?"

In lieu of a reply, he backs out of the yurt with a thoroughly self-pleased smirk.

I don't nap for very long, meaning I'm awake and looking at a field guide for the canyon when he re-enters a little under an hour later. The exact same expression is adorning his rugged, wonderful face.

"Good afternoon, Professor Maximus," I greet with a smile, though the temptations rises to drop it as he stops hard in place. Certain shadows take over his gaze, making me wish for another picnic table in the vicinity.

"Oh, sweet woman," he growls. "You look good enough to set me hunting for another picnic table."

I raise both hands, which lowers the sheet a good inch on my chest. "I'll bring the peanut butter if you handle the jelly. Or…we can just pretend to order in?"

His eyes darken by another shade as he jabs a finger toward the bed. "If we go there, we're not going to *leave* there."

If he thinks that command is going to steer me off the subject, the sun has fried a few of his brain cells. I tell him so with a tiny shimmy that drops the sheet below my hardening nipples.

"No." He slams his eyes shut. "No, no, *no*, you don't. We

have plans. You'll be very glad when we keep them."

I congratulate myself for expecting a comment in that vein. I'm more than ready with a convincing pout. "But what am I supposed to wear? Once the sun sets, I'll freeze in those shorts. So maybe we have no choice about—"

I have no idea that his march behind the room's dressing screen will yield his return with three dresses on padded hangers. They're flowy, flowery, and more than deserving of my gawking jaw.

"Madame Voracity sends her regards," he drawls. "Kell too. She kindly video-called to help me pick these out yesterday. You have the final selection, though. Whichever one you want. There are shoes and accessories behind the screen. Mix and match whatever you want."

"Seriously?" It's tight in my throat, clutched by rising emotions. And conflict.

I'm not new to this kind of gig or what to do. I've lost count of how many times I actually *have* done it for photo shoots of every ilk. But all of them were managed and planned because of some brand, even the one known as Kara Valari.

But all the preparation this man has taken…all the thought and care…

It's impossible to gulp down the tears anymore.

As a few break free and roll down my face, Maximus chucks the dresses to the foot of the bed and plummets to my side.

"Whoa. *Whoa*, little demon. What's this? Is the sprout making you feel gross?" He scoops my hand into his. "And it's okay if you hate the dresses. But Kell said that—"

I squeeze his fingers, adding adamant nail digs into the back of his hand. "And she was right. They're all stunning. I don't know how I'm going to decide."

He dips his head in, but it's not necessary. My senses are blinded with the ferocity of his scrutiny.

"Then…what is it?"

With my free hand, I wick away the stray drops on my cheeks. "Nobody's ever done this for me before. I mean… for *me*. Not for what I represent or for how many units my face can move of what they're selling. Even just now, I nearly started asking myself where you were coming from with this. What your angle could possibly be."

"My…angle?" The pause between his words is the framework for his stormy frown. Expecting it doesn't make me less frightened of it, especially its adjoining retort. "I don't have a damn *angle*, Kara."

"I know," I soothe. "I *know*—which is why I stopped the doubts before they started. The point I wanted to make is that this, tonight, is only us. Only *you*. The only thing you want to do with me is give *more* to me…and just when I think there can't be any more, there is…"

As I trail off, he pushes in. Our lips seek each other like the tide and moon, pulled beyond control, fulfilled beyond words. But somehow he finds some.

"And there always will be," he whispers into my parted mouth. "Always more, and always for you."

I slide my hand into his hair and drag him close again. His mouth is big and bold, conquering mine with stabs and slides that make me dizzy and needy. He doesn't protest when I work my way a little closer. Then closer. The sheets tangle between us as I wrap myself around him, following the call of the base desires that rise inside.

Higher…

Higher…

Until he yanks back with a tortured moan. But at the same time, a labored laugh. His chest is pumping as hard as mine. His gaze is hooded and hot.

"My love, if we keep this up much longer…"

"And that's a problem…why?" I challenge with matching spirit.

The corners of his eyes get new splays of tightness. Not his totally confrontational ones, though if he'd summoned me to his office with that look, I'd be fearing for my GPA. Maybe more. With more economy than his usual grace, he rolls back to his feet.

"Tick-tock, Cinderella. You'd best get up and pick your magical dress. The carriage will be here in half an hour."

Carriage?

I keep the demand out of my mouth and away from my face, figuring it'll get me *all will be revealed* again, or something just as cryptic. My delight in the Voracity originals has also taken over.

Short on time and seeing they're all in my size, I quickly pick a cream-colored knit with some delicate embroidery accents. It falls to my shins, which means a pair of wedge espadrilles is an ideal finish for the look. There's an assortment of hair ornaments in a basket near the washbasin and mirror, and I find a pretty pearl hair clip that helps to bring my air-dried lengths into some semblance of up-down order. After swiping on light bronzer and lip gloss, I'm a little more cleaned up and ready for Maximus's mysterious *carriage*.

"Oh…*my*."

The exclamation falls free before I can help it. I'm just shocked there isn't more to it, with some naughtier words attached for emphasis. But every one of them is certainly zinging through my mind, and I'd dare any female in this realm—in *any* of them—to deny herself the pleasure of letting them mentally scream away.

So…magnificent.

Not our conveyance, a golf cart that's romantically decked out with twinkle-lighted manzanita branches and velvet-padded seats.

My gasp is for *him*.

The man who steps to me now with his long fingers stretched and a smitten smile gleaming from the center of his beard. His hair is fully pulled back, tamed into a clean bun at the back of his head. He's changed into a pristine white button-down shirt and crisp khakis. The lighter attire causes the blue shades of his gaze to pop like waves on a Greek Island shore. They're intense, entrancing…

And they're focused only on me.

Always more. Always for you.

The man is obviously determined to prove that tonight.

And I'm absolutely inclined to let him.

CHAPTER 25

Maximus

I'M STILL AS STRESSED as a kid at prom.

Screw that.

I'm as neurotic as the full-grown man I am, wondering if my knees are about to give out when this woman finally hitches her hand into mine. Because right now, it's definitely going to happen…

And it does.

More vibrantly and searingly than ever before. The fierce electricity between us, like kerosene meets jet fuel meets nuclear reactor core. It burns white-hot within seconds but only perpetuates more energy, until it feels like real fission. The rest of the world sees us standing a foot apart, but we know differently. One fire. One heart. One soul.

"Hey. Why are you so tense?"

Of course she knows that as fact. Probably a lot more too. Thankfully, every self-control trick I've learned since boyhood is present, ready to be my wingman. With their help, I keep the most important details well away from Kara's mental reach.

"Not tense," I readily reply. "Just excited. I want you to love everything."

Her smile doles another agonizing but awesome gut punch. "I already do, Mr. Kane."

I motion to our driver, an affable resort staff guy who looks like he'd get along well with Gio, that we're ready to go. After helping Kara into the cart's back seat, I jog around and get in next to her. Though my nerves still feel like triple-wrapped barbed wire, I savor the profound peace of resting my lips in my woman's hair. The resort's eucalyptus and mint products are a perfect blend with the cinnamon notes that are natural for her skin and an aphrodisiac for the rest of my days.

I don't want these moments to end.

But they can't end fast enough.

Since arriving yesterday, I've been mentally preparing for the hundred ways the next hour can go. Not the ending—the surest thing about all this, thank God—just every tiny detail leading up to it. The minutiae over which I've obsessed more than any lecture or lesson plan.

For all the fixating, I've deliberately stopped short at several parts of the visions. Held back from anticipating one specific factor. Kara's reaction. I didn't want to build expectations that wouldn't become reality.

But after she emerged from our tent a few minutes back, more jaw-droppingly gorgeous than I ever could have imagined, more of my fantasies are escaping the mental border checks.

At the bottom of the hill, we take a mild turn off the main road and onto the nature trail that looks out toward the Channel Islands. Though there's some haze over the ocean, the prominent rises of San Miguel, Santa Rosa, and Santa Cruz can clearly be seen. Between us and them, there are miles of azure waters that ripple like a vast liquid firmament. Depths both stunning and frightening, demanding that a man gaze at them with nothing less than his grandest dreams.

Since I'm already living mine, there's a gigantic check mark for that box.

Not the best metaphor, since these moments belong to the limits of no boxes. Even the brackets of my chest feel too small for my heart as we reach a lone picnic table— fortunately still intact—positioned on a small rise toward the end of the greenbelt between a hiking trail and the beach. A white tablecloth is held down by arrangements of the wildflowers that I picked earlier in the afternoon and a pair of place settings is arranged, side by side, to allow clear views of the approaching sunset. The sky is already painted in watercolor-worthy hues of purple, orange, pink, and amber.

It's one of the most perfect sights of my existence.

But it doesn't take away half the breath that my woman does.

"Oh, *wow*," she rasps before I get one foot out onto the ground. Somehow both of *hers* are already there, and she's rushing around the front of the cart with a stare rivaling the sky for wide-open beauty. "You're really bucking for that *Best Boyfriend in the Universe* trophy, aren't you?"

"And *you* really want a lesson about waiting to be properly escorted to dinner, it seems." Unbelievably, I maintain the irked tone a good ten seconds longer than I expected—until the moment she windmills back with one arm, landing a chastising chuck to my right pectoral.

"You're kidding, right? Because you seriously don't mean I was supposed to wait on this."

My pique is officially torpedoed. I don't know what part of her debate has me more enchanted: the gutsy banter or the physicality she adds to it with that spirited stance into the wind. But I have no more time for this inner debate. Not when I can focus on savoring more of her gorgeousness. All of her energy and beauty, with the wind tugging at her hair. All of her light and life, with that dress molding to her figure.

The body in which she's nurturing a creation from our love.

Another miracle on a very long list.

An amazing catalog, but one that's out of order. A divergence I'm determined to fix, perhaps this very moment. It wasn't on my list of possibilities, but I'm willing to flex. The light is golden, the cart driver is gone, and the sweet demon of my dreams is reaching a hand back to take mine…

No.

To yank on me with unignorable intention.

"Come on!" She uses her free fingers to pull off one shoe and then the other. "Let's take a pre-dinner wade."

I match her tug, ensuring she pays attention this time.

"How about an after-dinner one? There's something I want to talk to you about."

"We'll have dinnertime to talk. The tide's coming in. Once the sun is all the way down, the water will get rougher."

I cock my head. "When did you switch to Marine Science for a major?"

"Careful. I might start spouting whale mating trivia too."

That catches me off guard enough to give in to a laugh. Equally huge mistake. The woman already feels my vacillation and takes advantage, hauling me closer to the water.

"All right, hold up. Do I have time to take off my sh—"

Fast answer to that? No. The Pacific tide makes that a hundred and fifty percent clear by inciting a forceful wave to charge the shore—and us. The eager roller hits me up to waist level, and lands at the center of Kara's bustline.

But the stampede of profanity in my mind is silenced by a bigger wallop. The delighted shrieks of my gorgeous, drenched girl.

By now, I really mean that last point.

After a stronger bomber courtesy of the sea, Kara loses her footing. I lunge and catch her, letting the choice obscenities have their way with my lips now. But not all. I'm sure she'll have a few too.

But the only sounds from the woman are more laughs. Higher and giddier. Curling over every lush curve of her mouth. Igniting new fires in her huge, expressive eyes. Blazes I've never witnessed there before. While her anger and arousal inspire flames that prowl at her irises, these torches are...dancing. Popping up and down as if moving to beats all their own.

The rhythm of her joy.

The cadence of her celebration.

A tempo I want in my life forever.

At first, I tell her that with the surge of my spirit. As soon as she feels all of it, I tell her again with a tuck of fingers beneath her chin. The waves are kinder now, having enjoyed their fierce flirtation with the shore, and undulate around us with their hypnotic flow.

Now.

This is the perfect moment. The *only* moment.

And I pull in a breath, getting ready. Summoning the words I've rehearsed so many times.

"Maximus?" Kara winds her arms around my neck, misreading the sudden lurch in my psyche. "What is it? I'm sorry I got us soaked. But look, it's such a nice day, and—"

"Marry me."

Her throat clutches. Her lips separate from each other. "Uh...huh?"

Her vacillation is a spur for my purpose. "We didn't do this thing true the first time. And to be honest, this wasn't how I planned things *this* time. But I know, with everything I am, it's the right time." I emphasize it by palming her head with my hands. "I've never been more in love with you, Kara Valari—and I want to spend a lifetime of getting soaked with you. Stunned by you. Best of all, loving you to the best of my ability."

I compel one of my hands to slip down, searching for the delicate metal circle that I stashed in my pocket while she changed her clothes in the yurt. It's a giant relief to find it there, tenaciously camping out in a wet corner.

When I lift it between our chests, I can't tell if Kara's expression is twisted from another surge of happiness or a fresh hit of discomfort.

Maybe that's a good thing. I was pretty confident about this part of the afternoon, if not the other components. But I've been wrong about some things before, and some of those things include women.

I probably should have researched this part of the subject better. Should have grilled Kell a little more about Kara's hopes for the things *other* than the wedding. But I got cocky, thinking my instincts were providing the best directionals. That something rustic and private would be the way my girl really wanted to do this. That she wouldn't care if my gold ring was borne by my fingers and not a velvet box.

At least I can address one odd factor about the jewelry. The fact that the prongs aren't holding a single diamond.

"It's not that fancy right now," I rush to say. "But I wanted you to have something unique, that'll be an emblem of us. I have a friend, a former student, who's now an artist in Ventura. He had this design, with the fire on one side and the stars on the other, and it felt right. But there's no stone because I want *you* to pick it for yourself. I thought we could hit his studio on the way back to LA. That's only if you want t—"

Her lips mash mine with intensity that surpasses table-breaking force. I clutch her close with one arm, taking care to hold the ring tight with the opposite hand. Neither grip comes close to the hold she's just taken of my heart. This realization… It hits me as if she's lined her spiritual fist with spikes. It's joy and pain. Gratitude but fear. This captivating creature has the power to fly me to new heights yet plummet me to the worst pain. It's all her choice. My whole soul is hers.

Facts that aren't exactly new.

Only now, as I pull away just far enough to slip the gold circle around her finger, it's official.

"It's beautiful," she breathes out as soon as the ring is settled. "The most perfect treasure of my life. I love you so much, Maximus."

"Not nearly as much as I love you."

Tears brim in her eyes—euphoric ones, I'm close to sure of it now—before leaping up to kiss me again. This time, she clenches her legs around my waist too. In the process she rips her drenched dress, but neither of us cares. Actually, as we make our way back up to shore, I'm adamantly looking forward to having dinner with a sea siren in an intriguingly cut outfit…

Though I also entertain the idea of just asking for the meal in takeout boxes…

A musing that never reaches a definitive conclusion.

It's slammed totally out of my head just like the air is beaten out of my lungs—as *I'm* whipped off my feet and down the beach by at least fifty yards.

"*What the living—*"

Though as soon I spew it, I question if *living* should still be a part of my vocabulary. After my forced flight along the narrow beach, I've kicked up enough sand and pebbles to resemble a blob of cookie dough rolled in stale rock candy. The shit jabs in as I swipe a rough hand across my pumping chest, fighting the onslaught of a million vehement questions.

Questions for which I refuse to await answers.

"Kara?" Question one, a thousand times more important than the rest. I bellow it as loud and desperately as I can, spinning around like I'm on a bad drug trip. If only that didn't feel so damn close to the truth… "Kara!"

"Here."

I startle, puzzling how she's snuck up against my side. Just as quickly, the confusion is eclipsed by unfiltered terror—and raw rage.

My bride-to-be looks as battered as I feel. Her limbs are dusted by thick sand. As that coating starts to fall off, I take in the dark-red splotches that appear along her skin. They're all over her, as vivid as the crimson storm clouding the edges of my vision.

"Holy shit."

"I'm okay."

"Holy *shit*."

"Maximus!" She whips a hand up to my wrist, which is still mercifully connected to the hand I'm using to wick her blood. "I'm okay. Sprout too. You've got to get it together. *Please*."

Her final rasp corresponds to a strange stare she's shooting over my right shoulder.

I scowl but pivot, following her gaze until I spot the explanation for this insanity.

I'm expecting a wild creature of some sort. Possibly— *probably*—not something from this realm. Maybe a hydra, considering our location—or Cerberus again, on a crazy recon quest from his ultimate master.

I'd prefer even the underworld hound over an actual beast charging up the beach in our direction. It takes a full beat, then another, for me to absorb that I'm truly seeing this. And then a third long pause to allow the depths of my throat to render their reaction.

"God damn it."

I yearn, more than anything, that the expression was only an idiom—and not a direct reference to the asshole in the boater hat who's still stomping straight at me.

CHAPTER 26

Maximus

Z COMES TO AN abrupt stop no more than three feet away, casting a wall of pebbled sand at us in the doing. The eco buckshot has me hauling Kara close, hunching low and tight to shield her as much as I can.

My new position has a secondary advantage. It's a better angle for hurling a hard glower at my sick sire—because that has to be the explanation for this. For why his eyes are rimmed in a shade of red that's too damn close to mine. For why the smoke around him is increasingly tainted with the same color. For why his whole posture is heaving like a wild boar with fifty arrows in its back.

Is he fucking kidding?

And what's his ultimate point? To intimidate me? If I weren't so furious, that'd earn him a long laugh. If anything, it triples my char.

"What. The. Fuck? Are you out of your mind, old man?"

"Are you out of *yours*?" he bellows back.

After tucking Kara behind me, I straighten to my full height. "What's that supposed to mean?"

Suddenly, there's something in his hand. It seems to appear from midair, but he's got to know his parlor tricks don't dazzle me like they do my mother.

I'm more concerned with the way he waves it at me so violently, the resulting *whoosh* lifts my wet hair off my shoulders. It's likely doing the same to Kara, since she shivers violently against my back. Protective anger comes in another consuming surge. I have to focus on whatever he's brandishing whether I like it or not.

I definitely don't like it.

Not when I can already see it's a print copy of some top Hollywood gossip magazine. And I know it's recent because it's flipped open to a half-page photo of Kara and me from the EmStars red carpet, just a couple of nights ago. It's the exact moment in which I dipped her down for that hot kiss, all but pounding my chest with the she-is-mine-see-it-now stunt.

Stupid, stupid, stupid.

Because the media scarfed that stuff up like boxes of extra creamy mac and cheese—and *especially* because one of those on-the-stick photographers caught the shot of a lifetime. A moment in which the corset under Kara's gown shifted in ways it wasn't supposed to.

Revealing what the magazine claims to be a "love glow" in her midsection.

While I keep gawking as if my stare will magically erase the image, Kara finally pushes in. "What…is… Oh, my

God," she croaks. "No. Oh, no, no, *no*." Her anxiety doesn't abate even after I gather her close again, rubbing firm fingers around the ball of her shoulder.

"Hey. *Hey*, beautiful. It's going to be okay."

"No," Z spits. "It's definitely *not* going to be okay."

"What? Why?" I volley. "Even if this is viral, it only looks like a trick of the bright lights on that carpet. The caption here is a bunch of word winks and innuendos."

My father rips the magazine from my hand. It vanishes as swiftly as he made it show up. "Winks and whispers, eh? You think that's it? Wait. Let's rephrase. *Is* that it, Maximus?"

Heat burns deeper into my face, and I'm gladder than ever that this grandiose asshole wasn't present as I grew up. It feels shitty enough to *feel* like a teenager on the verge of a year-long grounding. If he'd actually been around when I *was* one… I push down the sudden temptation to shudder.

But I'll give back as good as I get on his judge-and-jury glare. No way is he privileged to see my shame. Or my secrets.

"You know what, Pops? It's absolutely none of your business."

Z's nostrils flare. His lips part until I can see the white clench of his teeth. "Open your stubborn eyes, boy. It's *all* of my business."

I clench a fist. "Screw you."

"Damn it, Maximus. Did you knock her up or not?"

Tension takes over my own face, so brutal it hurts. Is the king of wandering cocks actually playing Saint Peter about where mine has been? I roll my wrist, already anticipating how satisfying it'll be to break his jaw for this, but fate intervenes with self-control I never knew I had.

I nearly crow with pride as I lower my arm. Granted, I'm slow about it. Very slow.

In corresponding measure, words seethe up my throat. "Were you listening? I said it's none of your bus—"

"Maximus." Kara's voice is quiet but as firm as her touch, palming wide on my chest. Fingers that start to visibly tremble. "He's…right."

I shake my head. "*What?*"

"I'm sorry." Tears push at her words. "But he is."

"What are you—"

"I grew up watching my mother having to handle situations like this." Inscrutable emotions pinch her face for a second. "We always tried to be conscious about hiding things. Concealing the parts that humans would never understand. We were more vigilant during high-volume photo shoots, but sometimes things slipped through. A comment we'd make or a look we'd give. The fires that snuck through in our eyes… Veronica would have to work with the underworld high council on plans to explain it away."

I hate that her confession makes sense. I hate it even more for the distress it keeps dunking her into. But there's a mild silver lining. The mollifying effect it brings to Z.

He doesn't relax all the way, but when he kicks the pebbled sand again, it's not directed at us. "This time, that council is the least of our worries."

More than Kara's face is tense now. "I was afraid you'd say that," she rasps.

Before she's done, I'm fighting for more air in my chest and calm in my veins. "Somebody want to shed some light for the clueless guy on the beach here?"

The incrimination continues across Z's face, but he's finally killed the tinge on the entrance smoke. "If I'm aware of this and have guessed what it really is, guess who else has?"

The rage leaves me like a lake bursting a dam. The bare bed in its wake is a sheet of mortified ice.

"Hecate."

A tight nod from Z. "And with your suspicions about what she's planning, what do you think she'll do with the information?"

"Oh, my God," Kara chokes out.

My father's face is back to a forbidding scowl. "If we're not careful, that's exactly what she'll become to you," he states. "All the stories relay that I elevated her because of my gratitude and awe. But the real reason? I knew I had to secure her loyalty, and nothing short of a grand gesture would do."

My own teeth clash with each other until my jaw aches. "And now that she's not happy with that…"

"She's committed to a cause that'll avenge her disappointment. And she's ready to do whatever it takes for success." His head ducks toward Kara. "Including measures to get to that magical little hybrid you're carrying."

"Who isn't popping out right this second," I say. "So we have time."

Z scoffs so hard, it's nearly a laugh. "We have nothing."

Kara stiffens. "What do you…"

"If that witch shows up, even in five *minutes*, she won't think twice about cutting that child from your womb where you stand. Then she'll leave you to bleed out on this beach while she spells the fetus into a fully formed adult, ready to do whatever she asks of it."

As quickly as she's tensed, Kara sags into me. "No!" she sobs.

The fear digs into me differently. All too quickly, it morphs into wrath like I've never known.

"That's not possible," I spew. "The baby wouldn't live through it. She can't demand devotion from a *thing*."

Zeus's new chuff is a gallon of alkaline blasting my gut's pond of acid. "Says the demigod about the goddess who rules the zombies?"

"*No!*" But Kara's outcry is the dagger that cuts me all the way open.

"If zombification isn't a solution, she also has Persephone at her fingertips," Z continues. "In this kind of situation, the goddess of rebirth is handy in the back pocket."

For the first time, Kara jerks away from me. She's not repelled; I already see that across her face. She's *com*pelled. Bursting with emotions that feel impossible to process.

I should know. Every one of them pummels me too.

"What do we do?" she pleads. "Maximus? What are we going to do?"

I brace one of her shoulders with patent command. "If she gets anywhere near you, I'll tear her apart with my bare hands."

"Which she'll already be anticipating, meaning she'll kill you first," my father states.

I wheel on him, calling on nearly every muscle in my being to help with my civility. "So your better plan would be what?"

"The only option you have available," he counters. "Both of you will leave this realm now, with me. You can live under my protection in Olympus."

Before I'm able to knot it back, a boom of a laugh escapes. "Oh, sure. Under your protection. In the realm that Hecate likely knows how to access from every direction. And even if those access points are sealed, I'm not sure your actual queen enjoyed it when Mom and I were there the *first* time."

"Hera will understand, considering these circumstances." His continuing cool, while not up to his usual urbanity, is starting to nettle. He's talking about our lives here. Our *child*. "She hates the idea of bowing to Hecate more than I do. And, as I've just told you—"

"Got it already," I retort. "It's our only option."

"Not your only one."

The assertion has all three of us jerking around, nerves pricked by its source. But not in the way I've been terrified about. The voice doesn't come close to a mesh of Zen mother and smooth jazz disc jockey. It's not even female. Hecate doesn't yet know we're onto her grand plan, so she'd have no reason to drain her energy by shapeshifting. Or so I hope.

For a handful of moments, that assurance is joined by

confusion. *If not Hecate, then who's here?*

My stress must be messing with my brain, because I swear by every pebble on this shore, it sounds like—

"Gramps?"

Holy. Shit.

Though not outwardly, I share the combination of delight and dread in Kara's shout.

Because sure enough, Giovani Valari is standing just fifteen feet away.

He looks the same, despite being clothed in the all-black gear of the underworld military. He even lifts a corner of his mouth with a smirk to rival many classic Hollywood stars as his gaze settles on his granddaughter. But he doesn't move to greet her.

Though it's clearly killing Kara, she doesn't run forward either.

No chance of that, considering the dark and decadent figure by Gio's side.

Beneath his breath, Zeus spits a string of filthy Greek.

I don't dare avert my focus to translate it all, especially because it doesn't matter. Not when I'm locking a glare on the unnervingly serene face of the god who kidnapped my fiancée ten days ago. A placidity into which Hades is well settled right now—which spikes my dread to an altitude that new clouds have started to populate.

"Hey, Gio," I call out. "We have to stop meeting like this."

The man jogs his head to acknowledge my line but moves little else. He looks ready to speak, but Z beats him to it.

"What the do you want, H?" He stalks around, moving between the pair of them and the pair of us. "Or should I just cut to the chase and ask what fuckery you're up to?"

Hades casually folds his hands. Though the clouds have heeded my psyche and form a dark celestial forest overhead, the dark-red stones along his fingers sparkle as if we're in full sun.

"Fuckery?" he croons. "Come now, brother. Is it really that if I can offer a constructive option to my nephew and his bride-to-be?"

I contain a growl in the column of my throat. Barely. *Options.* It's rapidly becoming a word I hate. A fate I fear.

"Why am I finding it hard to punch the *more information* button right now?" I insert.

"Maximus. Hear him out." Astoundingly, Gio appears to offer it with totally free will. "He truly means no harm."

My gruff grunt is a twin to Zeus's. I trade a swift glance with him too. His scowl confirms the motivation of mine. Gio's here as collateral to gain Kara's trust. I only hope she's smarter than that. I already *know* she is, but her adoration for her grandfather is a potentially gigantic override switch.

"What do you propose, Hades?"

And there she goes, flipping that lever.

"What do you *think*?" Zeus grumbles.

Still, Hades shores up his stance. Eyeballs me with unmistakable intent. "You can have free shelter in Dis, as well. A chateau just for the two of you." He holds up a hand as if swearing his nothing-but-the-truth to a bailiff. "I won't come anywhere near the place. Giovani and Charlena will head up your guard details."

"Why?" I bark at once. "What makes your offer any better than his?" I thumb toward my father. "Hecate can get into your realm just as easily as Olympus. And, just like there, my last visit wasn't so enjoyable."

"An unfortunate fact, but a fate that won't be waiting for you again. You have my word. Though Kara is only half-demon, that still makes her half our own. We won't turn our backs on her or you, especially in this time of extraordinary need. And unlike the troops of Olympus, my warriors aren't benefiting from Hecate's favor, or lack of it. That applies to Hecate and Persephone, as well. If they attempt any kind of a run on your place, my demons will cut off their heads, dice up their bodies, and give the pile to Charon for fish chum."

My air hitches as fast as Kara's. It's one thing, as a victim, to envision Hades's cruelty. It's bizarre to hear it as a pledge for my own safety. More vitally, for my woman's and child's.

Should we actually trust him? Or is he here, even with Gio in tow, as an elaborate hoax to lure us to hell again?

Or should we accept my father's offer to be harbored by the ramparts of Olympus? I could request Reg for my security team, and Mom would likely be nearby…though the threat of Hecate's incursion would be higher.

I don't get a chance to lay out the thoughts as neatly as I want.

Z's golf claps shake the tree line past the greenbelt. "Oh, well done," he sneers at Hades. "Now there's a marketing brochure for the ages. *Come to hell. We'll make you some chum.*"

To his credit, Hades doesn't chomp on that bait. But

to my alarm, he uses the time to chain me in another unfightable stare. A look that does little to prepare me for his deceivingly calm challenge.

"Night is almost here. Hecate will be at her strongest, especially under the full moon. Kara, Maximus…you must decide now. What are you going to do? Where are you going to go?"

Continue Reading in:

Edge of Stars
Blood of Zeus: Book Six

ACKNOWLEDGMENTS

It took a real village of amazing people to help with this part of Maximus and Kara's journey. I am so grateful to you all!

Most importantly, thank *you*: a reader who dared to take a chance on a twisty new concept in the mythology romance realm! You have welcomed the professor and his little demon deep into your heart, and it means the world that you've continued the journey this far! My heartfelt thanks for your brave spirit and open mind!

I am so thankful to the entire team at Waterhouse Press, who keep believing in this project and working on its elements with your dedication and creativity. I am beyond thankful for your support. (Scott Saunders, your steadfast wisdom has *jolted* me with gratitude! Sorry, dude…you just know I had to go there…)

So many thanks to Carey Sabala, Victoria Blue, Kika Medina, and Corinne Akers, for catching my tears, holding my hand, and keeping me sane on the days when it felt impossible to go on. You're all such beautiful gifts from the cosmos!

My endless love to Tom and Leo. You are, and always will be, the pillars that hold up my soul, guard my spirit, and make my heart fly. I love you both so much.

ABOUT ANGEL PAYNE

USA Today bestselling romance author Angel Payne loves to focus on high-heat romance starring memorable alpha men and the women who love them. She has numerous book series to her credit, including the action-packed Bolt Saga and Honor Bound series, Secrets of Stone series (with Victoria Blue), the intertwined Cimarron and Temptation Court series, the Suited for Sin series, and the Lords of Sin historicals, as well as several standalone titles.

Angel is a native Southern Californian, leading to her love of being in the outdoors, where she often reads and writes. She still lives in Southern California with her soul-mate husband and beautiful daughter, to whom she is a proud cosplay/culture con mom. Her passions also include whisky tasting, shoe shopping, and travel.

Visit her at AngelPayne.com

Photograph © Regina Wamba